Dedicated to all my fellow Dog Fashion Disco fans
and to the *real* Mushroom Cult.
(You all know who you are.)

Editor: Denise Barker
Chapter artwork: Amy Hunter
Author photo: Elisabeth B. Adams
1984 Handwriting insert: Ashley Mayer
Front Cover, Back Cover, & Title Page artwork,
and 4 adverts: Kyle Lechner

Published by Scout Media
www.ScoutMediaBooksMusic.com
Copyright 2019
ISBN: 978-0-9979485-6-1 (print)
978-0-9979485-7-8 (eBook)

July 12, 2018 – March 28, 2019
(Monterey, CA)

For more information on my books & music:
www.BrianPaone.com

Gardenia's
Family Restaurant

Devour the hour 'til there's nothing left

SMOLENS
20 CLASS A CIGARETTES

SMOLENS
Take a Trip

Warning: The Surgeon General has determined that cigarette smoking is dangerous to your health.

SALEM, MASSACHUSETTS; 1984

1: GARDENIA'S FAMILY RESTAURANT

Vicki rubbed her hands and bounced on her tiptoes, darting her eyes up and down the busy downtown Salem street. She shivered and tugged her overcoat snugger when the wind blustering from the water over Pickering Wharf prickled her skin. She returned to wringing her hands together, the skin on her knuckles cracking from exposure to the cold winter elements.

"I knew I'd be stood up," she said with a thick puff of steam exiting her mouth.

She shook her left hand so her watch would fall below her sleeve's seam.

"Yep. Ten minutes late. This is the *last* blind date I go on. I swear."

She kicked a dirty-gray snowball across the sidewalk and turned to head to her car in Gardenia's parking lot—the restaurant's sign illuminating her backside—but instead she collided into someone's chest.

Vicki stepped backward. "Oh, jeez, I'm sorry."

"Don't worry about it, kid," replied the old man wearing a trench coat. "Mind if I bum a smoke?"

Vicki shifted her weight from foot to foot. "I-I don't smoke. I'm sorry, mister."

"Bullshit. You bought your first pack today so your blind date might think you're cool." The old man's voice emphasized *cool* to sound like a melodramatic high-schooler.

Vicki's eyes grew wide.

The old man shuffled one step forward. "I believe your boss retained a new client today. An Eva Smith? Looking for her grandfather?"

Vicki placed a hand over her opened mouth. "The Wharf Killer. How do you know about that?"

The old man's index finger tapped his temple. "Because I'm smart."

Vicki glanced at the passing cars. *Too much traffic and too many people are about for him to snatch me in plain view, aren't there?*

Smith's wrinkled and weathered finger pointed to Vicki's jacket pocket. "A smoke, please?"

Vicki's shaking hand reached into her pocket and retrieved the box of Smolens. She unwrapped the cellophane and handed the box to the old man.

Smith lit a cigarette and exhaled a mixture of steam and unfiltered smoke. "Your blind date won't show tonight."

"Is it okay if I leave, mister? I just want to go home."

Smith extended his hand toward Vicki. "Are you scared of

me?"

She flinched and glanced over his shoulder at Gardenia's parking lot.

"Fine, fine. Go. It'll save you additional wasted time and any further embarrassment."

Vicki ducked her head as she stormed past the old man.

"Sorry it didn't work out for you, Vicki. He just wasn't ... right for you."

Smith stood in the same spot, puffing his cigarette, as he watched Vicki get into her car and exit the parking lot without checking the oncoming traffic. Her back tires squealed as they found traction in the snow-covered roadway.

Smith tossed the half-smoked Smolens into a snowbank and headed for the entrance to Gardenia's.

"Good evening, Mr. Smith," the hostess said.

Smith nodded and smiled. "Any room at the bar tonight?"

"Absolutely. Go right ahead."

The retired private eye tipped his fedora and moved past her toward the back of the restaurant. Just before he reached the red-cushioned bar, he detoured to the jukebox in the corner. He reached into his breast pocket and fished out two nickels. After he inserted them into the slot, he entered the memorized code for his song of choice.

"Smith!" the bartender yelled from behind the beer taps.

The detective flashed an open hand in lieu of a full-fledged wave. The jukebox played his chosen song, and the singer had just described Rockefellers walking with sticks and umbrellas when Smith reached an open seat at the bar.

"Fain, how are you, my good man?" Smith asked.

"Can't complain. The holidays have certainly helped business."

Smith nodded. "Something about the season brings out the

drunks in all of us."

Fain chuckled. "I'm not complaining. Your regular poison tonight?"

"Yes, sir. Double it up."

Fain poured two whiskeys, each straight up into a separate glass, and slid them toward Smith.

The detective removed his fedora and placed it on the threadbare stool next to him, then raised his glass. "To the holiday season."

Fain lifted his glass of water. "To job security!"

The two men toasted, and Fain flung his dish towel over his left shoulder. "How's Travis and his kids?"

"He dropped them off earlier today. Them grandkids are having a sleepover tonight at our place. Wynn's at home with them, making cookies."

"And you're here, drinking."

"I had some ... business to take care of tonight."

"You back *detecting?*"

"Is that even a word?" Smith asked, chuckling. "I guess you could say that, but, the real question is, have I really ever stopped?"

Smith finished his first glass of room-temperature whiskey just as the jukebox fell silent again before Billy Idol's "Rebel Yell" graced the restaurant with its sing-along chorus and loud guitar hooks.

Smith grimaced and shook his head. "Music these days, huh?"

"The world moves on, you know? Whether you move with it or not," Fain replied as he restocked the shelves with clean and dry martini glasses.

Smith took the first swig of his second glass and closed his eyes. "There was a band—a jazz band—that would play regularly at Rippetoe's, my go-to bar back home, a long time ago. The Anacostia Trio. Now *that's* what I call music. But I fear those days of live classy music in smoke-filled lounges are gone."

Fain shook his head. "It's a different time."

Smith removed his pocket watch and checked the time. "Well, sir, it's time to make my way to the homestead to play Grandpapa."

"Don't be a stranger."

Smith slid off his stool, finished his second glass in one gulp, and replaced his fedora on his head. He smacked his tongue against his lips to clear any residual alcohol and straightened his posture. "I won't, Fain. And merry Christmas, if I don't see you."

"And a happy New Year too."

"Yeah, yeah. Happy New Year and all that jazz. Good gravy, why don't we just wish each other a happy Valentine's Day too and make out while we're at it?"

"Get outta here, you old fogy."

Smith flipped Fain the middle finger as he turned toward the front of Gardenia's.

Fain chuckled behind him just as that pretty boy with the perma-sneer screamed through the jukebox speakers about how she wanted more, more, more.

Smith eased into the driver's seat of his Pinto and closed his eyes. The muffled sounds of traffic mixed with the giggles and cheer of the holiday-season pedestrians momentarily soothed his brain. After a moment of taking in the ambience of Gardenia's parking lot from inside his car, Smith opened his eyes and adjusted the rearview mirror, bringing into view the face of a decrepit witch from his back seat.

"For Pete's sake, Anya! I swear you'll be the death of me by showing up like that."

Anya leaned forward and raised the black veil covering her pale face and lifted it over her head. She cackled and slid between the front bucket seats and sat next to Smith.

"We've been working together for how many decades now? You'd think I wouldn't surprise you anymore."

"*Working* together." Smith chortled. "That's a good way of putting it."

Anya *tsk*ed at him and placed a bony hand on his knee.

"Who do you have out tonight?" he asked.

"A small crew. Cyana and Pum'kin are leading the charge in the red-light district."

"Mine's over there in the Dumpster." Smith used his chin to gesture toward the large green trash receptacle on the other side of the parking lot.

Anya leaned back into the passenger seat, removed her hand from his leg, and sighed.

"What?" Smith asked. "What is … Oh, don't fucking tell me—"

"I can't use him."

Smith twisted his body so his torso faced Anya. "What do you mean, you can't use him? Scumbag was using blind dates to prey on young girls. If anything, he's *exactly* who you can use."

"It's more complicated than that. I'm very selective of my choice of bantlings."

"Oh, this is just rich, Anya. I've helped you grow the Mushroom Cult into over one thousand strong, with no regard for how low of a bottom-feeder they are, and *now* you start having standards?"

Anya peered out the passenger window, remaining silent.

"What's wrong with him, Anya? Why isn't he worthy enough to be part of your pathetic coven?"

The witch returned her venomous gaze to Smith, peering at him. "God, I hate you. You'd think after all these years we've spent together and through the countless girls we've turned, you would've used some obvious common sense to notice there are no men within my ranks."

Smith glanced at his fingers and used his index finger to pick at a hanging cuticle on his thumb. "I've noticed. I just assumed you were sexist."

Anya reached into the back seat and retrieved the weathered hardbound book. Placing the large artifact in her lap, she petted the maroon-colored front cover, like it were a cat.

"The book is pretty specific about who the vultures will collect and return to me cleansed and reborn."

"Let me see."

"Excuse me?"

"Show me, Anya. For decades, I've obeyed blindly, never questioning what you tell me the book says. For all I know, the book's pages are blank, and you're just making up shit as it pleases you. Let me see where it says that."

Anya hugged the book against her black-laced garments and spat mockingly, "For one, *Detective*, if memory serves me correctly, you had the book for quite some time. So, if anyone should know these pages are not blank, it would be you. I'm still not sure how much of the book you actually read."

Smith remained silent, fiddling with the calloused skin around his cracked fingernails.

"Alright," Anya said. "I can see this conversation is pointless. Just as that young man's death was."

"That *young man* was using blind dates to drug and shack up with young girls. He sounds like grade-A prime meat for your cult, if you ask me."

"Has he killed any of these girls?"

Smith gripped the Pinto's steering wheel with both hands. "I-I can't be 100 percent sure. I've been tailing him for a few weeks, and I only seem to track him after he's left the girl unconscious and raped or after the room has been destroyed with no one left inside."

Anya slid closer to Smith. "Do you think it was in those times when he killed the girls?"

"Why do you care so much all of a sudden?"

"Well, if you were smarter, you could've pinned the Wharf Killer moniker on him. Let everyone think he's the one doing your work ..." Anya's voice trailed off. "Well, speak of the devil."

Smith glanced in his rearview mirror and saw a Salem Police Department cruiser enter Gardenia's parking lot.

"They're getting closer to finding out the truth, Smith. It won't be much longer before the fuzz put two and two together, or you get careless and leave bread crumbs right to your front door. And how will Wynn react to the SWAT team kicking in her front door and face-planting her elderly husband into the Oriental rug at gunpoint? You had a scapegoat—a perfect person to frame—right at your fingertips, and your fucking pathetic righteousness got in the way. Again."

Smith's gaze followed the squad car as it pulled into an empty slot and as its taillights went dark.

"Will you give him to me then?" Smith asked.

"*Ho-ho-ho!* So, Mr. Holier Than Thou has turned on his own convictions, has he?"

Smith, without removing his attention from the officers

exiting the patrol car, placed a hand on Anya's bony thigh. "You know as well as I do that my days are short. Eighty-five is just around the bend and through the first door on the right. I can feel it in my bones. Plus I can only imagine how spending forty years with the likes of you has shaved a decade off my life. I'm asking this one favor, Anya. Give me the boy. Give me the boy and get Stepp to buy into the cult, and I'll disappear from our partnership forever."

"Take Wynn on that Alaskan cruise she's been begging you for since the sixties?"

Smith chuckled. "You're such a wench."

"Who is it?" Anya craned her neck to see out the back window.

"Taylor and Raynard."

"Business? Or are they getting drinks on duty again?"

"Can't tell."

"They have to walk right past that Dumpster. You sure he's concealed well enough inside? I'd hate for this to be the way the fuzz finally brings you down."

"He's hidden. Don't worry about that. Just summon the vultures and let me have him."

Smith redirected his gaze from the rearview mirror and startled when he looked out his driver's side window. Nikki and Candy stood next to his car, their decrepit fingers slowly caressing the closed window.

Anya leaned forward and signaled for the two ghouls to disappear.

"Okay, just this once, Smith. But I'll have to wait until Gardenia's closed. Too many lookie-loos around to smuggle the body from the Dumpster, and certainly too many people around for the vultures to make their descent here."

"Thank you."

"He'll be ready by tomorrow night for you. I'll even hand deliver him."

Smith rolled his eyes. "Don't overexert yourself."

"Night's still young, Smith. Still time to head to Hypnotic Encounters and get me a proper one. Just sayin'."

Smith shook his head and pointed the Pinto homeward as Anya and the book vanished from his passenger seat, leaving her trademarked residual stench of mildew and decay.

Officer Taylor paid his and Officer Raynard's tab at Gardenia's bar and headed toward the exit.

"Good evening, officers."

"Good ta see ya, Rex!" Officer Raynard replied and stopped.

"All quiet on the eastern front tonight, I hope?"

"So far, so good. Just came in for a midshift refreshment."

Rex grabbed Taylor's arm and guided the officer downward to whisper, "Any leads on the Wharf Killer? The mayor has been all over my ass about getting this guy locked up so he'll get out of the fucking nightly news. It's killing the tourist business."

Taylor cleared his throat. "I know, sir. Chief McBrayer has a few task forces in plan to blanket the city at night. Plainclothes officers."

"When's he gonna roll that out? Just so I have something to tell the mayor in tomorrow's city council meeting."

"He said after New Year's," Raynard answered.

"Maybe I'll come to the station and chat with the chief myself. I just pray every night that one of youse guys catch the killer before we find *another* mutilated girl."

Taylor scanned the restaurant. "Doesn't seem to be hurting business in here."

"Safety in numbers. People feel secure among a crowd. But take a stroll on the wharf after sunset on any given night? Fucking crickets. And don't give me that bullshit about it being winter. Downtown commerce has seen a 30 percent decline in sales since this fucktard started leaving girls strewn around the wharf."

"Don't worry, Rex. It's only a matter of time," Raynard replied.

"That's what I'm afraid of."

Taylor's portable radio chirped, and he raised a finger to silence Rex from speaking.

"Is it for us?" Raynard asked.

"Nah. Something on the west side."

Raynard slapped Rex on the shoulder. "Take care. Have a merry Christmas if I don't see you before then."

"You too, gentlemen. Tell the missus I said hello."

"I will," Raynard said, and the two officers left the restaurant just as "Blue Christmas" emanated from the jukebox speakers.

Duston's infection in his right foot hurt more tonight than it had in recent weeks. He had to use both hands, wrapped around his right knee, to help drudge his leg forward, just to take each step.

The cold pierced through his ragged and unwashed clothes and froze his skin. His stomach growled louder than the passing cars, all spraying gray snow filled with salt and dirt.

"Settle d-d-down in there. Just a few more s-s-steps. Gardenia's is r-r-right up ahead, and I'm sure their D-D-Dumpster is full tonight."

Duston's mouth watered when thinking about the unfinished steak dinners and all the trimmings he'd find discarded inside the massive trash receptacle alongside the building. He propelled his leg to take a few steps through the slush on the sidewalk unaided by his helping hands so he could warm his exposed fingertips. He beat together the threadbare remnants of his mittens to create some warmth as Gardenia's roadside sign now came into view.

After shambling forward a few more moments, Duston entered the restaurant's curtilage and spotted the parked police cruiser. He stopped and hesitated.

"Well, w-w-we's gotsta eat. Hopefully they the friendlies."

Duston's ripped and tattered coat opened in the oceanside wind, and he turned his back to the building to shield his front side from the gust. From behind, he heard the two officers exit the restaurant and head toward their cruiser.

Duston felt relief when he turned around and saw who they were.

"Yep, it's a g-g-good thing it *is* the friendlies workin' tah-night," he mumbled.

"Duston!" Officer Taylor called from the walkway that connected the front doors to the parking lot.

Duston raised his right hand in a meek hello gesture, then crammed it inside his jacket for warmth.

"No shelter tonight?" Raynard asked as they approached.

"All f-f-full, Off-f-ficer Raynard, s-sir."

"You aren't gonna sleep out here on the wharf, are you?"

"N-n-no, sir. Just want to eat f-f-first, then might s-s-see if M-M-Ma is alone tonight."

Taylor sighed. "Would you like me to buy you dinner? No reason for you to go Dumpster-diving tonight. Plus that Dumpster"—Taylor glanced at the receptacle alongside the building—"has probably seen more sanitized days."

"Oh, n-n-no, Mr. Taylor, s-s-sir. I'd feel too bad to t-t-take youse monies. But that's mighty n-n-nice of ya."

"Alright, Duston. Listen. See that pay phone across the street in front of the Witch Museum? If you can't find anywhere to go, use that phone to call 9-1-1. This is our beat all night, so it'll be us who gets dispatched to you. We'll help you find somewhere cozy, if you run out of options."

Duston tried to smile but the cold only allowed one side of his frozen lips to rise. He nodded and gave a short embarrassed wave before turning toward the Dumpster that hopefully held tonight's dinner.

Taylor and Raynard shuttled into their patrol car, trying to keep the blustery night air outside the vehicle. Taylor started the car and activated the window defogger. They could barely decipher Duston's blue jeans as he scaled the top lip of the Dumpster through the layers of fog blanketing the glass.

Duston landed with a wet *thwap!* inside the blue Dumpster. A mound of boxes cascaded downward, like a too-tall tower of sand on a beach. Wilted lettuce, bruised fruit, and decaying fungi rolled on top of him. Pain seared through his lame foot, but he gritted his teeth and bore the pain.

He stuffed his exposed fingers into the trash heap below him and shoveled aside as many cardboard boxes as he could, scavenging for any real food—a half-eaten kid's chicken-finger platter would even suffice at this point.

On his hands and knees, Duston grazed a thick french fry underneath a mound of food-stained napkins.

"Bingo," he whispered, his breath creating a rolling mushroom cloud of moisture.

He grabbed the fry and yanked. When the fry wouldn't budge, he sifted away more debris from the pile.

And noticed his prized potato slice donned a fingernail.

"Do ya hear something?" Raynard asked.

Taylor leaned forward and wiped the remaining fog from the windshield with the cuff of his uniform jacket.

"Shit! That's Duston!" Raynard flung open the car door.

Raynard could hear Duston's stuttered screams clearer now as the two officers sprinted toward him.

"Are you hurt? I've told you to stop climbing over—"

"Th-th-th-th-there's s-s-s-s-s ..."

"Okay, slow down," Taylor said as he reached Duston. "Just tell us what happened."

Duston swallowed hard and composed himself as a spinach leaf slid off his shoulder. "I think a b-b-body's in there."

"In ... the Dumpster?"

Duston nodded.

"Why don't you take a seat in the back of the cruiser? We'll check it out," Raynard said.

The two officers exchanged a how-much-has-he-had-to-drink-tonight glance before heading toward the Dumpster. The squad car's door closed behind them, and Taylor thought, *At least he'll be warm for a few minutes.*

Raynard was the first to reach the Dumpster, when Rex called out to them from the front of Gardenia's, "Everything kosher, guys?"

Taylor quickly exhaled in disgust. "Everything's fine, Rex. Go home. Nothing to see here."

Rex was already halfway to the Dumpster. "I'm not going anywhere until I make sure whatever it is your noses have picked up isn't another dead girl."

"Fucking great," Raynard mumbled as he went head over feet into the pile of food waste.

Taylor stayed planted to intercept Rex's prying eyes. "Look, Rex. Let us do our job. Go home. I promise you'll be the first one we call if we find anything."

"Rex! Honey! Are you coming? I'm freezing!" his wife yelled from the walkway to the parking lot.

Rex turned to answer her just in time to see her stumble off the concrete path and catch her balance in the crunchy slush covering the dead grass.

"Aww, shit. Looks like I gotta babysit my fucking wife now. Goddamn drunk."

Raynard remained motionless inside the Dumpster after uncovering half of a male face underneath the rubbish. "Well, Taylor …"

"Yeah, buddy?"

"It's nothing! Just some punk's book bag," he said loud enough for Rex to hear.

Taylor shrugged, as if to say, *See? I told you so. Now off you go to take care of the grown woman you married.*

"Fine!" Rex spat, defeated. "Jen, I'm coming. Stay there!"

Rex's wife attempted to find the concrete pathway again but lost her balance and fell face-first into the snow.

"*Jennayy!* Are you okay?" he yelled. Then, in a whisper, he added, "You dumb bitch."

Taylor waited to make sure Rex and *Jennayy* were snug inside Rex's vehicle before speaking. "Find anything?"

"They gone?"

"Uh-huh."

"Call Sergeant. Tell him to get down here. Don't put this over the net."

"What'chya got?"

"Another body."

"Fuck! I knew there'd be another girl before Christmas. I could just feel it in my—"

"It's a male."

Sergeant Santana instructed Taylor to go inside Gardenia's to order Fain to close the restaurant posthaste. "This is now a crime scene" was his ending statement.

Flashing blue lights and strobing red ones littered the Salem night sky. Two rookie officers had been posted at the parking lot entrance to deny any further patrons from entering. Santana had encircled the building with yellow crime-scene tape. Every officer on duty was on scene, regardless if they were out of their assigned patrol zone or not.

"This would be a perfect time for someone to rob a bank," Taylor whispered to Raynard before he headed inside Gardenia's.

Fain met the officer at the front door. "I've already made an announcement that no more food would be served and for everyone to finish their meals as fast as possible."

"Anyone complain?"

"Just one toddler who had pooped himself."

Taylor laughed and shook his head.

"I offered everyone inside a complimentary meal for their next visit," Fain added.

"Smart man."

"Minus alcohol."

"Ha! I knew there had to be a catch," Taylor said. "Okay, so we really gotta get these people out. We aren't even touching the package until the premise is completely vacated."

"I'll get them out."

"And that means you too."

"Ah, shucks, man. Throw me a bone?" Fain asked.

"No can do, boss man."

"But it's *my* place. I can be the media-relations guy—or whatever the official term is—when the reporters arrive. I can plug Gardenia's on prime-time news as well as give them nothing about what you guys found. It's a win-win."

Taylor walked away from Fain without indulging in any further conversation.

The last patron left less than fifteen minutes later.

Raynard glanced at their cruiser and wondered how long the on-call detective planned on interviewing—interrogating—Duston.

"They don't think he killed the guy, do they?" Taylor asked Raynard.

"Nah. But they have to be thorough."

"Jeez, if anything, we could be considered alibis for Duston, since we saw him go into the Dumpster."

Raynard shook his head. "Just stay close, and stop thinkin'

so much."

Duston stood from the back seat of the cruiser and approached the two officers as the suit-wearing detective walked toward Chief McBrayer.

"Well, f-f-fellas. I'm free to go."

Taylor scowled in the detective's direction. "I hope he went easy on you."

"Oh, he w-w-was very professional. Either of you have a s-s-smoke I can bum?"

Raynard leaned inside the squad car and grabbed his pack of Smolens from the center console.

"Here ya go, pal."

Duston nodded in thanks and placed the cigarette between his lips. "What a f-f-fucking night, huh, guys?"

Just then the detectives exhumed the cadaver from the Dumpster in a not-so-graceful fashion; his body bounced like a dead fish when it hit the parking lot's asphalt. John Doe came to rest, dead eyes still open, facing the rows of police cars and emergency personnel.

"As soon as the medical examiner arrives, we can get the fuck back to a normal night," Taylor said.

Raynard opened his mouth to reply, but the sound of a dozen flapping wings made him pause.

"Nothing about tonight is normal," he finally said, searching an empty sky for what seemed to be an invisible flock of birds.

2: EN LA NOCHE

Vicki maneuvered her car into the only open space outside Hypnotic Encounters. The flashing neon sign, depicting a naked lady falling into a martini glass, illuminated the slush-covered front entrance.

She slipped on a patch of ice as she reached to open the front doors to the club and her hand slid right off, breaking one of her Pampering Pink–colored fingernails. She flapped her hand to help lessen the sting. When the pain subsided, she opened the door, and a large man in a blue shirt adorned with the strip club's girl-in-a-martini logo greeted her, the ear-piercing thump of "When Doves Cry" filling the venue as Vicki could see the profile of a girl grinding on the pole to the beat.

"ID, please," he said.

Vicki reached into her back pocket—her broken nail snagging on the fabric of her tight jeans—and retrieved her driver's license.

The bouncer glanced at it and handed it back to her. "First time here?"

"What makes you ask that?" Vicki asked, while returning the license into her pocket.

"Says you just turned twenty-one this month."

Vicki blushed. "I'm here to see my friend. She's working tonight."

"Oh? And who's that?"

"Caitlin."

The bouncer chuckled. "Look, girl. Real names mean nothing to me. In here, they only go by their stage names."

"I think she picked Aurora. She's new. Last night was her first night."

The bouncer leaned backward and folded his arms. "And it was her last night too."

Vicki furrowed her brows and shook her head. "I'm not following."

"Aurora—Caitlin—had a meltdown onstage. Froze like a two-bit whore in church. One of our regulars actually had to talk her down. Pissed off the boss. Gramps not only talked her down, he talked her right into getting dressed and quitting. We tossed out the old man on his bony, frail ass."

Vicki snickered and raised her hand to cover her mouth. The idea of Caitlin paralyzed with fear onstage for her first night as a stripper filled Vicki with childlike glee. And she had no idea why.

Vicki thanked the bouncer for the information and headed toward her car in the parking lot, the muffled sounds of Prince trapped inside the smoke-filled den for the perverted.

After she had merged with the commuter traffic, she pointed her car toward Caitlin's house in Lynn. Keeping her eyes on the road, Vicki rummaged through the messy pile of cassette tapes scattered on the passenger seat. When a red traffic light forced her to stop, she located the album she had been looking for. She inserted Side B of the white cassette into the deck and let the radio autoplay the first track.

With the intention of distracting herself until she could vent to her best friend about her blind date blowing her off, she turned the music louder and drummed on the steering wheel, while her favorite rock star serenaded her with wanting flesh for fantasy.

"So I made a fool of myself tonight. Twice!" Vicki said, when Caitlin opened the door. Without waiting for an invitation, Vicki rushed past her best friend into the living room.

"*Umm*, come in," Caitlin said, snickering at her friend's unabashed entrance, and closed the front door.

"Wait. Are your parents home?"

"Nope. They won advanced-screening tickets on the radio for some movie that doesn't come out until next week. *Johnny Dangerously* or something like that."

"Grody to the max. I hate old detective tales."

Caitlin chortled. "You mean, crime-noir?"

Vicki inserted her index finger into her mouth and made a gagging gesture. "Yeah. So boring."

"But it does have Michael Keaton in it."

"Yeah, he can be my Mr. Mom any day."

Caitlin rolled her eyes and grabbed Vicki's hand, pulling her toward her bedroom.

"When are you moving out?" Vicki asked. "You're twenty-one now. It's kind of embarrassing."

"That's why I took the job at Hypnotic Encounters. Was gonna save up to get my own place. I've been keeping my eye on some really cheap places over in Parkview."

"Well, that leads me to one of the things that happened to me tonight."

"Wait." Caitlin stopped. "Wasn't tonight your blind date with … with … What was his name?"

"Tony. Donna never told me his last name. Just told me how hot he was, used to be the star quarterback in high school, yada-yada-yada. Doesn't matter anymore anyway."

Caitlin nodded. "I can only imagine the reason why you're here instead of there is because he was a real jerk."

"I think I'd take a jerk over being stood up."

"Bastard," Caitlin said under her breath. "Come in here. Let me show you what I got today."

Caitlin dragged Vicki by the wrist into her purple-vomited-everywhere bedroom and handed her a vinyl album cover.

"My parents hate her, so I had to hide it. I played it as soon as they left." Caitlin reached across her vanity and replaced the gramophone's needle on the first song. Madonna's voice filled the room.

"So I went by to see you dance after I left the restaurant. Thought maybe a good laugh would cheer me up."

Caitlin shot her friend a fake-angry glare and then laughed. "I don't know what happened. I hit the stage for my first dance, cowboy hat and all. 'Hold Me Now' to boot."

"By the Thompson Twins? *Eww*. I *hate* that song. You should've used this song." Vicki gestured to the record player. "*This* sounds like your personal theme song. No wonder you were fired."

"I was *not* fired! And are you calling me *material?*" Caitlin teased and shot a glance at the speakers. "I don't know what happened, Vic. Stage fright? Regret? Shyness?"

"An awful song?"

Caitlin punched Vicki in the arm. "I just froze. I couldn't stop staring at that pole, like it'd have some transcendent wisdom for me or something. Some old guy snapped me out of it and put a lot of things into perspective. He was tossed, but I feel like I was saved. In more ways than one last night."

"What'd you do?"

"Chucked my cowboy hat in the trash and came home. But that's so sweet you tried to see me dance."

"I only agreed to go out with Tony to make Stepp jealous."

"Girl, you got it bad! I've never seen you have the hots for anyone this bad before. And I've known you for more than half your life."

"He's just so hot. It doesn't matter if he's paying me a compliment or yelling at me from his office about something I royally fucked up. Both make me flustered. I break out in a sweat every morning he shows up. I try to get to the office before eight so I can open it up, and I make sure I'm there to have his coffee ready."

"Isn't he married?"

"Divorced." Vicki went off into her la-la land daydreaming.

"Aren't you curious about his first wife?"

Vicki frowned. "Why?"

"To see what kind of woman he fancies?"

"And then divorces," Vicki reminded Caitlin.

"Still," Caitlin continued, "what broke them up?"

Vicki tilted her head.

"If you know what broke them up, then you'd know better how to handle him—or if you should even be dating him."

Vicki sighed loudly. "I wish he'd look at me just once like I could be more than his secretary."

"He *is* a sharp dresser."

"And he wears those suits so well. I just hate it when he

calls me Mouse."

"Mouse?"

"It's a stupid pet name he has for me. His little mouse. But I can swallow that if we were, you know, *together* together."

"Hey, in five weeks, it'll be a new year. You never know what the future holds. You want a drink?"

Caitlin reached behind her row of hanging jean jackets and retrieved a duffel bag. She opened it and removed two unopened nips of vodka. She twisted the lid off them and handed one to Vicki.

"Here's to us, Vic. That 1985 will bring me my own apartment and bring you a roll in the hay with your hunk of a boss."

The two girls took a warm swig from their small glass bottles.

The record player needle glided from track two into the beginning of the third song.

"This song is so bitchin'," Caitlin said when Madonna sang her most-current hit.

"Totally. I know who I'd like to touch me for the very first time."

The two girls *clinked* their nips together in agreement.

Smith unlocked the front door to his house. Sci-fi sound effects and giggles floated from the living room. He took a deep breath and held it before subjecting himself to the almost-violent barrage of affection he knew he was about to receive. When he felt he was ready for the chaos, he entered.

"Grandpapa!" Addie yelled and flung herself at his legs.

"Hiya, sweet pea," he replied and rubbed her shoulders.

His only grandson bolted at him and collided with Smith's stomach, an audible *Oomph!* escaping his lips. His oldest granddaughter sat on the couch, somewhat unfazed at his arrival and not removing her gaze from the *Dr. Who* episode on the television.

"We made you cookies!" Addie yelled in excitement.

"You did? Well, good thing I'm hungry!"

"Mel spilled the whole bowl of eggs and flour on the floor. It was such a mess!" his grandson added.

"Shut up, Shaun. You're such a tattletale."

"Okay, Melissa," Smith said. "That's enough. Don't talk to your brother like that."

"Little twerp," she whispered before returning her attention to the television.

"So where are these cookies?" Smith asked his two grandkids still attached to his legs.

Addie took his hand and led him toward the kitchen. "C'mon, Grandpapa. In here!"

"Isn't it too late for you guys to still be up?"

"Well ..." Addie said, "I already had *my* beauty rest when I took a nap today. I think Mel could use some beauty rest too!"

"I heard that!" Melissa yelled from the other room.

Smith reached for the cellophane-wrapped plate of cookies on the table.

"Grandpapa? Why are your fingers so dirty?" Shaun asked.

Smith glanced at his hands and saw Blind-Date Guy's dried blood trapped underneath his fingernails and caked into the wrinkles of all his knuckles. "Let me just wash my hands before I touch any food. Did you guys wash your hands before you made the food?"

"*Uh-huh.* Grandma made us."

Smith scrubbed the blood from his skin under the running sink faucet, more to race against Wynn entering the room and seeing his hands than for any sanitary purposes.

Addie and Shaun each grabbed a cookie and handed both to Smith.

"Well, thank you."

Addie curtsied in acknowledgment of her grandfather's gratitude.

Smith bent to meet their faces. "You guys don't really like *Dr. Who*, do you?"

Addie shook her head. "Mel picked it."

"At least it wasn't stupid *Grease* again," Shaun added.

"How about we go back in there and pick something we all like?"

Smith's two grandchildren nodded, eyes wide, and grabbed just enough cookies for themselves, leaving Melissa's share resting on the plate.

"The committee has deliberated and unanimously agreed," Smith announced when he entered the living room. "*Dr. Who* has been voted off the tube to make way for something the young'ins might like instead."

"Who's the committee?" Melissa asked with a sourpuss scowl.

"Me and the kids."

"Fine. Whatever. I'm going to the basement," Melissa retorted and stormed from the room.

No one spoke as she barreled past her brother and sister.

"You know what? She's getting too old for these sleepovers," Wynn said, joining the rest of them in the living room. "She's hitting the age where she'd rather be at the mall with her friends on the weekends than hanging out with her younger siblings and two old farts like us."

Smith took his first bite of cookie and laughed. "*Old farts.* That certainly describes us, all right."

"Your farts are old!" Addie said, and Shaun giggled.

Smith approached the large cable box sitting on top of the television. "C'mon, kids. Go sit with Grandma. Let's see what's on."

Addie and Shaun snuggled on either side of Wynn with their cookies, and Smith pushed the row of buttons in order, navigating through the channels.

"There! That! That!" Addie yelled.

Smith clicked the button for the next channel. His reflexes to stop moved slower than his repetitive motion.

"No, Grandpapa! Go back!"

Smith pushed the previous tab–like button. "This?"

Both grandkids nodded.

Smith walked across the living room toward the couch with the opening theme song to *Fraggle Rock* entering its final chorus behind him.

Melissa reached the makeshift bedroom in the finished basement. Her grandparents had assembled three cots that surrounded her grandfather's pool table, which sat dead center in the room. She flung herself on her cot and grabbed for her Walkman. After placing the foam headphones over her ears, she pressed Play. She closed her eyes and let the room disappear underneath the magical sounds of Wham! singing about never dancing again after a night of infidelity.

Melissa rocked her head back and forth on her pillow to the beat. Just as the world had finally disappeared and she had forgotten that she was spending another lame weekend with her grandparents instead of playing tonsil hockey with Graham, someone ripped her headphones from her ears. She opened her eyes, ready to shove whichever of her two younger siblings had the gall to act so immature and to interrupt the dreamy sounds of her favorite band.

The room was empty.

Then a hand grazed Melissa's stomach, and she jumped clear out of her cot, almost landing on the pool table.

"Oh, it's you. You have to stop doing that to me. You're seriously gonna give me a heart attack one day."

"You know what's funny? Someone else has been saying something like that to me for almost forty years now." The witch stepped forward from the shadows and raised her black veil to expose her face. "Come. Sit, child. I can sense frustration in you."

"Who are you? Yoda?"

The witch furrowed her brows. "I do not know this Yoda."

Melissa snickered at her friend's lack of understanding pop-culture references.

Her friend had been in her life for as long as Melissa could remember, going back to toddlerhood. In fact, she can't even remember a time when Pale Witch—Melissa didn't know her real name—wasn't around. She knew her friend hadn't shown herself to Melissa's siblings or parents; Melissa liked to think of her friend as her own childhood imaginary friend, one who just so happened to not-be-so imaginary. It wasn't until Melissa had become interested in Salem's deeper history and folklore—and began studying Wicca after school at Madam Hapney's shop on Pickering Wharf—when her friend had allowed Melissa to flip through the Mushroom Cult book.

Melissa sat up on her cot, the music of Wham! sounding distant and tinny as George Michael's voice came from the discarded headphones.

"Not in the mood to partake in wholesome family time?" Pale Witch asked, running her decrepit finger along one leg of Melissa's jeans.

"They're so retarded. I hate it here. But Dad said they won't be around much longer and that I should spend as much time with them as possible now, while they're still alive."

"You'd rather be somewhere else?"

Melissa reached for her Walkman to stop the music. "Anywhere but here."

Pale Witch stood and towered over Melissa. "Would you like to accompany me tonight? I have business on the other side of town."

Melissa jumped up from the cot. "Really? You'd let me tag along?"

Pale Witch nodded.

"And what are we gonna do?"

"We have to keep the promise of a favor. And I think it's time you met the vultures."

Melissa slipped on her Keds and grabbed her winter jacket. "What if someone comes to check on me? Or it's time to put Addie and Shaun to bed? I'll be in deep shit not only with my grandparents but with my dad too."

"Don't worry about that. It'll all be taken care of. You're in no jeopardy of being caught."

"Wait. How do we get there? Do you drive or something?"

Pale Witch shushed her and stepped forward. Holding the

antique book in her left hand—pulled out of nowhere—she spread the fingers on her right hand and placed it over Melissa's face, like a grotesque spider hugging a larger prey.

A flash of light illuminated the basement, leaving the room void of anyone—human or ghoul.

"Did you hear that?" Wynn asked.

"Yeah. It sounded like a *pop*, … like a firecracker went off downstairs," Smith replied. "I'll go make sure Mel is okay."

Smith stood from the couch, placed his hands on his lower back and stretched backward, and then headed for the staircase leading to the basement. He descended the stairs one at a time, using the handrail for balance. When he turned the corner into the basement, he saw Melissa's feet sticking out from behind the obstructed view of the pool table.

"Melissa?"

No answer.

"Melissa?"

No answer.

He stepped forward to round the corner of the pool table.

"Mel?"

No answer.

Smith sighed, half in relief and half in slight annoyance at the typical teenage behavior. He stood and watched his granddaughter, her eyes closed and listening to her Walkman. He wasn't sure if she was sleeping, and, if she was, he didn't know if he should turn off her music. Was listening to such horrid music that loud while asleep damaging to a young person's eardrums?

Smith decided to leave her be and headed back upstairs. When he entered the living room, *Fraggle Rock* had ended, and he approached the cable box.

"Alright, children. It's time for your grandpapa to watch his news."

Addie and Shaun grumbled in protest.

"Go downstairs and get in your pajamas," Wynn said. "I'll make you some hot milk, and you can have one more cookie before bed."

The kids squealed in excitement and bolted for the staircase.

"Be quiet!" Smith yelled. "Your sister is down there sleeping!"

Smith and Wynn heard pitter-patter noises as the kids raced down the staircase. They returned like a tornado, even before Smith could press the Channel 5 tab on the cable box. The channel was in a commercial break, and Smith ambled to his favorite La-Z-Boy.

Before he reached the burnt-orange recliner, he heard a sampled beat with what sounded like talk-singing—something the kids called "rap."

"*Ooh! Ooh!* I wanna see this movie!" Shaun said and clapped his hands once.

Smith placed both hands on the recliner's armrests and eased himself into the cushions. His gaze fell upon the television screen, and he saw a group of inner-city youths dressed as if spray-paint cans had exploded all over their clothes, dancing and flipping and spinning on their backs, like an overturned turtle in a gale.

"What is this crap?" Smith asked, pointing at the screen.

"Dear!" Wynn scolded.

"It's not crap, Grandpapa. It's a break-dancing movie."

Smith reached for his pack of Smolens. "Whatever happened to the good ole-fashion jazz movies?"

Wynn chuckled. "There never were any good jazz movies."

"Says you," Smith retorted as the movie trailer ended. "And what on God's green Earth is an electric boogaloo?"

"It's, like, dancing or something."

"Well, you can ask your dad to take you to that," Smith said to his grandson. "No way you're catching me at the theater, watching something called *Breakin' 2: Electric Boogaloo*. And it's a sequel. Have you even seen the first one, Shaun?"

Addie rolled her eyes. "Watches it every day."

"I think it's time for that warm milk and cookies," Wynn said to the kids, "before your grandfather starts a fight with someone over a silly dancing movie."

"Love you too, hon."

Wynn glanced back and winked at her husband.

The commercials ended—the number of adverts for children's toys became a constant reminder that the most wonderful time of the year had its hand on all parents' shoulders—and the news resumed. Before Smith tuned out the hubbub coming from the kitchen, he heard Addie ask if she could drink her warm milk from her favorite mug.

He knew in a few moments his Top Gun For Hire mug would be full of warm milk, and the baby of the family would be sipping gleefully. He just hoped she couldn't taste the decades of whiskey that mug had held.

Smith heard Wynn speaking—"I bought that mug for Grandpapa way before we were even boyfriend and girlfriend"—and returned his attention to the nightly news.

"Police are not revealing the identity of a male found in a Dumpster on Gardenia's Family Restaurant's property earlier this evening ..."

Melissa felt a sensation as if her solar plexus had imploded and then burst outward with unmeasurable force. She imagined it was probably how the big bang may have felt, if experienced by a human. Faster than she could say "Careless Whisper," she had been transported from her grandparents' basement to now standing in a white room with a metal table. As soon as the shock of the jaunt dissipated, she realized a cadaver rested on the metal table. "W-Where are we?"

Pale Witch walked halfway around the table, stopping at the corpse's foot and peeking at the tag hanging off his big toe. "City morgue."

"Who is that?"

The witch released the tag, letting it swing from the digit. "Says his name is Anthony Birch, age twenty-three. Does that ring a bell?"

Melissa shook her head.

"I'd assume not. Freshmen don't ever fraternize with adult men, do they?" Pale Witch shot Melissa an accusatory glare.

"I-I don't know what you're implying, but—"

"Last time I checked, your beau is college-graduate age. In fact, I think a Mr. Graham Shiavo is old enough to go to jail, if anyone were to find out about you two, that is."

Melissa shook her head, confused why her childhood *friend* was treating her like this—it was the first time the witch had ever been mean.

"I'd like you to meet some of my friends," Pale Witch said, her tone still scolding the young teenager.

Melissa heard low guttural and raspy breathing behind her. And it sounded like more than one *thing* was panting. Her feet remained planted where she stood, her knees wobbled, and she couldn't will herself to turn around.

A hand touched her shoulder, and she spun around, looking straight into the eyes of four female ghouls, faces half rotting and wounds visible, like a roadmap of the trauma that had originally sent them to their deaths. Melissa took a step backward toward the slab holding the dead Tony Birch.

"Oh, knock it off, girls. Don't worry, Mel. They're harmless. Unless I don't want them to be, that is."

"What are they?" Melissa extended her pointer finger at one of the ghouls and tried to poke it, like someone not wanting to touch slime but whose curiosity wins over her disgust.

"They are my generals in the Mushroom Cult. Mel, meet Cyana, Pum'kin, Nikki, and Candy."

Melissa spun her head to look at her friend. "You mean, that's a real thing?"

"In the flesh, in front of you."

"All these years, I just thought that was some spooky story you had created for me."

Pale Witch lifted the book from her side and placed it on the metal table next to Tony's leg. "This book isn't just filled with fairy tales and fables. This is the Mushroom Cult book. It contains everything that keeps me alive, keeps my coven growing, keeps the vultures doing my bidding, and, most important, holds the riddle for how I can attain immortality. I was close once—or so I thought. That snot-nosed rug rat didn't need to die, after all. And my power waned because of my miscalculations, and it took years for me to regain my strength. But that was a long time ago, and no new potential prospects have surfaced throughout the years. Until now."

"All snuggled like bugs," Wynn said as she crawled between the sheets next to Smith.

"Everyone asleep?"

"Out cold. Mel didn't stir either."

"Did she still have her headphones on?"

"Yep. I turned off the music but left them on her head."

"I dunno, Wynn. I think maybe we should cut back on these weekend excursions to Grandma's house. The kids are getting older. It's apparent Mel wants to be here as much as I want to see that *Electric Boogaloo* movie. They aren't babies anymore."

"I know, but it's only one weekend every few months. I don't get to see them otherwise. Plus it gives Travis and Gwen a weekend to do grown-up stuff."

"We never got to do grown-up stuff when Travis was little."

"That's because you dragged me from where we are both from to here."

"Touché. I'm gonna turn out the light."

"I'll do it. I want to read a bit before going to sleep," Wynn said and reached for her hardcover copy of Stephen King's *The Talisman* from the nightstand.

Smith rolled over, facing the far wall, and hoped Anya would come through with his request. By this time tomorrow night, he wanted to have the first reborn member of his own personal Mushroom Cult.

I'll have to come up with a different name for my coven, he thought as he drifted off to sleep.

Pale Witch slammed the book shut, and Melissa startled in fright.

"So they're witches? Like you?"

"Oh, child, you have so much to learn. Let's just say they're part of the hive mind. Ghouls who exist only to please me. Harmless to you. Friends even."

Melissa only slightly relaxed, then nervously chuckled. "Hi. Nice to meet you."

Candy gurgled something unintelligible.

"Don't even try. Think of them as newborns," Pale Witch said. "But here's the real reason we are here. ... Him." The witch looked at Blind-Date-and-Dead Tony. "Would you like to see some real witchery?"

Melissa nodded.

"And not that phony shit Madam Hapney has sold to you either," she added.

"How did you know—"

The witch pointed to her temple. "Because I'm smaaaaaart."

The four ghouls stepped forward and made a circle around Tony's corpse.

"Pum'kin, would you like to do the honors tonight?"

The ghoul nodded and rocked back and forth, shifting her weight from her right foot to her left foot and back again. Pum'kin hummed something that sounded like a chant but without any real or cohesive words.

"Tonight is a big night, girls!" Pale Witch said. "Tonight the vultures will turn a male specimen for the first time. Tonight a scum of the earth will be cleansed and reborn. Resurrected.

And this gift"—the witch directed her gaze right at Melissa—"is at the request of Detective Smith. For he wants to also build a grand army of ghouls."

Melissa took a step backward. "What?"

"Oh, you didn't know? Your grandpapa is the Wharf Killer. Your grandpapa has been collecting girls for me for almost forty years. Your grandpapa was in cahoots with the Boulevard Killer from the forties back in Vegas. Why do you think your grandparents moved to Salem and left their family behind? They fled. They *raaaaaan*. You are a direct descendent of the most prolific curator I have ever had the pleasure of working with." Pale Witch took a step forward, and Melissa cowered. "And that is why you'll bring me the ultimate prize."

"Grandpapa knows about you?"

"You'll bring me the coveted virgin that'll make me immortal," the witch continued. "I found her in the most ironic of places. I made a fatal mistake decades ago but not this time. This time I knew it was her the moment I smelled her."

"I-I don't even know what you are talking about."

Pale Witch flew across the table—above the deceased Tony—and opened her mouth to reveal three rows of fangs. She landed so close to Melissa that the witch's black dress tickled Melissa's exposed skin.

"You stupid little cunt. I've been nurturing and prepping you since you were an infant. Of course you know what I'm talking about. You've always known. You've always known there would be a payback time. Who do you think took care of the bullies on the playground? Who do you think flipped that car your ex-boyfriend was in after he broke your heart? Who do you think burned down that McDonald's when they didn't have the fucking Happy Meal toy you wanted? You think that was all coincidence? I have been sweeping away people and places who have wronged you your whole life. Now all I ask is one simple fucking favor, and you pretend like you have no idea what I'm talking about."

Melissa choked on the witch's rotting breath, and she took a trembling step backward to distance herself from the unexpected anger. Melissa wrung her hands together so tightly she thought she had drawn blood and realized she needed to pretend like she knew what Pale Witch was talking about, and hopefully that would lead her down the path of *actually knowing* what Anya was talking about. "You're right. I'm sorry. I didn't mean to be so ungrateful."

"That's better. That's the nice little girl I always knew you were."

Melissa relaxed, thinking she had thwarted her friend's temper.

"Vicki. Her name is Vicki. She's Detective Stepp's secretary. I don't know how or why she's the Chosen One, but the moment I walked into his office this week to get him interested in investigating your grandpapa as the Wharf Killer, I—"

"You did *what?*"

"Oh, child. Your grandfather needs a successor, and I need someone to continue feeding the Mushroom Cult's ranks. Smith won't be around much longer, and I can't have him check out without having his understudy in place and ready to go."

Melissa had to dig deep to find the courage to ask the next question. "Was my grandfather someone's … understudy?"

"A long time ago, yes. A Mr. George Covington. Now it's time for Smith to pass the torch, and we both picked Detective Stepp. Who would've known his lily-white secretary would also prove to be the one to bring me immortality?"

Admitting to herself that she still didn't really understand anything being said, Melissa was just happy to have settled Pale Witch's rage for the time being.

"If you help me"—the witch held up the book—"I'll share some of the Mushroom Cult's deepest secrets. Secrets that will wow even Madam Hapney and her clan of two-bit psychics on the wharf."

Melissa licked her lips as she looked at the metal and maroon leather-bound book.

"Alright, let's do it."

The witch patted Melissa's hand. "That's a good girl. But first, let's finish our business here." Pale Witch pulled her black veil over her pale face, like a shield from what's to come. "Pum'kin, call the vultures."

Melissa screamed when the morgue's window shattered, and black feathers and the flapping wings of birds of prey filled the room.

3: APPROACH AND RECEDE

Melissa awoke the next morning snug in her cot. Her headphones still rested over her ears, but the Walkman had either run out of battery power at some point during the night or someone had shut it off for her. She rubbed the slumber boogers from her eyes and looked at her two sleeping siblings. She didn't know whether she felt excited or terrified about meeting the results of last night's ritual in the morgue face-to-face. Would Tony look and act the same way the female ghouls did? Or would he have a completely different set of attributes altogether?

Then her thoughts drifted to the woman who Anya wanted Melissa to befriend—some secretary named Vicki. But how would Melissa get an adult to hang out with a high-school freshman?

Her grandparents were already awake and bustling around upstairs. She grinned when she thought about the newfound respect she now had for her grandfather—him being the Wharf Killer and wanting his own army of ghouls.

How wickedly wicked, she thought.

She scooted down her covers with her legs and crept off the cot to not wake Addie and Shaun. An old piece of parchment fluttered to the floor from the creases of her blanket. Melissa noticed old calligraphy-style writing adorned the paper and bent to retrieve it from the floor. It felt brittle, and she was afraid it would crumble if she held it too tightly, like a dead leaf in late autumn.

Gingerly picking up the paper, she could decipher the writing better. In black-ink cursive, Pale Witch reassured Melissa a whole unexplored world awaited her, if she would help her friend in her quest. At the bottom of the page, the witch had ended her correspondence with *In an act of good faith, I have given you a deposit of sorts. Turn over.*

Melissa flipped the parchment, and the other side contained a string of words she did not recognize; she didn't even recognize what language the words were written in. At the bottom of the small foreign-tongued paragraph, Pale Witch had scribbled *Don't say these aloud unless you mean it. You'll know what they're for when the time comes.*

Addie stirred and yawned.

Melissa jammed the parchment into her overnight bag, between her clothes for today and her makeup bag.

"Good morning, Mel."

"It sure is," Melissa answered and headed up the stairs, whistling the melody of the chorus to "Wake Me Up Before You Go-Go" and leaving her baby sister with a dumbfounded look on her face.

Vicki had just spread the cream cheese on her bagel when the TV news anchor spoke. The butter knife fell from her grasp. She rose from her kitchen table, zombielike—numb of all feeling and unknowing of her actions. She finally swallowed to break the catatonia her body had involuntarily entered when hearing the report of a body found at Gardenia's last night.

Vicki pointed at the small screen with a shaking finger, as if the reporter could see her. The blood drained from Vicki's face when the television screen cut to a picture of the victim. His name was posted in an orange graphics bar underneath the photo of him, alive and kicking, from his high-school football days.

Tony Birch.

The anchor continued to report how police believe Tony had been slain before being discarded into the Dumpster at Gardenia's last night. Then an eight-hundred number scrolled along the bottom of the screen—a number the Salem Police had obtained for any tips from citizens regarding the Wharf Killer's identity. The reporter stressed how the police are not ready to jump to conclusions that Tony Birch is another victim of the Wharf Killer's spree, but they aren't ruling it out either—until now only females needed to be frightened at night.

Vicki ran to her telephone hanging on the kitchen wall, disregarding her uneaten breakfast, and called Caitlin.

Vicki didn't wait for Caitlin to say hello before she spoke. "Caitlin, we need to meet. Now. It's super-fucking-important."

"Who's this?"

Vicki slapped her forehead with her palm. "Sorry, Mrs. O'Keeffe. I figured Caitlin would pick up. It's Vicki."

"I'll get her for you."

Vicki heard a twinge of disgust in Mrs. O'Keeffe's voice for being cussed at this early in the day.

"What's up, Vick-O-Rama?" Caitlin greeted her friend when she got to the phone.

"I gotta see you. It's about last night. Something about my blind date. Are you free for lunch?"

"*Um*, let me check to make sure Mom doesn't—"

"I'm totally freaking out, Cait. Please."

"Can't you just tell me over the phone?"

"I'm too freaked out to be alone right now."

"Yikes. Okay, girlie. Meet me at Liberty Tree in an hour. We'll grab lunch."

Vicki replaced the receiver on the cradle and headed to the shower. Her hands were still shaking forty-five minutes later when she pulled out of her driveway and headed to the mall.

Melissa grabbed her grandfather's TOP GUN FOR HIRE mug from the drying rack as the Mr. Coffee percolated its warm black existence. She drummed her fingertips on the counter and glanced at the sun-shaped clock twice.

"Are you the only one up yet?" Smith asked, entering the kitchen in his Eeyore pajamas he only wore when Addie slept over—his last year's Christmas present from his youngest granddaughter.

"Yep."

"You went to bed early last night. Didn't you want to see what happened last night on *Fraggle Rock*?"

Melissa smirked and nudged her grandfather in the arm. "You sly devil, you."

Smith donned his poker face and eyed his granddaughter. "Excuse me?"

The Mr. Coffee released its last drip into the pot, and Melissa filled her grandfather's mug to the top. Without adding milk or sugar, she grabbed the mug with both hands and took a sip—the temperature not seeming to bother her lips.

"She told me who you really are. And I wonder who else knows. Does Grandma know?"

"Who told you what? And what does Grandma know … or not know? Mel, what are you talking about? You feel okay?"

Melissa sat at the floral-printed Formica-topped table and swiveled the yellow-cushioned chair to face him. "*She.* Your friend. At least I thought she was only *my* friend—a childhood imaginary friend who turned out to be real—but it seems you've been in cahoots with her for a long, long time."

Smith wrung his hands together and rubbed the back of his neck. Anger welled in him, but he couldn't dam it. "Listen, kid. I don't know what you're talking about, but speaking such nonsense like this is really fucking—"

"Whoa! Grandpapa, I've never heard you talk like this before. Did I hit a nerve or something?"

Smith grabbed the other chair and flung it out enough so he could sit across from his granddaughter. He leaned forward, peered into her eyes with a cold stare, and pointed a finger at her chest.

"I don't know if you think you're being funny or if you're just a stupid ninny, but knock it off now. Whatever game you think you're playing with me—"

Wynn entered the kitchen, her slippers making a *swish-swoosh* sound with every step.

"Good morning, Mel. Sleep okay?"

"Like a rock."

"Do you want a bagel and cream cheese? Or I can make waffles."

Melissa locked her gaze on Smith's face. "I'm just gonna have my coffee, Grandma. Thanks though."

Wynn turned her back to the kitchen to open the refrigerator.

Melissa leaned forward, closer to her grandfather, and mouthed *She doesn't know about you!*

Smith pursed his lips and slid his hands back and forth on his Eeyore pajama pants.

Wynn closed the refrigerator, holding a small container of half-and-half. She opened the cabinet above the toaster and removed a *Wizard of Oz* promotional coffee mug—also a Christmas gift—and filled the cup.

Melissa shook her head at how long it took for her grandmother to pour a cup of coffee and to get the fuck out of the kitchen so her and the Wharf Killer could continue their palaver. Every move Wynn made grated on Melissa's nerves.

"How about some Saturday morning cartoons while we have our coffee?" Wynn suggested and approached the small kitchen television.

"No!" both Smith and Melissa said in unison.

Wynn took a step backward and placed a hand on her chest. "Well, excuse me. I guess I'll leave you two to it and go take a shower."

Melissa and Smith remained silent until they heard Wynn closing the en suite bathroom door in the master bedroom. Then Smith scowled, and he stared at Melissa. "Start talking."

"I don't know what her name is or if she has a name at all. When I was a kid and talked about her, Mom would tell me that she was just my imaginary friend. But she isn't imaginary. She has never gone away. She's some sort of scary fairy godmother who has looked out for me my whole life."

Smith vigorously rubbed his face in anxiety and

frustration—one of his worst fears realized. "Anya."

"Huh?" Melissa asked.

"Her name is Anya."

"Ha!" Melissa stood from her chair, knocking it into the television stand behind her. "I knew it!"

"Just hush. Calm down. She's not any kind of fairy godmother. Trust me on that."

Melissa sat down and wrapped her fingers around the handle of the mug. "She brought me to see a dead body last night and then told me that you are the Wharf Killer. Afterward I met some of her friends, and then I saw vultures—"

"Mel, hold on. I have to ask you some serious questions. I need you to drop the tough-girl act for a moment and answer me. Okay?"

Melissa nodded.

"Be careful what you say. She hears everything."

Smith didn't even know where to start with his interrogation. There were just so many things Melissa might know—so many awful, awful things.

Liberty Tree Mall burst at the seams with Christmas shoppers. Large bright banners adorned almost every business, advertising their holiday deals. The Muzak piped a continuous stream of poorly reconstructed classic Christmas carols through the mall speaker system.

Vicki unwrapped her crunchy taco and scoffed at the amount of lettuce and grated cheese that had fallen from the shell during transport from the Taco Bell storefront to an available table in the food court.

"Alright, we're here. Spill the beans," Caitlin said and bit into her soft taco.

"I feel better already, just being out in public and with someone." Vicki took a long sip of her Tab. "Did you see the news this morning?"

"Who watches the news? Lame! Who are you, my dad?"

Vicki set her cup on the table and shook her head. "Dammit, Caitlin. When are you gonna grow up? For Christ's sake, you got a job as a stripper … a *stripper* … so you could afford to get your own place! And you quit that job after one night. Some of us are working to be actual adults." Vicki's outburst surprised even herself.

Caitlin unwrapped her second taco without making eye contact with Vicki and used the only ammunition she had against her best friend's tirade. "Look who's talking. At least I'm not a virgin at twenty-one."

Vicki slammed her taco onto the table. "That is not fair, nor relevant. I'm the one having the crisis here. They found my blind date in a Dumpster next to Gardenia's. They think he's a victim of the Wharf Killer."

"Shut. Up!" Caitlin replied. "Are you"—she leaned in closer—"fucking kidding me?"

"The morning news announced his name and showed his high-school jock photo. It was him. *My* fucking blind date. Killed, … mutilated in the parking lot."

"Now I know why you're freaking out."

"That's not all of it. You know how I know it was the Wharf Killer? Because he stopped and talked to me."

"Wait. What?" Caitlin asked, taking a bite of the taco as lettuce and shredded cheese tumbled onto the table.

"Cait, this is no joke. I mean, I could've died last night. Ever since I saw the news this morning, all I keep thinking about is that I might be dead too if so many people hadn't been around."

"What did the killer say to you?"

"Well, that's the even freakier part. He asked to bum a smoke, and, when I told him I didn't have one, he then told me that he knew I had bought a pack that day and that I was waiting for a blind date *and* that we had a new client come into the office yesterday morning. I didn't connect the dots last night until the news this morning. He knew about the new client because she came in to talk to Stepp about the Wharf Killer. He knew that because he *is* the killer."

"Do you remember everything about the way he looked?"

"Pretty much."

"We need to go to the police right now so you can give them a—"

"Hey, ladies!" a teenager said as he forced himself onto Caitlin's chair.

Caitlin had to slide over to share the seat with her younger brother. She used her right leg as a crutch to not fall off the side while their shoulders pressed against each other.

"Aren't you supposed to be working?" Caitlin asked. "We're kinda having girl's time right now, if you don't mind."

"I'm on lunch break. And, no, I don't mind at all," Benji said and smiled at Vicki. "How you doin', girl?"

Vicki rolled her eyes at Caitlin's brother's pathetic attempt at flirting.

"Well, you can't eat with us," Caitlin said.

"C'mon, Cait. Not a single table is free, and I hate eating in the breakroom. The old ladies I work with smell like mothballs. Gross!"

"Maybe he should know too," Vicki said.

"*Ooh*, I get to hear some girl gossip? Let me grab some

food first, and I'll be right back."

Benji maneuvered through the gaggle of hungry Christmas shoppers toward a Chinese food storefront with a long line, then veered toward McDonald's.

"I think we should go right to the police station from here," Caitlin continued.

"My only reservation with that is, it might conflict with Stepp's investigation. I don't want to step—no pun intended— on his toes or do anything that looks like I'm undermining him or going over his head. He was hired by the Wharf Killer's granddaughter, Eva Smith."

"Admit it, Vicki. You're more afraid to piss him off, ruining any chance of getting into his pants, than you are of actually jeopardizing your job."

Vicki giggled and shook her arm to adjust her jelly bracelets.

Caitlin took a sip of her Tab. "Okay. Well, my suggestion is, call your boss right now and ask to meet with him and tell him everything. Then at least the information is no longer on your shoulders, and he can decide if the police should be involved. Plus that gives you two some off-the-clock alone time. Personally I don't think that's the ethical thing to do. I'd go straight to the cops. But I also understand the predicament you're in."

Vicki nodded. She hadn't realized her heart rate had increased when Caitlin had suggested Vicki meet Stepp outside of the workplace. She reached for a hot sauce packet and noticed her hands shaking.

"You okay?" Caitlin asked, her gaze fixated on the trembling sauce packet.

"I don't know if I'm more terrified about what happened last night or about calling Stepp on a weekend to ask to meet with him."

"Girl, it's not like you're asking him out on a date. Plus, something like this might bring you two closer."

"I'm back. Miss me?" Benji asked and turned to the family sitting at the next table, pointing at an empty chair. "You using this?"

The father at the table shook his head, and Benji slid the empty chair to his sister's and Vicki's table.

"I think I'll call him now," Vicki said. "Before I lose my nerve."

"Call who?" Benji asked with a twinge of nervous jealousy.

"Her boss," Caitlin answered.

Benji nodded in relief—he didn't think that schmuck was any competition—and freed his Big Mac from its Styrofoam clamshell container.

"Isn't there a pay phone near Marshall's?"

"If you need a phone, I can let you use the one in our back room," Benji offered, hoping to score extra bonus points.

"Your boss won't mind? Sounds like that's gotta be some kind of store policy violation."

"He's running around the sales floor like a chicken with its head cut off. He won't even notice. He's such a dweeb. Plus, if I get caught, it'd be worth it, helping you out."

Caitlin rolled her eyes. "Put that thing away before you hurt someone with it, Romeo."

Vicki giggled, and Benji mumbled, "I hate you, Cait."

"Well, finish up. I don't think you should be sitting on this information," Caitlin suggested.

The trio scarfed their lunches and tossed their trash into the nearest waste bin and headed toward Anne & Hope at the far end of the mall.

"I'm gonna come too, if that's all right," Caitlin said.

Vicki nodded. "Yeah, I might need you there for moral support."

"Would anyone like to tell me what's going on?" Benji asked. "Since I am sticking out my future-in-retail-career neck for you."

"Vicki thinks the Wharf Killer harassed her last night at Gardenia's and killed her blind date."

Benji stopped walking. "No fucking shit! That's so fucking gnarly. Mad props!"

"This isn't a joke."

"You're right. I just, never in my wildest dreams, thought *that* was what you were going to say. I mean, this is like *huuuuuge*. Vic, you could be a fucking hero if you're the one who blows his identity. I even think the cops have put a bounty on his head."

They reached the center atrium, where a large white tree made from ceramic tiles adorned the floor of the mall's main intersection. A young boy, running as fast as he could, tripped and launched headlong into all three of them and landed on his face.

"Oh, jeez. I'm so sorry," Vicki said as she reached down to pick up the boy from the floor. "Are you okay?"

He nodded and looked behind him.

Vicki followed his gaze and saw someone who must be his grandmother, doing her best impression of a run to get to the boy at their feet.

"Are you sure you're okay?" Caitlin asked.

The boy then grabbed his left knee and winced without

answering her. They stayed for the few moments it took for the hobbling woman to reach the boy, apologized just to be respectful, and turned right toward Anne & Hope—Liberty Tree's most-beloved anchor department store. Navigating through the swarms of bustling and frantic shoppers attempting to locate that one last *Transformers* Bumblebee or Optimus Prime action figure, the trio entered Benji's workplace.

Benji led his sister and her best friend toward the back room. "Stay here a sec." Benji opened the Employees Only door and peeked inside the room. "Okay, all clear. If anyone on the management team comes back here, I'll tell them that you're my sister and that you're my girlfriend and that there's an emergency at home."

Vicki chortled. "You wish, flyboy."

The girls followed Benji to the red telephone sitting on a desk blanketed by scattered papers, spreadsheets, sales reports, and unreviewed seasonal employee applications.

Vicki took a deep breath and exhaled as she shook her wrist to use gravity to slide her jelly bracelets toward her elbow before picking up the receiver. She dialed her boss's home phone number she had memorized, and her stomach flipped when she heard the first ring.

"Yello?" a voice asked, scratchy and gruff.

"Mr. Stepp?"

"*Hmm?*"

"Oh, my God. Did I wake you? I'm so wicked sorry."

"Mouse?" Stepp cleared his throat. "Yeah, but it's okay. Had a late night. What time is it?"

Vicki glanced at her Swatch watch. "Just past noon."

"Jesus. Is everything okay?"

"I was wondering if, ... *um*, you might, ... *um*, well, if you could or had the ability to, and you weren't busy, to maybe—"

Caitlin shoved Vicki in the shoulder blade in a *get on with it* gesture.

Vicki closed her eyes to summon the courage and blurted out, "Are you available to meet with me today?" She exhaled the rest of the air in her lungs, and her heart thumped in her eardrums. "I'm sorry to call and bother you, but it's super-duper important. It's about the Wharf Killer."

Vicki heard Stepp rustling around.

After a moment of silence, Stepp asked slowly, "What about the Wharf Killer?"

"I think, ... I think I know who he is. Or at least what he looks like."

"Vic, not to burst your pretty little bubble, but I know what he looks like. I was given a recent Polaroid of him. I was also told his name. My new client gave me everything at our first appointment yesterday morning."

"I-I'm sorry to have bothered you. I'll see you Monday morning," Vicki finished with clear disappointment in her voice.

She removed the receiver from her ear and reached to replace it on the cradle when she heard her boss's voice again.

"Vic, wait!"

Vicki returned the receiver to her ear so fast that she misjudged and smashed its plastic into her temple. "I'm here!"

"I'd like to know how *you* got this information."

"Have you heard about the body found outside Gardenia's last night?"

"No," he replied, and she heard him turn on his television.

"The cops found a dead body in the Dumpster. It was my blind date. Remember how I told you about that and how you said blind dates never work? Well, it was his body they found, and then the Wharf Killer met me out front. He knew way too much about me. I think he's been stalking me."

"His name is Smith."

Vicki rolled her eyes. "Well, that narrows it down."

"Todd Smith. Although Eva said he uses Arbuckle as a last-name alias sometimes."

Vicki recalled Eva's appearance as soon as Stepp mentioned her name. Vicki remembered thinking how Eva's skin was so blemish free that the woman looked like an animated mannequin—almost *House of Wax* fake.

"I was thinking of going to the police with his description but—"

"Don't you dare even think of doing anything of the kind. This is my fucking case, and I have more information on Smith than the cops even do. I am two steps ahead of them, and I will be the one who brings him down. Not some rootin'-tootin' rookie hotshot."

Vicki giggled. "You said *rootin'-tootin'*."

Stepp laughed. "See? You get me all worked up, and who knows what's gonna come flying out of my mouth."

Vicki blushed and gripped the receiver tighter. "So can we meet today, or do you want to wait until Monday?" She crossed her fingers.

"Let's meet in an hour. There's a new coffee shop at Redman's Place that I've been dying to try."

Vicki hopped once onto her tiptoes and made a victorious fist with her free hand. "Sure. Sounds great. I'm in Danvers now, so I can make it to Parkview in time. Which coffee shop is it?"

"Sweet Insani-Tea."

After they exchanged good bye pleasantries, Vicki spun to face Caitlin and her brother.

"Sounds like everything is falling into place," Caitlin said.

"I'd love to stay and hang some more, but, you know, destiny awaits."

"Glad I could help you," Benji muttered, keeping his gaze on his mandated work shoes.

"You're the best too!" Vicki landed a peck on Benji's cheek.

She strutted to her car in the parking lot and didn't care that the perma-smile on her face hurt her cheeks. She pointed her car toward the Parkview border and merged with the holiday traffic.

Wynn unbelted her two youngest grandchildren from their booster seats in the back seat of Smith's Pinto.

"I think this is the first time Mel has ever bowed out of a trip to the mall. I guess it's official now. She's all grown up."

"Don't take it personally," Smith replied, recalling the morning's kitchen conversation. "She doesn't want to chance running into any of her friends while hanging out with her boring grandparents. At her age, that embarrassment is probably worse than death."

As they headed toward the Liberty Tree Mall's main entrance—the two grandkids in between their grandparents, holding hands—Smith thought about how much he would have to discuss with Anya later tonight when she, hopefully, delivered his first bantling. He held open the left side of the double-glass doors for his wife and grandchildren and then entered the mall behind them.

Shaun sprinted ahead toward the toy store on the corner of the main intersection. As he entered the mall's atrium—with the decorative tiled tree on the floor—he tripped and launched headlong into a trio of shoppers, landing on his face.

"Oh, jeez. I'm so sorry," the pretty girl said as she reached down to pick Shaun from the floor. "Are you okay?"

Smith noted Shaun looking behind him to make sure one of his grandparents were en route to rescue and to coddle him. While Wynn trotted toward him, Shaun grabbed his left knee and winced. Smith shook his head. Shaun was shooting for one or two scoops of mint chocolate chip ice cream later.

Then Smith slowed down. He felt the last forty years of hiding his secret from his wife and from extended family potentially fall apart as he recognized Vicki and Caitlin—aka stripper Aurora—walking together. Either one of them could recognize him, and both would have their own reaction and story to tell. Both of which could be equally devastating to his harmonious family life.

How would Smith explain what he had been doing at the strip club, talking to the dancers, when he was supposed to be in bed next to his wife? And what had he been doing out killing people for the past four decades? And did the two fit together to form a complete puzzle?

He grabbed Addie and ducked into Deja View Computers.

"Grandpapa, what are you doing?" Addie exclaimed as he yanked her into a store.

Smith was sure his youngest grandchild had no notion as to the contents, even the half-looking typewriters she probably didn't understand.

Some of the holiday shoppers turned their suspicious attention to the little girl who had yelled louder than Smith would have liked.

"It's okay, baby. I just want to check the prices of their computers. Thinking of getting one, you know? Might sit down and try to write that great American novel everyone aspires to do."

"You're weird, Grandpapa," Addie said and giggled. "Look! This one has games!" She sprinted to a display computer where a simulation of a man on a tractor had to be moved around a maze to find the pixelated rabbit who kept stealing his carrots. "I wanna play! How do you play?"

Smith looked over his shoulder through the large storefront windows to see when Aurora aka Caitlin and Stepp's secretary would be out of sight. Only then would he relax.

"I don't know, baby. Maybe you use these buttons to move the little man?" He pointed to the four arrow buttons, all pointing in a different direction.

Addie clapped in glee as she controlled the man on the tractor chasing the bunny.

"There you are!" Wynn said as she entered Deja View. "We had no idea where you went."

She held Shaun's hand.

Smith noted that Shaun was whimpering and milking the incident as long as he could; ice cream was at stake.

"Sorry, hon. I saw the new computers, and we wanted to check them out. What happened, Shaun?"

"He fell," Wynn said. "Ran straight into some teenager. Full speed, trying to get to a silly toy store."

"You all right?"

Shaun nodded.

Smith grabbed his grandson's hand. "I think we should get you a triple scoop of ice cream."

They left Deja View with a smile on Shaun's face stretching

from ear to ear.

Vicki pulled into the parking lot of Redman's Place Mall off Main Street in Parkview. Before she exited her car, she pulled down her rearview mirror so her entire face was visible in the reflection. She applied bright-pink lipstick and used her finger to touch up her mascara. She looked at her jelly bracelets and sighed. Her boss might find these particular accessories juvenile and not very sexy, so she stripped them off and placed them in her vehicle's center console.

She exited her car and headed toward the entrance situated next to Neptune's Cellar department store. She passed Stepp's already parked red T-top IROC—the windows all down and the rooftop ones removed, his vanity Massachusetts license plate GUN-4HR gleaming in the sun. Knowing he had gotten here first had her quickstepping toward the doors and sent her pulse soaring.

Maybe he was anxious to see her outside of workplace hours too.

She stopped at the mall directory to find the location of this new coffee shop. She found Sweet Insani-Tea in between Baskin Robbins and Poof & Snoofin's Boutique and headed in that direction. When she approached the shop's entrance, she cleared her throat, pulled her shirt taut, and flicked back her hair. She wished she had applied some lotion to her skin.

Stepp was seated in the far corner. Vicki swallowed hard when she saw him dressed in a white Armani suit jacket—unbuttoned—and an exposed baby-blue T-shirt hugging his chest. If he had been totting a gun and badge, he would've looked just like one of the characters from that new television show about undercover Miami detectives that had aired since September.

"Hey, boss," she said. She couldn't think of what else to call him. She had never referred to him otherwise at work—that would be inappropriate—but, out here in public, it seemed silly to refer to him as Detective Stepp.

"Ah, Mouse. I waited to order. Let's get some good java and chat." He stood from the chair and placed his hand on her lower back to guide her to the barista line.

She felt as if his touch sent actual electric sparks up her spine that then exploded inside her head.

"What can I get you folks?" the male barista asked when they reached the counter.

"I'll have a black coffee," Stepp said, "and whatever the little lady fancies."

Vicki smirked. "I'd like a Jasmine tea."

The barista nodded and turned his back to them to make their drinks.

Vicki drummed her fingertips on the counter and tapped her foot, feeling every silent second that passed.

"Here ya go," the barista said and handed them their drinks.

Vicki reached into her pocket.

"I got it," Stepp said and pulled out a money-clipped wad of one-hundred-dollar bills.

Vicki placed a hand over her chest in an *oh my* gesture.

They walked with their respective drinks to the table Stepp had already claimed.

"First, let me say, it's nice to see you outside of the office," Stepp said. "I think if we're going to be closer working partners, it's important that I see who you really are."

Vicki looked down into her cup of Jasmine tea.

"I can tell you're nervous, for whatever reason I have no idea, so let's get to know each other better first. Then, all the awkwardness can be left outside in the cold. Sound okay?"

Vicki nodded.

"I'll go first. Favorite movie?"

"*Flashdance.*"

Stepp jutted his bottom lip and nodded in approval. "Mine's *Dirty Harry.*"

"Never seen it."

"Looks like we'll be making some extracurricular time to watch it."

Vicki smiled, unsure if he was suggesting they were getting together to watch *Dirty Harry* as a romantic endeavor or just for her to broaden her cinematic horizons.

"My turn," she said. "Favorite book?"

"I don't read. Always hated it. Don't have time for it."

Vicki leaned back in her chair and folded her arms, feeling empowered for the first time around him. "Well, I'll tell you that you are certainly missing out, mister!"

Stepp laughed. "Okay, bookworm, tell me what your favorite book is, and maybe I'll take another stab at this reading thing. Convince me and change my mind."

Vicki realized how double-edged that order really was. Was he only talking about reading, or was he implying something more intimate with her?

"No. You'll just make fun of me. Plus you probably wouldn't like it anyway," she said, batting her eyelashes and adding as many flirtatious moments as she could.

Stepp took a sip of his black coffee. "This is why I've always liked you, Vic. Feisty. Alright, favorite artist?"

"Billy Idol."

Stepp rolled his eyes.

Vicki took the first sip of her tea. "And yours, Mr. Detective?"

"Duran Duran."

Vicki nodded, not wanting her facial expression to reveal that she'd rather be deaf than listen to any of their songs; however, she felt she needed to say something in reply. "So, are you hungry like that wolf too?"

As soon as the words left her mouth, she wanted to curl into a ball and die. No, better yet, she wished she could find some Time Transporter 4000 and zip backward about ten seconds to stop herself from being so lame. Vicki placed her forehead in her palm, her elbow on the table for support, and shook her head.

Stepp belly-laughed and sunk deep into the cushion. "*Smooth* is not your middle name, is it, Mouse?"

If Vicki hadn't wanted to disappear before, his comment sealed the deal.

"That's okay. I still think you're adorable as hell."

Vicki elevated her gaze above her hand. *Did he just call me adorable?*

Stepp waved his hand in front of his face as if he were swatting a fly. "Okay, okay. The pleasantries are over. You love girls in leotards, sliding across the dance floor, and I love a man with a big gun. You love a man with bleached-blond hair, and I love a British band in tight pants. Now we're acquainted." Stepp took a sip of his coffee. "Tell me what happened last night."

"Okay, so, I agreed to that blind date and—"

"Blind dates never work."

"Yeah, you've said that. A few times now. So I was waiting outside Gardenia's. We had agreed to meet on the sidewalk right at the entrance. My date was late—later than I think is appropriate—so I turned to walk back to my car and bumped into this old dude. I apologized, and he asked for a cigarette. When I told him that I didn't smoke, he said all this crazy stuff about me."

"Like what?"

"He knew that, ... um, that I had bought a pack of cigarettes—"

"But, Vic, you don't smoke!"

Vicki shrugged her shoulders as high as they could go and gave Stepp the cutest and most innocent smirk she could muster. "I was trying to impress my date."

"Are you really that hard-up"—Stepp fiddled with his coffee mug—"that you need to conform to what you think your fucking blind date might be into?"

Vicki swallowed hard and hoped he couldn't see her cheeks burning red.

"You are so much better than that. Any guy would be lucky to get you just the way you are."

Vicki giggled and flipped her wrist out of pure habit, trying to readjust the absent jelly bracelets that had been left in her vehicle. "Then he started talking about that woman who came to see you."

Stepp smiled, his eyes looking past Vicki into some other realm. "Aah, yes. Eva." Vicki didn't like that look. It was threatening. It was ... making her jealous.

Stepp snapped his attention to Vicki and his coffee. "Okay, so what did he look like?"

Vicki described Smith to a T, based on the man who appeared in the Polaroid which Stepp had been given.

"Yep, that's definitely him."

"And then Tony was found in the Dumpster afterward."

"Hate to scare you any more than you already are, kid, but

I'm pretty sure you chatted with the Wharf Killer just moments after he had killed your boyfriend."

"He wasn't my boyfriend!" Vicki razzed and then felt guilty for turning some young man's death into a flirtatious moment. "The Wharf Killer knows who I am. I feel like he knows a lot about me."

"If Smith was going to kill you, he would've either done it by now or wouldn't be chatting with you. But this is a huge crack in the case."

"How so?"

"I hadn't figured out how to track him down yet. Now I have a starting point. Your boyfriend might not have died in vain. Would you like to meet me at Gardenia's tonight for a drink and a chat with the bartender about our Wharf Killer's behavior and patterns of activity?"

Vicki had to place her hands in her lap so Stepp couldn't see the excited and nervous tic she did with her fingertips, since she didn't have her jelly bracelets to help relieve the anxious tension.

"Name the time, and I'm all yours."

"How about eight o'clock?"

"I'll be there."

"It's a date then!"

Those four words replayed themselves in Vicki's ears over and over throughout the rest of the day.

4: LAST NIGHT NEVER HAPPENED

Vicki stood in front of her full-length mirror while "White Wedding" blasted from her boom box. She jutted and raised her chin, proud of the wardrobe ensemble she had chosen to wear when she met with Stepp—classy yet provocative.

She checked her Swatch watch, and her heartbeat quickened when she realized she had somehow fallen five minutes behind in her preparation. Fully aware this might be the only chance she'd ever get to woo her boss outside of work, she felt she could justify a five-minute delay. She turned sideways so the mirror reflected her complete profile.

"Yeah, I'd do me," she said, pleased with her efforts as the boombox transitioned into "Hot in the City."

She eyed her stack of jelly bracelets as she exited her bedroom. "Not tonight, girls."

Vicki noticed Stepp's IROC idling in the open-air parking lot when she entered the nearby empty parking slot. She saw his silhouette focusing on his hair through the reflection of his rearview mirror.

Vicki tapped on his driver's side window. "Hey there, top gun for hour."

Stepp's face scrunched in confusion. "Huh?"

"Oh, nothing. Making a joke about your license plate."

Stepp threw back his head and roared with laughter. Every fiber of his suit vibrated with his body as he belly-laughed.

Vicki took a step backward and gulped as she glanced up and down the main road, not knowing where to place her gaze, fully aware now she had made some terrible and embarrassing mistake.

"Did you, *hahahahaha*, think that, *hehehehehe*, my license plate actually said, *baaaaahahahaha*, top gun for *hour*?"

Vicki swallowed and wished she wore a pair of magical ruby slippers—there's no place like home, there's no place like home, there's no place like …

"It's top gun for *hire*, you ditz! You've been working for me for how long? And you didn't know my plate said TOP GUN FOR HIRE? What the hell is a top gun for hour? Am I some kind of hooker-detective?"

Vicki's backside struck the car parked in the slot next to the IROC. If the parking lot had been free of vehicles, she would have kept walking backward until she had entered Salem's commuter traffic, where she would welcome her guts and entrails to be splattered across the roadway.

She placed her forehead into her palm. "I'm so stupid."

Stepp stopped laughing. "Honest mistake, I guess. But you gotta admit, it is pretty funny."

Vicki didn't feel like admitting anything right now.

"C'mon, Mouse. Let's go in, have a few drinks, and get some intel on Smith's behavior and schedule."

Her boss sounding like a detective again made her collect her composure. "Sounds perfect."

Stepp exited the red IROC and escorted his secretary along the walkway from the parking lot toward Gardenia's front entrance. Just before they reached the double-glass doors, he placed his hand on her lower back and opened the door for her.

Stepp's touch felt like electricity shooting through her veins; she could feel the heat emanating from his fingers through her jean jacket.

"We'll find a spot at the bar," he said to the hostess before she could even inquire about how many were in his party, and they breezed by her as if she were the most insignificant human on Earth.

Stepp guided Vicki through the tables full of families, elderly couples, and businessmen elongating a night with coworkers before they had to return home to their mundane lives and nagging wives. When Stepp and Vicki reached the bar at the back of the restaurant, he offered a stool to Vicki before taking a seat himself.

Hearing two stools slide from underneath the counter, the bartender spun around. "Good evening, folks. What'll it be?"

"Whiskey for me, Fain. On the rocks. And whatever the little lady wants."

Vicki bit her bottom lip, realizing her choice of drink could say so much about her and her possible intentions with her boss. *Choose carefully, Vicki.*

"Long Island iced tea."

Stepp nodded in approval. "I like it. Go right for the gold." Then he fell silent.

Vicki glanced at him, curious about what he was doing—

what his method was.

Stepp studied Fain's movements. He watched the way the bartender tilted the glass to drop in the ice for his whiskey. He scrutinized the manner in which the barkeep held the whiskey bottle; there had to be some tell that Stepp could use as a door to open a conversation. So far, Fain had completed each movement of preparing the drinks in a methodical and normal fashion.

John Denver's "Twelve Days of Christmas" played on the jukebox, and Stepp noticed a nanosecond of disgust flash across the bartender's face.

"Hate this song too, huh?"

Fain glanced at his patron. "What makes you say that?"

"I noticed you cringed a bit when the song started."

Fain placed the whiskey on ice in front of Stepp and moved on to mixing Vicki's Long Island iced tea. "What are you, some kind of psychic?"

"In a town built on snake charmers and charlatans, I don't think there's any more room left for smoke and mirrors."

Vicki raised one eyebrow and leered at Stepp, as if he had just spoken Latin.

Stepp patted her thigh under the counter as if to say, *It's all part of the plan.*

"No, sir," Stepp continued. "I can just spot someone who is sick of hearing the same song played a hundred times a day—a song that might drudge up some not-so-pleasant childhood memories of the holidays."

Fain took a step backward.

"Didn't mean to scare you. You must not remember me. I'm a detective. Reading people's faces is my business. Name's Stepp."

Fain tossed his dish towel over his shoulder and shook Stepp's hand.

Vicki giggled. "I apologize for my boss. He can be ... intense at times."

Stepp slipped his business card across the bar. "What do you know of Mr. Smith? Elderly gentleman. Frequents here. Granddaughter named Eva."

Fain pursed his lips and shook his head. "I only know of one Smith, and he's been coming here for years. Usually comes for our Monday night's three-for-one special on house liquor. Doesn't have a granddaughter named Eva though. If you'll excuse me ..."

Fain attended to a small gathering of men, all pining for his attention.

"What do you think?" Vicki asked, drinking more of her iced tea a bit too fast and coughed.

Stepp bounced his fist off the bar counter. "Someone is lying. Either the bartender is protecting Smith, or his granddaughter gave me a fake name."

Stepp considered the possible scenarios.

Vicki shifted in the stool.

Stepp didn't need her trying to distract him right now with her nervous fidgeting. Stepp knocked back his whiskey in one gulp and slammed the empty glass on the bar, the remaining ice cubes clinking. "Fucker is lying."

Vicki glanced at him from the corner of her eyes, afraid to look at him dead-on. "Why do you say that?"

"He thinks he's being a fucking hero by covering for his—"

"Another drink?" Fain asked as he returned to Stepp and

his secretary.

Stepp nodded and used a single finger to push his empty glass toward the bartender.

Fain filled the glass without adding additional ice cubes and turned.

"I'll be honest with you," Vicki said to Fain, stopping him in his tracks. "I had a blind date set up last night. We were gonna have dinner here. I waited for him outside until an elderly man, whom I have never met before, told me that my date wouldn't show. And then this man said things as if he had been spying on me all day."

"Did your date ever show up?" Fain asked.

"Her date was Tony Birch," Stepp said.

Fain placed a hand over his chest and stepped backward. "Oh my."

"Now you can see why we're so interested in this Mr. Smith."

"Why do you think it was Mr. Smith who had killed Tony?"

Stepp took a long gulp of his whiskey and leaned across the bar to make sure no eavesdroppers could hear him. "Because Vicki's description of this elderly gentleman matches a Polaroid I was given by Smith's granddaughter when she came to my office to hire me to track him down."

"Why would his granddaughter hire you to track him down?"

"Because she believes he is the Wharf Killer."

Fain's eyes darted back and forth. "There's no way Smith is the Wharf Killer, is there?"

"I chatted with the Wharf Killer right after he had murdered my date," Vicki said. "Let that sink in."

She took another sip of her drink and smiled at the look on

Stepp's face.

Stepp rested his hand on her knee.

She quickly drank numerous gulps, obviously nervous at his touch.

Stepp reached into his Armani suit jacket and retrieved the Polaroid. He slapped it on the bar counter and gave Vicki's knee an additional squeeze. "Feast your eyes. I'm sure that dude is a regular of yours."

The Polaroid stopped skidding across the bar and came to rest against a bowl of peanuts.

Fain grabbed the photograph and laughed. His bellowing made Stepp and Vicki exchange concerned glances.

"How much have you guys had to drink before you came in here?" Fain asked after he caught his breath.

Stepp's hand slid from Vicki's knee as he tensed up and donned his who-the-fuck-do-you-think-you-are mask.

Fain flicked the Polaroid back at Stepp. "You really had me going there for a minute. Thanks for suckering me in. I always enjoy a good ruse. Next round is on the house."

Stepp grabbed the Polaroid and looked at the blank, undeveloped piece of synthetic plastic. He leaped to his feet from the stool and his half-drank whiskey tipped over, sending a small tributary of alcohol traversing the grooves in the well-worn bar counter.

"What the fuck?" Stepp exclaimed, unfazed by his spilt drink.

Vicki remained silent but glanced over his hand at the blank Polaroid.

Stepp placed one foot behind him to brace his unsteady wobble. "There was a picture here! I swear! It was Smith standing in front of the Desert Palms Motel. *Your* customer. Smith. The fucking Wharf Killer!"

When Fain never responded, Stepp heard the eerie quiet in the place. Looking over his shoulder, Stepp noted how the Gardenia's patrons had stopped their idle chatter and food consumption to stare at the obvious drunk lunatic at the bar.

Vicki stood. "C'mon," she whispered to Stepp.

He glared at her like a caged tiger and grabbed her almost empty Long Island iced tea. He stuffed the now-blank Polaroid into the ice cubes and chucked the glass against the mirror behind Fain's head. The bartender ducked as the glass shattered, raining shards into his reservoir of liquor bottles.

"Let's go," Stepp ordered Vicki.

He placed his hand on her lower back to help her move faster out of the restaurant. When they passed through Gardenia's front doors, they slowed their pace as they walked along the pathway to the parking lot. Stepp kept his hand on Vicki's back.

Vicki wondered how long he would keep his hand there, reveling in every moment he touched her. If he never touched her again, she at least could resort to this touch in her fantasies.

They entered the parking lot, and she felt like she had lost control of her limbs. The iced tea warmed her veins and seemed to have lightened gravity.

Stepp slid his hand from the small of her back and tested his chances by resting it on the undercurve of her butt.

Vicki swallowed the saliva that had collected in her mouth and decided to play it cool regardless of the tingling sensation consuming every fiber of her being. She flaunted a sashay as she walked, hoping he would find the additional friction on his hand enticing.

They reached his IROC, and he removed his hand. Vicki felt an automatic sense of void when his hand no longer cupped her, like a cord had been severed, and endless possibilities were now squelched back to fantasies and late-night sequestered desires.

"I'm sorry I lost my temper."

Vicki smiled, realizing he had only apologized for losing his temper, and not for placing his hand on her buttocks. "It's okay. The whole thing was pretty weird." Her head swam from the mixed drink, and she had to place a hand on his car to steady herself.

"Are you okay to drive home?"

Vicki felt a pang of disappointment as she realized he was ending their night here. "Why? Do you want to take me home and tuck me in?"

Stepp glanced at the steady traffic passing Gardenia's. "I would, Vic, but I have a meeting that I can't miss tonight." Stepp glanced at his Rolex. "In fact, I should get going if I'm to make it in time."

Vicki burped. "I understand. I'll see you Monday morning? I hope I helped you in some way."

Stepp unlocked the IROC. "You have been amazing, Mouse."

"Aw, shucks. You're always amazing."

"Go home and get some sleep. We'll chat Monday morning."

"Yes, sir," Vicki said and gave a stumbling half salute. She turned and faced the rest of the parking lot. *Now, if I could only remember where I had parked.*

Smith checked his watch and lit a Smolens.

"Have somewhere to be?" Baron asked.

"Nervous habit."

"You? The self-proclaimed bulletproof detective? The top gun for hire? The invincible dick? Nervous?"

A ruckus exploded behind Smith elsewhere in the bar. Three men had sprung to their feet, and one had a fistful of another's shirt.

"Be right back," Baron said, and Smith nodded.

The bartender reached under the sink and retrieved a wooden baseball bat with the word Peacekeeper written in black marker down its shaft. Keeping the bat by his leg, Baron exited from behind the bar and maneuvered around the billiard table toward the open patron area of the Pale Horse. He raised the bat as an extension of his pointer finger when he talked.

"Look here, Mr. Wackenhut. I've given you your fourth, fifth, and sixth warning this month alone. Do I need to call Mrs. Wackenhut and tell her to come get you because you won't play nice in the sandbox with the other kids?"

Wackenhut cowered and released the gentleman's shirt from his grip. "No, Baron. I'll quit it."

"You fellas, please get along. I don't feel like having to unleash the beast."

Smith chuckled from his stool, his back facing the melee behind him.

Baron returned to his post behind his bar and leaned forward, using his elbows and forearms as support.

"Unleash the beast?" Smith asked, his chuckle turning into a full-fledged laugh.

"These fuckers. Especially *that* one. You know? I bought the Pale Horse from Moe when he wanted to open Sneakers in Parkview in '76, and, through all these years of bar fights and shitheads, no one has been more of a thorn in my side than Wackenhut over the past year."

Smith finished his whiskey and pushed the glass toward the Pale Horse's barkeep.

Baron instinctively turned to grab a bottle of the house whiskey. "I still want to hear about what's making you nervous, but I need to show you something first. I'm gonna start selling these on New Year's Eve." Baron disappeared from Smith's sight below the counter. He popped back up, holding two pint-size beer steins. "Limited edition Pale Horse memorabilia."

Baron handed one to Smith.

The detective turned it over in his hand and traced the Pale Horse logo engraved on a gold plaque attached to the glass stein.

"Here's my idea. People can buy a stein for one hundred dollars, and then all their drinks are half off throughout the entire year."

"Like renting a drinking space."

"Right. And their passport to the half off is their stein. The lease, if you will, runs from New Year's Day to New Year's Eve. And I'll only have fifty available each year."

"They'll sell like hotcakes. Hotcakes, I tell ya!"

Baron replaced the two steins underneath the counter. "So, go on. Why are you nervous, Mr. Stoic?"

"That body they found outside Gardenia's last night? That was my handiwork."

"Ya know? A tiny piece of me thought that might've been the Wharf Killer, but then I said, *nah*. You've never targeted a male before."

Smith took a sip from his refilled whiskey. "This chap had

it coming. He was preying on young women, using blind dates as his vehicle for meeting them."

Baron poured himself a gin and tonic. "What did your priestess have to say about that?"

"She refused to take him. Something about him not fitting in with the Mushroom Cult because of his gender."

"She's a fucking sexist cunt."

Smith laughed and raised his glass. "I'll drink to that!"

"Hey, B. You got change for a buck for the jukebox?" a man wearing a *Dark Side of the Moon* T-shirt asked, leaning forward across the bar next to Smith. He propped his pool stick against an empty stool.

Baron opened the cash till with a *cha-ching!* and handed the man ten dimes, then returned to Smith. "You sure you don't want me to educate you in the voodoo arts?"

Smith shook his head. "This place never ceases to amaze me. With all you guys, it's all about mystics and psychics and voodoo and witchcraft. Does it ever end with you people?"

"Welcome to Salem!" Baron said and took a sip of his gin and tonic.

"Salem welcomed me decades ago. She just hasn't stopped the celebration."

"Back on track …"

Smith wagged his finger in the air as he took another gulp. "I chatted with the girl who he was going to meet for a bit."

"Getting risky in your old age."

"Something just felt different about the whole thing. Finally tracking him down and disposing of him. I felt like I needed to say … *something* to the girl whose life I had just saved."

"The Blind-Date Killer!"

"Why does it always sound like I'm watching an episode of

Batman whenever I talk to you?"

Baron laughed and pointed to his head. "You just can't stop the genius that's trapped up in here!"

From behind them, the jukebox played a familiar acoustic guitar riff, masking some of the *clack*ing sounds of billiard balls striking each other as the male singer asked the casual listener if they could tell the difference between Heaven and Hell or blue skies from pain.

"Figures the dude wearing a Pink Floyd shirt would play this. So fucking cliché."

Smith eyed Baron with a hint of confusion, not completely understanding what a Pink Floyd was. "I've never approached or conversed with any of the people involved with Anya's bantlings. Not since my days in Vegas. And it almost bit me in the arse. Earlier today Wynn and I took the younger two grandkids to the mall, and Shaun accidentally ran into the young lady from last night. I mean, literally. Smashed right into her. If she had noticed or recognized me, I'd be answering decades of questions from Wynn."

"Getting sloppy in your twilight years, eh?"

"So now you think I'm a cunt, do you, barkeep?" Anya asked from behind Smith, placing a cold hand on the detective's shoulder.

"Party's over," Baron said and stood upright. "The bitch is back."

Anya slid from behind Smith and took a seat in the empty stool beside him.

"Can I get you something to drink?" Baron asked. "Or is dining on the souls of misguided girls enough to fill your dirty black heart?"

"Always a gentleman," she replied, then to Smith said, "I only stopped by to tell you that your requested recruit should be ready for you."

Smith shifted in his stool and glanced at Baron before addressing Anya. "Thank you. Can we talk later about it?"

"Don't want your little boyfriend to know, is that it? *Hrm?*"

Baron flicked the top of his fingers under his chin toward Anya.

A female approached the bar and wedged herself between the empty stool where Anya sat and Smith's stool, separating them to create enough space to press her stomach against the counter. "Two margaritas, please."

Baron nodded and watched as the girl put her hand straight through Anya's neck to rest her hand on the back of the stool for support. He reveled in the look of disgust on the witch's face as his patron unknowingly violated Anya.

"Hey, it's you!" she said to Smith, a smile growing from ear to ear.

Smith took a longer look at the female. "Caitlin, aka Aurora the Pole Starer! How are you?"

Caitlin hopped into the empty stool next to Smith, right into Anya's invisible lap.

Baron stifled a chortle and had to turn away from his customers. Watching Anya make an *Oomph!* face when Aurora landed on her lap was just too much.

Anya scowled and hissed at Caitlin, then flashed her three rows of fangs at the back of the woman's head in an invisible gesture of frustration.

Caitlin leaned back in the stool, swiveling it so she could face Smith.

"I just wanted to thank you again for saving me from that wretched place. I don't know what I was thinking."

"What *were* you thinking? You know Hypnotic

Encounters' specialty is their erotic massage add-on in the VIP rooms," Smith replied, watching Anya wring her hands together in front of Caitlin's unsuspecting face.

"I'm just trying to save up some moolah to get my own place."

Anya squinted at Smith, resembling something close to giving him the evil eye, and disappeared from the stool she was sharing with the failed stripper.

"There are more respectable ways to earn money than shaking your rump to complete strangers."

Baron placed two margaritas in front of Caitlin.

"I'm sure there are. I heard Sweet Insani-Tea is looking for baristas."

"There ya go," Smith said to her. "Always another opportunity just around the bend."

"Thanks again, mister."

Pink Floyd finished on the jukebox, and the sound of a synthetic piano over an infectious disco beat flooded the bar.

"*Gah!* This is my song!" Caitlin screamed and sashayed the drinks to her table as her hips bounced to the beat, belting out the first few lines with the singer's initial verse about dancing and jiving.

Smith nonchalantly glanced at Caitlin's companions and sighed a breath of relief when he saw Vicki was absent.

"She was at the mall today with that girl from Gardenia's."

Baron took a step backward and framed his mouth with his index finger and thumb. "So, both girls know you—but for different reasons—and probably haven't realized you are the same person. Playing with fire, Smith. Playing with fire."

"How could you keep a straight face when she sat right in Anya's lap?"

"How could *you?* That shit was hysterical."

"I love watching Anya squirm like that."

"Yeah. And, buddy? What did she mean about your recruit should be ready?"

Smith took a long gulp of his whiskey. "I think it's getting late."

Baron drummed his fingers on the bar counter. "*You* want your own clan of broods! That's some dangerous creeks you're swimming in. Don't fuck with her magic. You leave that shit at the door! Nothing good can come of what you're thinking about."

Smith stared at his cracked fingernails.

"Look at me, *dee-teck-tive*. Nothing good! This is a fire you don't know how to control, and a lot more people than you are liable to get burned."

"I knew coming in here and talking to you was a bad idea." Smith tossed a one-hundred-dollar bill on the bar. "Keep the change, as well as your opinions."

After the door to the Pale Horse had closed behind him, even after he had reached the Pinto's on-street parking spot, Smith could still hear Caitlin's high-pitched and drunken voice trying to stay in tune as she sang along with the song's chorus.

A seventeen-year-old dancing queen, Smith thought as he paid attention to the lyrics of Caitlin's shrill attempt at matching the female's voice coming from the jukebox. *Sounds like a recipe for a future bantling.*

The shadows reached their long fingers toward the two men acting inconspicuous in the parking garage corner.

"It's all there," Stepp said, watching the albino man count

the wad of bills.

"I don't trust a man who wears a powder-pink suit," the man replied as he reached the last ten-dollar bill in the roll.

"What did you bring me tonight?"

The man glanced at his Buick behind him, and his gaze fell on the silhouette sitting in the passenger seat. "A redhead."

"Perfect."

The man reached into his jacket pocket and handed Stepp a bag of a white powdery substance, matching the man's skin tone and lack of pigment in every visible strand of his hair.

Stepp shoved the bag into a satchel slung over his shoulder as his dealer whistled three short bursts. The albino's Buick door opened, and the redhead exited the car, swinging her hips as she approached the two men.

"Amber, this is Mr. Stepp. Please make sure you take good care of him tonight."

Stepp let his gaze eat up her black thigh-high boots and fishnet stockings.

"Bring her back in one piece," Rhino said, noticing Stepp lick his lips.

Amber took Stepp's hand, and he escorted her to his IROC as Rhino placed his jet-black sunglasses over his eyes.

Who the fuck wears sunglasses at night? Weirdo, Stepp thought before calling out, "Hey, Corey Hart!"

The albino man glanced, unamused, over the top of his Buick at the not-very-funny detective and his rented date.

"Where am I dropping this one off when we're done?"

"On the wharf. Behind Madam Hapney's shop. That'll be walking distance from her place."

Stepp nodded and opened the car door for Amber, like a true gentleman.

Stepp snorted another line of cocaine through a rolled hundred-dollar bill—this line twice as long as the first one. He lifted his head from the Carriage House Motel's small end table next to the bed and inhaled as much air as he could handle through his nose. When his lungs were filled to capacity, he grunted and expelled the air through his mouth.

"You want a hit of this?" he asked Amber, who sat behind him on the bed, rubbing his back.

Stepp prepared another line and handed her the rolled-up bill.

She leaned forward, propping herself up in the doggy-style position to reach the cocaine.

"Good, huh? Rhino always has the best shit in the North Shore. Both drugs and girls."

Stepp pinned Amber's red hair behind her head and forced his lips on hers as his fingers danced over the thin webbing of fabric covering her milky-white thighs.

"*Woo!* That is some good shit!" he yelled into the pay-by-the-hour motel room.

A cockroach scampered over the dresser from Stepp's jubilant outburst.

Amber leaned forward again, grabbed the bag from the end table, and tapped some sprinkles of cocaine over her cleavage, the crystals sticking to the mixture of sweat and cheap perfume already clinging to her skin.

Stepp's eyes widened as he buried his face in her bosom, collecting as much of the powder and her taste as he could with his flicking tongue. He reached his hand between her legs, finding the bull's eye.

Amber lay back on the bed, and Stepp slithered the length of her body, rubbing himself along her. His heartbeat accelerated, and he placed one hand underneath her miniskirt, grabbing her buttocks as hard as he could while unzipping his suit pants.

She grabbed the back of his head and pulled his mouth to hers and then swiped his hand from his zipper so she could free him herself.

He used his now-free hand to fondle one breast with such gusto that she flinched.

Amber guided him into her and let the drug do its job, hoping the deed would be finished sooner rather than later.

All she needed to do was outlast him and then strike when he had passed out.

"You and your little voodoo priest think you're so funny," Anya said, appearing behind Smith while he brushed his teeth. "You just love it when I look like a fool."

Instead of turning around, he glanced up from the sink to meet her gaze in her reflection in the mirror. "I have a bone to pick with you."

"Oh, this should be good."

Smith spat, wiped his mouth, and turned to face the witch. "Who in the Sam Hell do you think you are? Hanging around my granddaughter since she was a child? I should sever this partnership right now."

Anya pulled the black veil from her pale face and took an aggressive step forward. "And I should sever your fucking breath."

"You stay away from my family. That was *never* part of our deal. The last time you meddled with one of your curator's family members, a little girl was sacrificed on a cross. Remember Rose? I surely do. Every day of my life I think about that little girl burning in flames. All because *you* got involved."

"You know very well *why* that happened. And it was in error."

"An error that burned a little girl alive. Stay away from my—"

Knock! Knock!

"You okay in there, hun?"

"Yeah, Wynn. I'm fine. Just talking to myself. Was I too loud?" Smith glared at Anya to be silent.

"Sounded like you were arguing with someone."

"I'm right as rain. Gonna take a shower. My hair smells like cigarette smoke from the Pale Horse, and I know how much you hate sleeping next to that smell."

Wynn giggled from the other side of the door. "Love you."

"Love you more."

When Wynn's footsteps had faded to the backside of the house, Anya pointed her bony and crooked finger into Smith's chest. "I just came here to tell you where you can retrieve your package."

"You mean Tony? Is that how you think of your girls? As packages?"

"Don't compare your one insignificant bantling to my grand army."

"I gotta wait until Wynn falls asleep anyway, so I can sneak out of the house."

"He'll wait for you. In fact, he won't know how to go anywhere without you. He'll be in the small toolshed behind the House of the Seven Gables."

Smith nodded.

"Have you thought about what you'll name your little coterie?"

"I'm not so hard-up for power that I need a name. Plus, who says I want any more than just him?"

"You'll see. You won't stop once you start. Don't you think the Mushroom Cult started with just one girl? After you control that first one, you can't dam the urges for more."

"I'll be fine."

"Yeah, you'll be fine. You and your magical band of fools. Regardless, he's ready now."

"Thank you. But stay away from my family. All of them. Especially Melissa. If you don't do anything else ever again for me, please leave her be."

"Saying *please* has never swayed my decisions. In fact, begging makes you look weak."

A wave of nausea hit Smith's intestines like a ton of bricks. He doubled over, placing his face in the toilet bowl.

Anya laughed as she faded from the bathroom.

The nausea evaporated when the last remnant of her image had evanesced.

Amber slid from the bed and placed one foot on the stained and threadbare motel carpet. She paused, keeping that one foot on the floor and the rest of her body dangling off the side of the bed. She studied Stepp's breathing. It hadn't changed.

She slid her other foot off the bed and planted it next to the first. Then she wormed over the edge until her body was free of the mattress. She stood and tiptoed around the bed toward the end table, noting the dead mouse in that corner of the room.

Stepp snorted and coughed, and Amber froze. She caught a glimpse of herself in the mirror—fishnet tights ripped, mascara smearing her cheeks, red hair disheveled, one bra strap clinging to her elbow. When she felt sure Stepp was not about to wake up, she continued her journey toward his wallet and the remaining cocaine.

The black wallet felt heavy in her hand when she flipped it open. Her fingers danced along the edges of the bills inside, and she smiled. Tonight was a good score. She shoved the wad of hundred-dollar bills between her breasts, letting the lacy bra act as a money hammock. She crammed the remaining cocaine into her miniskirt's back pocket and turned toward the door. Amber's knee struck the corner of the dresser, making all the dangling drawer handles rattle against the wood.

Stepp vigorously wiped underneath his nostrils with the topside of his index finger and rolled over, pulling her side of the sheets on top of him.

Amber placed a hand over her thumping heart and swallowed. She counted to sixty, and, when the man hadn't stirred again, she moved toward the door. She wrapped her fingers around the doorknob and ever-so-slowly freed the chain lock. The small tab reached the larger opening, and she let the chain fall against the door. She turned the knob and pulled. Light from the parking lot widened across the carpet, like a pie slice.

Amber placed her foot in the opening to keep the door from creaking and slid her body through the small crack. The box springs creaked behind her, and she turned her head toward the sleeping john.

Amber only had time to blink once as five splayed fingers struck her face with enough force to bounce her skull off the doorjamb. She fell to the shaggy carpet and landed on all fours, like an infant trying to crawl.

The man's shin connected with the side of her jaw, flipping her onto her back. She grabbed her cheek and rolled away from the attack.

Stepp closed the door and reached down, grabbing Amber by her red hair. He dragged her to her feet as she flailed, trying to strike him somewhere ... anywhere. He turned her so she faced the wall-hanging mirror and pinned her hands behind her back by wrapping his fingers around her wrists. He pulled her close so her backside pressed against his chest and her trapped hands grazed his groin.

He peered over her left shoulder, so he could see both of their reflections in the mirror. "Gonna rob me blind and take my shit, you filthy whore?"

Amber squeaked and shook her head in short bursts.

Stepp pulled her wrists down, the momentum bending her body backward, her lower back arching.

"Do you even know who I am? People don't steal from me. I steal from *them*. I take what I want. And I am invincible."

Amber's eyes widened. "Please, mister. I-I'll give it back."

Stepp freed one of his hands from her wrists and caressed the length of a handful of her hair. "Of course you will. You'll give it *all* back, you dirty fuck. And who the hell steals all of someone's money *and* their drugs? Now *that's* pretty fucking low."

Stepp felt Amber's body shake and shiver.

"My-my kid is sick. She might die if we don't get her treatment. I-I only do this for her hospital bills. No one will hire me and pay me what I need to cover her bills because I dropped out of school when I was pregnant with her, and I hate myself every fucking night for having to put out for limp dicks like you just so she can get—"

Stepp smashed Amber's face into the mirror and released her wrists. She crumpled to the carpet in a heap and landed with her eyes open and her right arm draped unnaturally across her torso.

"Fucking pig, trying to steal my fucking money," he said to Amber's lifeless body and spat on her face.

Stepp turned from her and collected his personal affects. "I can't believe this happened *again!*"

He slipped on his shoes and stuffed his socks into his pocket. "When will these little piggies learn?"

He bent and withdrew his wad of cash from Amber's cleavage and quickly counted it. "Need to make sure you didn't hide a few extra bills somewhere else, you whorebag."

He pinched the corner of the baggie sticking out from her back pocket and retrieved his leftover cocaine. "It's not enough to take all my cash, but you gotta take my drugs too? Party's over, cum-catcher."

He crammed the bills into his wallet and stuffed the baggie into the opposite pocket from the socks. He made a fist and placed it against his forehead, pacing the room in small circles. "Dammit! Why'd you make me do it? Why'd you make me do it again? I mean—" He stopped pacing and pointed a finger at the corpse. "All you had to do was take your payment—what you were worth—and go on your way in the morning." He retracted his finger and paced again. "But, *no.* You had to walk your greedy fucking fingers into my wallet and take what you hadn't earned. And … And … And! I even shared my coke with you! And *this* is the thanks I get?"

Stepp stopped pacing and placed his forehead into his open hand. "Jesus! Is it that fucking hard?"

He stumbled and grabbed the corner of the dresser to steady himself. He extended his other hand and held it in the air, trying to slow down the spinning of the room. "Maybe ..."

He walked hunchbacked toward the bed, each step a struggle. "Maybe ..."

He crawled over the disheveled blanket and dirty sheets toward the pillow against the wall. "Maybe I'll take a little rest before I vacate the premises."

Stepp rolled over on his side—the pocketed-socks side—and curled into the fetal position and closed his eyes.

Amber's eyes remained open as her lifeless body lay on the floor in front of the mirror.

A deep hush fell over the room, and all was silent ... until the motel door swung open, pulling a swirl of dried and dead leaves into the room.

No one stirred. Not even the dead mouse.

Anya entered the motel room as a gust of leaves whirlpooled around her ankles. "Okay, girls. Let's make this quick."

Four ghouls entered the room behind their witch and headed straight for Amber's corpse. Each grabbed a limb and dragged her toward the door.

Anya approached Stepp, asleep on the bed, facing the end table. She petted his feathered hair with her bony fingers. She knelt so she was nose to nose with him. "You didn't disappoint me, Detective." She ran one finger the length of his manicured eyebrow. "This is just the start of a beautiful friendship." Anya clapped in excitement. "I can just feel it!"

Stepp cleared his throat and turned over.

Anya stood and glanced at her girls.

Candy grumbled incoherent guttural sounds.

Anya nodded. "That's right. Get her outside. The vultures will do the rest."

Candy slapped Cyana's decayed hand to get her to move faster. Cyana bared her rotting teeth and made snapping gestures with her mouth, like a rabid dog.

"Girls! Girls! Stay focused."

Cyana closed her mouth and grunted as the four ghouls continued the extraction of Amber from the motel room.

Anya held open the door for her generals and scanned the parking for any loitering lookie-loos.

"What the … *fuck* is this?"

Anya snapped her attention toward the bed.

Stepp sat upright with his back against the wall and his knees pulled against his chest.

"Shit," Anya muttered and stepped into the room.

Stepp wiped his face with the palm of both hands with such vigor that Anya thought initially he was brushing creepy-crawlers off his skin.

Pum'kin dropped her assigned limb and hissed at the disoriented detective.

Anya raised her hand and shushed her ghoul. Anya took a step toward the bed, and Stepp cowered. She lifted the black veil from her pale face, letting the lace drape over the top of her head.

Stepp's eyes darted back and forth between the witch at the foot of the bed and Amber's dragged body. He touched the baggie in his pocket and swallowed hard.

"It was laced, right?" He tilted his head. "I mean, you're

not real. She's not really dead. I'm not really here. Fucker laced my shit." Stepp removed the baggie and violently shook the contents onto the bedspread. "That's gotta be it. Laced."

Anya glided from the foot of the bed to Stepp's side quicker than he could blink and react. She placed one sprawled hand over his face. "Sleep," she whispered.

Stepp's head rolled to one side, and his body slumped onto the mattress.

"Get the bitch outta here now!"

The four Mushroom Cult ghouls quickstepped from the motel, raking Amber across the parking lot's bumpy and broken asphalt.

"Bring her into the woods."

By the time the small coven reached the wood line, Amber's face had been tenderized from the rough asphalt— pieces of her flesh abandoned along the escape route from the motel.

"Hide her under those leaves and bushes, and then, Nikki, you can do the honors."

Nikki clapped and assisted her three comrades in hiding Amber's body. When the ghouls' work satisfied Anya, she stepped backward and spread her arms as if hanging on a crucifix. One hand held the good book—the metallic-adorned maroon leather-bound one—as she looked into the night sky and chanted.

She finished repeating the familiar spell to summon the birds of prey, yet the sky remained empty. She shot her gaze left, right, up, down. Nothing. She slowly lowered her arms, as if gravity had become too heavy, and the book rested against her thigh.

Candy grunted one short burst of sound in confusion.

"*Shh!*" Anya barked. Straining her ears to hear any signs of her abettors and not wanting to believe just yet that they had finally abandoned her after all these centuries, Anya held her breath so the sound wouldn't mask any shred of possible resonance from the vultures. Nothing but ...

Crickets.

Distant rumbles of car engines traveling Route 1.

Muffled voices from a television.

No flapping of wings.

Then ... snow.

Anya continued staring into the empty sky as large puffy flakes floated earthbound and landed on her face and black garb. Within moments, snow covered the landscape and the undead—and the real dead.

"What did I do wrong?" she asked the book.

She opened to the pages detailing the summoning of the vultures and read the same words she had been reading—and had memorized—for hundreds of years. She closed the book, and snowflakes covered the one-eyed triangular symbol on the cover.

The four ghouls took a step backward and glanced over Anya's shoulder into the parking lot.

Anya's brows furrowed in suspicion when she noticed the ghouls' faces elongate in fear. Anya took a deep breath to collect herself before turning around to face whatever waited behind her.

Pum'kin took an additional frightful step backward, and Anya clenched the book to her chest.

Anya spun around and gasped.

Smith took one final glance up and down Turner Street to confirm no traffic or late-night pedestrians crept along the streets and then opened the unsecured toolshed at the back of the House of Seven Gables' property.

The flimsy wooden door creaked on its hinges, and Smith entered. He reached up for the chain on the overhead bulb. Light flooded the small space, washing over a sheet outlining a human form underneath. Smith grabbed a handful of fabric and yanked, like someone removing a tablecloth without disturbing the arranged china.

He kneeled to study the sleeping ghoul's face. "So, Tony …" Smith grabbed the corpse's cold hand. "You're mine now."

Tony's eyes flung open, and he gasped for air, arching his back and clawing at the toolshed's walls.

Smith cradled Tony into his chest like a newborn. "It's okay. It's okay. I got you."

Tony's breathing slowed, and Smith felt him relax. He put Tony at an arm's length and brushed the bantling's hair from his forehead.

"Tonight is my retirement party, thanks to you," Smith said. "My change of command, if you will."

Tony's gaze darted from tool to tool, not giving any indication he was listening to Smith—or even if he understood words yet.

"You'll be released into the city to continue the cleansing I started so, so many years ago."

Tony grappled at a hanging garden shovel, like a cat playing with a ball of yarn.

"I can't do it anymore. I don't *want* to do it anymore. And, from what I've learned about that Stepp guy, I don't think he'll be a worthy successor. I need to walk away from this business and know it's in good hands. Do you think you can do that for me?"

Tony stopped swatting at an extension cord and, for the first time, looked at Smith with a sense of understanding. He opened his mouth to speak, but only gurgling moans escaped. A wave of panic and sadness washed over his face.

"I know. It's a learning curve, but, from what I've seen with Anya's girls, you'll learn very quickly how to understand and to communicate with those sounds."

Smith sat next to Tony, their backs against the wall. Smith patted Tony's knee. "You were a bad man. You know that?"

Tony looked at Smith and grunted.

"Yeah. You liked to kill dames on blind dates. They even tried pinning some of your victims on me. But you have moxie, kid. I saw that right from the beginning. Your intentions were all wrong, but your gumption is what got you this job."

Tony played with a small pile of dirt that had fallen from the wheelbarrow nearby.

"I'm going home to my wife and a regular life, while you, my friend, will continue the mission. Wipe the bottom-feeders from the streets—the druggies, the hookers, the pimps, the pushers ..." Smith snapped his fingers in rapid succession in front of Tony's eyes. "Hey, you listening to me? I don't want you to resort to your old ways. It's important that your targets are worthy of the slaughter."

Tony nodded, already showing signs of the rapid intellectual growth from being reanimated that Smith had seen the Mushroom Cult exhibit.

"Those vultures are something, aren't they?"

Smith startled when the toolshed door swung open, and a man stumbled inside. He sat across from Tony and Smith, his head hanging between his knees as he shivered. He shook the light dusting of snow from his coat and coughed.

Tony clapped like a child receiving a gift, and the man scurried on all fours.

"Oh, j-j-jeez. I-I-I didn't know anyone w-w-was in here. S-s-sorry, guys."

"It's okay, Duston. Having a hard time finding a warm place tonight?"

"S-S-Smith? Oh, am I g-g-glad it's someone I know! It's s-s-snowing out there now."

"We've been lucky. It's been a mild winter."

"S-s-so far. Who's your friend?"

"This is Tony."

Duston leaned forward on his hands to bridge the distance between them, so he could shake the newcomer's hand.

Tony's face lit up with glee that he had someone new to play with. He leaned forward to smell the strange man's hand.

Duston froze, and his eyes widened. He recoiled to the wall and jumped to his feet, then wagged his finger at Tony. "Tha-tha-that ..."

Smith stood to meet Duston's height. "You okay, Duston?"

"I f-f-fell on h-h-him."

"Fell on Tony? Now that's preposterous. How do you think you fell on my friend here?"

"In the D-D-Dumpster. He wa-wa-wa-wa-wa-wa-wa ..." Duston cleared his throat. "He was *dead!*"

"Oh, good gravy," Smith muttered and turned to his bantling. "Tony, he's all yours."

As if a switch had been flipped, Tony shed all the infant-like clumsiness and gained controlled dexterity. He opened his mouth to reveal six sharp fangs and sprung upon Duston.

Smith saw a flash of Duston raising his hands in defense, and then ... it was over.

Tony stepped back from his first kill and looked at his

master, awaiting the next command.

"This was *not* the way I had envisioned our first night together."

"What is all this peekaboo cavalry business?" Anya spat at the endless rows of vultures in the Carriage House Motel parking lot, all facing her in perfect ranks. Their numbers extended as far back as the edge of the building and started just a few feet from her. They blanketed the few parked cars in the lot, making the rooftop lumps look like dunes on a desert of black feathers. She couldn't see a single speck of asphalt; the birds were crammed together, wing to wing, tail to beak.

Anya took a step toward the ocean of black feathers and beady eyes all focused on her. "What is all this about? I hold the book! That means I hold all of you. How dare you defy me and not come when called."

She stopped and surveyed the impressive gathering of birds.

Movement within the back of the meadow of black caught her eye. The vultures bisected, splitting apart to create a circle around something and then filling in the space behind it as it moved forward. The moving circle inched closer to Anya, and she could see a small sleeping child—a girl. Six vultures carried the sleeping child on their shoulders and placed her at Anya's feet, the circle filling in behind them.

"What's ... Who's this?"

The lead vulture gestured its head toward the child.

"I don't understand."

The vulture opened its beak and hissed. It flapped its wings and rose off the ground just high enough to tap Anya's hand with its beak and then landed to nudge the girl's arm with its beak.

"You want me to … touch the child?"

The lead vulture lowered its head in a respectful bow.

Anya scanned the parking lot. Every vulture, for as far as she could see, made the same bowing gesture. Anya knelt before the child and placed her cold withered hand on the girl's forearm. She gasped as a tunnel of light filled her vision.

Voices collided with other voices, faster and faster, swirling around her head, until they became one mushed-together conversation:

I'm sorry, but she only has one year to live if she can't receive treatment.

I don't know where I'll get the money, Mom.

We lost all our insurance.

Mommy, it huuuurts!

Is this your first time hooking?

I need the money.

Mommy, I love you.

Squeeze my balls, bitch.

Work for me, and I'll get you the best clients—

I love you too, baby.

—the clients who pay the most … for your girl.

Am I going to die, Mommy?

I don't do anal.

You do now, whore!

I'm gonna take care of you, baby doll.

The window to begin treatment is closing on your little girl.

That's it. Suck it like you want it!

I'm sorry, miss, but you need at least a GED to apply here.

Read me another story, Mommy.

Bring her back in one piece.

I hate myself every fucking night for having to put out for limp dicks like you just so she can get—

Anya jumped back, the tips of her finger scorched from the sleeping child's skin. The witch put her fingers in her mouth to soothe the burning sensation. She glared across the sea of parking-lot squatters.

The vultures stood motionless, blinking in tandem, casting their judgment on her. And she could feel it. She felt it on her singed fingertips as well as inside her rotting chest cavity.

"Oh, c'mon! Don't tell me your pea brains have finally dialed into some fucking moral compass!"

The gaze from their beady eyes held steady on her.

"Her mother was a woman of the night! A vixen! I didn't know there was a clause about the *reason why* she was hooking, didn't know there were exceptions to your fucking rule. The black and white of it is, she was whoring herself and spreading her filth across the city. Stepp terminated her, fair and square, and now it's up to you—all of you—to fulfill the process that the book demands."

The birds of prey did not falter. Not a single beak or wing moved as the snow fell on their feathery coats, turning their color to a shade of ashen black.

Anya looked at the sleeping girl. "And what about her? So it's okay to kidnap a sleeping child—a sleeping *sick* child—just to highlight that you disagree? Put her back in bed, then come and give me my bantling."

Anya turned her back to the committee and faced her four ghouls standing in fear, their backs pressed against tree trunks. Anya glanced at Amber's corpse, snow catching in her red hair, and sighed.

"Fine," she mumbled with her back remaining to the

parking lot, relinquishing to the vultures. "Have it your way. Do as you think is fair to right my wrong. But"—she spun around to face the committee—"the next one he kills is mine, no matter what pathetic excuse she may have for defiling the streets and for tainting the goodness of society."

Anya flipped her black veil from her head over her pale face and disappeared into the woods. Her four Mushroom Cult generals turned and followed in a methodical systematic line.

Cyana took one last quick glance at the scene behind them before the ghouls vanished into the Mushroom Cult's own special netherworld. The parking lot was empty, sans a handful of parked cars. The sleeping child was gone. And not a single remnant of Amber's corpse remained.

The vultures had reversed the wrong.

Again.

5: SWEET NOTHINGS

Vicki arrived at the office even earlier than normal on Monday morning. She had spent way too much of her Sunday closing her eyes and replaying the feel of Stepp's hand on the backside of her jeans in Gardenia's parking lot. A few times during her reminiscing, she would allow herself to delve into furthering the moment—Stepp would press his body against hers, trapping her against his IROC. The world would disappear as they panted, and she would feel how he just couldn't resist her anymore, how he wanted to eat her up, how he wanted to drink her up, how he wanted to ravish all of her. And then her eyes would snap open, and she'd be looking at her boring and lonely apartment, Billy Idol's voice floating from the 8-track player on the kitchen counter.

Vicki unlocked Stepp's office door and skipped toward the light switches, then headed for the Mr. Coffee. After getting the first pot of the day brewing, she sat in her desk chair and wiggled her bum to situate herself. She readjusted the bronze horse paperweight so it sat flush against the appointment calendar on her desk. The grin that had started when she had woken up this morning with the thought of seeing her boss today still hadn't faltered when the Mr. Coffee had finished filling the pot with its warm black existence.

Vicki filled her Scooby-Doo mug with coffee, then added cream and sugar.

Vicki, you're twenty-one years old and going to work for an actual detective. Why do you want your Scooby-Doo mug at the office?

Because, Mom, Scrappy-Doo is just so darned cute!

She turned on the office radio and tuned it to her favorite news-music channel. She glanced at the clock and thought the minute hand must have slowed down.

She closed her eyes and allowed herself one last fantasy before her boss arrived. *If there is a God, this'll be the last time these images only exist inside my head.*

Stepp escorted his new client out of the office and turned to his secretary. "I need to see you in my office. Now." Vicki stood from her desk, leaving her Scooby-Doo mug of coffee half empty and stealthily checking her breath by using a cupped palm against her mouth. She followed Stepp into his office, and, when he kicked the door closed behind her, she didn't even realize her blouse had been ripped open until she heard the buttons bounce off the hardwood floor. She closed her eyes as his lips started at her neck and quickly trailed between—

"Vicki! Jesus!"

Vicki almost fell backward in her desk chair when Stepp's voice had to rise above a yell to get her attention. She jerked her hand away from inside her waistband and turned her back to him.

"You know what? I'm all for getting yourself off, but can you *not* do it here?"

Vicki kept her back turned to him and squeezed her eyelids as tight as they could go. She clicked her heels together three times, just in case that really did work. She even tried to sink her neck and head into her blouse, as if it could magically turn into a turtle shell.

The office was silent except for the sounds of Stepp pouring himself his first cup of coffee and the bridge to Yes's "Owner of a Lonely Heart" blanketing the room from the in-wall speakers.

Vicki peeked at Stepp from the corner of her eye. Embarrassment had just annihilated any desire she'd had to playfully mention his parking-lot groping. She didn't even know if she could look him in the eye for at least … forever.

"Any appointments this morning?" he asked, continuing with mundane Monday morning tasks, as if he hadn't sent any signals Saturday night and hadn't just caught her masturbating in his front office.

His stoic demeanor made it easier for Vicki to compose herself. "One at ten o'clock. Some guy—a …" She rifled through the daily planner. "Mr. Arends. He wanted to discuss that he thinks his neighbor is, oh my, catching and eating the neighborhood pets."

"For Christ's sake. Where do you find these people?"

"Me? They call here looking for you. I don't *find* them."

Stepp leaned against the folding table that hosted the Mr. Coffee and various accompaniments for his clients while they waited. He tilted his head and approached the gaudy fake Christmas tree in the corner.

"Did you decorate that?"

Vicki smiled and smoothed her blouse, raising her chin slightly. "I certainly did."

"Well, it looks like shit," he said and stormed past her

toward his office.

Vicki startled when his door slammed. She grabbed a pen and fiddled with it, trying to keep the welling tears from leaking onto her cheeks. She tapped the pen on her desk—*rata tat tat*—trying to comprehend why he was acting like such a dick. She laughed when she thought about saying out loud, "No pun intended," but chose not to.

She had been so sure—unequivocally certain—that things would be completely different this morning. She had theorized how Stepp's not-so-modest sign of affection Saturday night was the possible beginnings of something more—a lot more. Gentle kisses in the reception area, rough sex in his office, snuggling and movies on Friday nights, movie and dinner Saturday nights, hand-holding at Topsfield Fair next October, sweet nothings whispered to get her to laugh and to relax when she meets his parents for the first time at Easter …

"Vicki!"

Stepp's bark snapped her from her life planning, and she quickstepped down the hallway toward his office. She peeked only her head inside when she reached the opened door.

"Where the fuck is the key to my wet bar?"

Vicki stood motionless and silent. She had no idea he even had a key to his liquor cabinet. "I-I don't know—"

"*I don't know?*" he repeated, contorting his voice to sound like a whiny brat and mocking her tone. "Jesus fuck, Vic, what good are you? And will you get the goddamn phone please?"

Vicki glanced down the hallway and hadn't realized the office phone was ringing. She galloped toward her desk—her stomach in knots and her head confused.

"Detective Stepp's office, always one step ahead."

"Put J. on."

"May I ask who's calling?" Vicki asked.

"Just put him on, bitch."

Vicki pulled the receiver from her ear in alarm. She flicked her free hand's wrist to organize her jelly bracelets and to help compose herself. "He does not take anonymous calls, sir."

"Fine. Tell him it's Rhino."

"As in, Mr. Rhino? That's your last name?"

"Yeah. That's my last name. And my first name. And my motherfucking middle name. Tell him that goddamn Mr. Rhino Rhino Rhino is on the motherfucking phone."

Vicki placed the phone on her desk and scampered down the hallway. She knocked on Stepp's still-opened door.

"What?" he yelled from underneath his desk, on his hands and knees. "It better be an important call. This key is gone."

"He says his name is Mr. Rhino Rhino Rhino. But it sounds like a fake name, if you ask—"

Stepp slammed his head on the underside of his desk when he tried to leap to his feet after hearing who was on the phone.

Vicki took a step forward, hoping to comfort his injury. "You okay?"

"I'm fine," he said and swatted her away like a pesky mosquito. "Transfer him in."

Vicki stood somewhat shell-shocked at the events that had unfolded in such a short amount of time—events that were *exactly* the opposite of how she had fantasized about this morning playing out.

"Did I stutter? Fucking, move!"

"Yes, sir," Vicki answered and returned to her desk.

Stepp's door slammed closed right after she had heard him answer the transferred call. He began with, "Hey! Buddy, ol' pal …"

Stepp placed his palm to his forehead and used his elbow as a crutch to prop his head on his desk. He closed his eyes and waited for Rhino to finish berating him. *Where was that fucking key? If I ever needed a drink before in my life …*

"And Amber says *you* are the reason why she is quitting working for me—working for anyone, for that matter. Says you guys spent all night talking, and you convinced her to get her ass off the street and to do something respectful to help her sick kid. Says that your 'warm heart' and 'fatherly kindness' was the wake-up call she needed to get her head back on straight."

Stepp lifted his head and stared at the locked wet bar. *Wait. What the fuck did I do?*

"She was my number one source of income. She was my hot shining star. She has a goddamn waiting list of clients who want to 'fuck the new redhead.' I only let you skip the line because I knew, once you got a taste of her, you'd be a repeat customer too. She was bringing in more than half the Benjamins that all my other girls were bringing in combined! And you go and get all self-righteous and give her a moment of clarity? Who the fuck do you think you are?"

"I-I have no idea what you're talking about, Rhino. We snorted the coke and then fucked. I passed out, had some fucked-up dreams, and, when I woke, she was gone. We didn't talk at all. About anything."

"Lying prick. If I ever see you again—Oh, man, you'll regret ever meeting Amber. I should come over there right now and make you pay for all the lost wages I'll endure because of your fuckery. You dicked me out of a new Buick, you douchebag. It's not easy getting new girls, with the Wharf Killer still on the loose and all. Especially pieces of ass like Amber."

"I know who he is."

"Come again?"

"The Wharf Killer. I know who he is. I know his name, what he looks like, and I know where he frequents every Monday night."

"How will this help you help me?"

"I'll pay him a visit tonight. Wipe him like a turd off the face of the planet. Potential new recruits will feel safe again."

Rhino remained silent.

"I'll talk with Amber. Tell her there isn't any other way to get as much money and as fast as she does than by working for you."

"It's a start," Rhino grumbled.

Stepp spotted the key to the wet bar on the windowsill. "Rhino, as much as I'd love to keep chatting, I gotta go."

"Stepp, if you fail to take down the Wharf Killer or to bring Amber back to the family, I'll mutilate your genitals."

"Always a pleasure, Rhino. Good day, sir," Stepp retorted and slammed the receiver into the phone cradle.

He practically leaped across the room and grabbed the key. He unlocked the wet bar and grabbed a half-empty bottle of scotch.

"Vicki!" he called through his closed office door. "Cancel my ten o'clock appointment. Tell that fruitcake I got some other shit to take care of. And don't let him reschedule."

Stepp slid to the floor, his back against the wall, and took his first swig of many that day.

Vicki had been staring out the office window in turmoil when she heard Stepp's office door open a few moments after she had hung up from canceling Mr. Arends's appointment. She quickly scattered some papers around her desk and wrote the lyrics to "Rebel Yell" on a legal pad so she would appear busy. The knot in her stomach grew tauter.

Stepp stormed past without acknowledging her. An invisible wave of alcoholic odor followed in his path. Vicki thought, if she could see the scent, it wouldn't look too much different than the dust cloud that follows Pig-Pen in the *Peanuts* cartoons.

"Mouse, where's the sugar?"

Vicki ran around her desk and scampered to help him, so maybe his tirade would calm.

"I don't need your help!" He shoved her backward. "I just need the fucking sugar to be in the sugar holder where it's supposed to be. If *I* can't find it, how in the hell are my clients supposed to? Huh? You ever think of that?"

Vicki cowered at her desk and ran her fingertip along the length of the bronze horse paperweight sitting next to the desk calendar.

Stepp raised his hands in defeat and marched back to his office.

Vicki shook her jelly bracelets to her elbow as paranoia set in. *Had I done something wrong? Should I have made the first real move? Maybe he was waiting for me to kiss him. Maybe he's been thinking of me the same way I've been thinking of him and is feeling frustrated that he gave me a clear-cut signal that he wanted me, and I didn't follow through. Yeah, that's the ticket. That's gotta be what it is.*

Vicki giggled when the term "emotional blue balls" popped into her head. She returned to staring out the window, only this time, she felt much better about Stepp's manic behavior toward her; she now knew it was because she didn't act on her urges to give him what he wanted.

Melissa Smith entered Salem High's cafeteria and headed straight for the lunch line without scanning the large room. No reason to search for friends or classmates to sit with; she had never joined anyone at lunchtime, and no one had ever invited her to sit with them—either in the cafeteria or outside during free time.

She grabbed the top red tray from the stack and got in line behind some obnoxious football jocks, punching and giving each other noogies.

"Get a room," she muttered.

One turned to face her and studied her school attire, starting with her black headband and finishing with her black Keds.

"Freak," he retorted.

Melissa accepted the usual lunch slop and found an empty table next to the restroom. Across from her sat a small gaggle of seniors, yoking it up and having a grand old time, as if life was just peachy. Melissa bit into her bacon cheeseburger and stopped chewing almost immediately. "The Wharf Killer" floated from one of the seniors' mouths across the aisle and into her ears. She strained her hearing to decipher what they were saying about her grandfather.

"So I let my sister's best friend use the phone in the back room at work to call her boss and to tell him about how she thinks she chatted with the Wharf Killer in front of the restaurant."

The two younger girls, who Melissa now determined were not seniors, giggled and put their hands over their mouths in an exaggerated *Oh my* gesture. Melissa sipped on her chocolate milk as she leaned closer to hear better.

"My sis's best friend is a detective's secretary. I guess he was hired privately to hunt down the killer. I don't know anything else about that, but I think she may have helped crack the case."

"That is so rad," one of the girls swooned and batted her eyelashes.

"What's even radder, is that I was standing there when it all went down! I mean, I might get some reward or something—helping deliver information that leads to the capture of the dreaded Wharf Killer. Or some of the fame too, you know? If this is ever made into a movie or something."

The other girl placed her hand on his forearm. "It's like, you're kinda like a hero or something, Benji."

Benji smiled and looked at the tiled ceiling. "Yeah. I guess I might be. You want my autograph now or later?"

Melissa rolled her eyes as the girls giggled again.

Benji shoved a spoonful of banana pudding into his mouth. "I think my sister's friend will help her boss stake out the killer or something crazy like that. Maybe she'll take me with them."

"Who's her boss?" asked the girl who donned the waist-length French braid.

"His name is like Stand or Skip or ... something like that."

"Detective Stand?" the other asked and giggled.

Melissa froze midbite. The french fry pinched between her two fingers hung in the air. *Does he mean Stepp? Is he talking about Stepp's secretary, Vicki? Anya's main target? And she's this dweeb's sister's best friend? All too easy ...*

Melissa chomped her fry with determination, an evil smirk

across her face. *Like taking candy from a baby.*

The bell rang to announce the end of lunch and the handful of transitional minutes before her next class started. She stood and made sure she fell in line behind Benji, studying his movements and mannerisms as he cleared his leftover food into the wastebasket and placed his tray in the receptacle area at the front of the cafeteria. She stayed in close proximity behind him until the corridor split in opposite directions, and she needed to head left to geometry. Benji veered right toward whatever class he had next.

While her gaze focused on the corridor in front of her, Melissa's thoughts swarmed like a hurricane at all the possibilities and variables she needed to explore to infiltrate the senior's circle of friends and family, leading her organically— hopefully—to meet Anya's mark. It couldn't feel forced, and she had been racking her brain all weekend, devising a feasible plan; she couldn't just loiter unsolicited at Stepp's office and try to befriend his secretary. Even the ditziest broads' red flags would signal something was awry. But now a natural path to reach Vicki had possibly emerged, where suspicions would not arise.

As Melissa turned into Room 242 for geometry, she thought she heard Anya cackle and say, "That's my good girl. I knew you'd find a way."

"Line 'em up, and I'll knock 'em down," Smith said to Fain.

The bartender set three shot glasses in front of Smith as the usual Gardenia's clientele ate their family-style dinners behind him. Fain turned toward the shelves of spirits and removed the house whiskey.

Smith wagged a finger in the air. "Give me the good stuff tonight."

Fain placed both palms on the counter and leaned over the whiskey bottle toward Smith. "What are we celebrating? You dying on me or something?"

"Let's just say, I handed over the torch last night and have a new lease on life."

"You know what I respect about you?"

"*Hmm?*"

"Even at your age, you still find ways to spice things up. Never stagnant. You're not one to roll over and to play dead. And you know Monday's three-for-one deal is on house liquor only."

"I'm splurging tonight."

Fain pushed the three full shot glasses of top-shelf whiskey—no ice—toward his customer.

Smith held one in the air as a few drops spilled over the edge. "*Salud!*" He tossed back his head and drained the glass into his open mouth.

A large, rotund man took the empty stool next to Smith and nodded at him in greeting. "Hey, Fain. What's this MTV crap you have on the boob tube?"

Fain glanced at the television screen nestled between stein glasses. "Dunno, Chief. One of the waitresses must have put it on."

"Bunch of pansies jumping around in ladies' leotards. And girls think that's manly?" Chief McBrayer said. "Can't believe we're watching A Flock of Pigeons—or whatever they're called—instead of the game."

Fain reached up and turned the knob to Monday Night Football.

"Damn Dolphins," Chief McBrayer said, while staring at

the Miami-Dallas game. "The Pats will never get to a Super Bowl now, with that Marino kid playing in our division. What'chya say, partner?" He slapped Smith in the arm. "You got money on this game?"

Smith rubbed his shoulder and returned to his shot glasses.

"Smith, have you ever met our illustrious chief of police?" Fain asked.

"Can't say I've had the pleasure," Smith said and shook the chief's hand.

"What brings you in here, Chief?" Fain asked.

"Well, with the Wharf Killer's latest victim being found in your Dumpster on Friday night, I thought I'd take a casual gander around the neighborhood. Gonna start the night off right with a drink. For warmth, you know. Plus Rex and the mayor had my balls in a vise today down at city hall over this fucker."

Fain pointed at Smith. "That reminds me. I totally forgot. Some private eye was in here Saturday afternoon with a female, asking questions about you."

McBrayer glanced at Smith, and the detective darted his eyes back and forth between the two men.

"Well, not *you* specifically," Fain continued. "They were looking for an older man with the same last name but with a granddaughter named Eva. Said they have proof he's the Wharf Killer, and they are tracking him. I guess it pays to have the most common last name in all the Western world, huh? Almost an automatic alibi. I told him that you came in here every Monday night for happy hour."

"Wait," Chief McBrayer said. "Someone was in here, a detective no less, and claimed to know who the Wharf Killer is, and you didn't call the fucking station?" He slammed his fist on the bar, and liquid splashed from both Smith's and the chief's glasses. "I should lock you up for obstruction of justice, Fain!"

"He didn't have anything. He told me how he had a photograph of the Wharf Killer. When I questioned him about it, he tossed it across the bar at me."

"Holy baby Jesus on a popsicle stick! You even saw a photograph of the killer? That's it. I'm gonna kick your ass right here." Chief McBrayer slid off his stool.

"Hold on! He slid me a Polaroid, and it was blank. An undeveloped, unused Polaroid. Like it was some kind of sick joke. That's why I didn't call. Guy was a fucking looney tune."

Smith wiped the perspiration from his forehead.

"You don't have a granddaughter named Eva, do ya, Pops?" the chief asked.

Smith shook his head. "No, sir. I have two granddaughters, and the eldest is a freshman at Salem High. Her name is Melissa. The baby is Addie."

"See?" Fain said, pointing at Smith with all five fingers splayed. "The most common last name in the world, a joke photograph, and a granddaughter named Eva. That's all I got. That's why I didn't call."

"Do you remember who he was at least?" McBrayer grumbled.

"Said his name was Stepp. Had his secretary with him."

"*Aah*, yes. J. Stepp on Combs Avenue. Our narcotics task force has had him on their radar for a few months now."

Smith placed his shot glass on the bar, his ears tuned with curiosity. He needed to make sure he didn't seem overzealous to dig for more information on Anya's number one pick to carry on the family business. If only Fain would ask, it would make the conversation seem so much less—

"What do you guys think he's into?" Fain asked the chief.

Oh, thank God.

"We've been trying to get close to the North Shore's main supplier of coke, and we know Stepp is a customer. We just can't seem to ever pinpoint their meeting places. If we can put the squeeze on Stepp, the weasel might roll over on his dealer. Stepp is just a minnow. We're looking for the bigger fish. I wouldn't take anything that so-called dick says seriously. In fact, I might pay him a visit tomorrow. See if he'll divulge any of this info."

Smith felt a weight lift from his shoulders and got lost in the realization that, if Fain had told Stepp that Smith came here every Monday night, Stepp might be preparing to confront Smith here tonight. Smith entertained other scenarios that could unfold as early as right now, but then Chief McBrayer slammed his fist on the bar and screamed at the TV, "Throw the fucking flag, ref! Even I could see the hold from here!"

Smith jumped and spilled half a shot of top-shelf whiskey on his fedora sitting next to him.

Stepp had found a place in Salem Commons by the Witch Museum where he felt comfortable hiding himself. From this location, he could see all of Gardenia's parking lot, as well as everyone who entered and exited the restaurant. He would watch and wait for Smith to go inside for his weekly Monday drinks and then wait for him to come out to confront him.

Stepp's plan felt easy enough, if only he knew what kind of car Smith drove. He realized the elderly man might not even be here yet, and, if he was, Stepp wouldn't know it. He was basing this entire stakeout on Vicki's description—and that's assuming she remembered what Smith looked like.

"Dumb broad," Stepp whispered and chuckled.

Stepp leaned his back against the gazebo and reached for a cigarette. When he removed an empty package of Smolens from his back pocket, he crumpled it in his hand with one flex of his fist and searched his interior suit jacket pocket for his backup pack—the disgusting and only-use-for-emergencies pack of Brandts.

He balanced one between his lips, letting the chapped skin hold the cigarette in place, and used a match to light it. After taking three short puffs, he scowled and pursed his lips. "*Gah. Fucking gross!*" He placed the cigarette between his lips, more to satisfy an oral fixation than for feeding his nicotine craving.

Stepp pushed himself upright when he saw an elderly gentleman exit through Gardenia's doors. Stepp squinted, focusing better on the man's features, not sure if they matched Vicki's description.

Christ, every old geezer looks the same.

Then the elderly man held open the door for his wife— most likely—and they walked hand in hand toward a Porsche in the parking lot.

"Ain't no way in hell Smith brings his old lady out drinking on a Monday night, and ain't *no way* in hell he drives a Porsche."

Stepp relaxed against the gazebo's white latticework again. He took another drag of the Brandt and saw Chief McBrayer hold the doors open for a family of four.

"*Aww,* shit."

Stepp swung his body around to the far side of the gazebo, out of the line of sight from anyone on Gardenia's property. He kept his head down and waited for much longer than he felt it would take the chief to get himself into his car and to drive away. Stepp continued to stare at the patches of gray dirt-stained snow scattered throughout the commons.

"Official business?" asked a man with a gruff voice.

Stepp almost choked on his Brandt.

When Stepp didn't respond, the man continued. "A little birdie told me that you might have a description of the Wharf Killer. And I didn't know you were a magician, tossing around disappearing Polaroids at people."

Stepp refused to make eye contact. "I don't have anything on the killer, Chief."

"Oh, no? So my little birdie must be a big fat liar. I'll make sure I tell him that. What *are* you doing here? Loitering after sundown is a ticketable offense."

Stepp mustered the courage to meet the chief's gaze. "Client thinks her husband's cheating on her. Got a tip he's in there with his mistress right now. Gonna try to get some proof for the missus."

"Uh-huh," Chief McBrayer replied, nodding and not buying a single word. Then, surveying the commons, he asked, "You're not waiting for someone else, are you?"

"I don't even know who the Wharf Killer is, never mind where he might—"

"I'm not talking about the killer, J. I'm talking about your extracurricular activities."

Stepp bought himself some time by puffing on the Brandt while images of Amber and him snorting cocaine fluttered through his mind. After he figured taking any longer to smoke the cigarette would look like blatant stalling, he said, "I don't know what you're talking about."

"Sure you don't. You're not the only one keeping an eye on someone around here. Have a safe night, J."

Chief McBrayer walked away toward his parked personal vehicle hidden in the shadows between two lampposts.

Stepp turned toward Gardenia's again and sighed, wondering how much longer he would have to wait to see someone who might possibly be his mark. He directed his gaze over the top of a beat-up Pinto pulling out of the parking lot and onto the front door of the restaurant again.

Smith returned to the parking garage across from Gardenia's with Tony in the passenger seat. "We'll sit here and see if Stepp is as predictable as I think he is."

Tony grunted and clapped twice.

"What a nitwit Anya picked this time." Smith leaned forward to increase the fan speed on the heating system. "I'm cold. You cold?" he asked Tony. "Hey, look! There's the nitwit now. Man, either he makes this profession look bad or I just make it look that easy."

Smith and Tony watched Stepp jog across the street and barrel through Gardenia's front door.

"Guarantee you that he's too anxious to do a stakeout properly, and he'll head straight for the bar, loaded with questions. *Rookie.*"

Tony placed his palm on the passenger side window.

"Patience, young grasshopper. He won't get any further information from Fain. And, even if he stays to try to 'catch me,' he's too impatient to wait all night. He'll be leaving sooner rather than later. We just need to sit tight."

Tony relaxed and made a sound that resembled a cross between a cat's hiss and a dolphin's cry.

"Fine. You want some music? Here." Smith turned on the radio and tuned to his favorite AM jazz station. "These were the days, Tony. Nothing like a Friday night at Rippetoe's with the Anacostia Trio playing in the corner. Everything seemed simpler then. Well, before I met George Covington, that is. Don't you think it's getting a little blasé that, whenever there's a string of murders, we always get a moniker based on a location? The Boulevard Killer, the Wharf Killer, the Boston Strangler, the Muswell Hill Murderer, the Whitechapel Murderer—better known as Jack the Ripper of course."

Tony grabbed Smith's arm with his decaying and rotting ghoulish hand and then pointed.

Smith squinted to make out the person leaving Gardenia's. "That's not him, my friend. Don't worry. Time is on our side." Smith increased the volume of the Benny Goodman song coming from the car's speakers. "But I can't help but feel like I'm the mouse chasing the cat who's chasing the mouse."

Stepp used both palms to shove open Gardenia's front doors to exaggerate his frustration as he left the restaurant and bar.

"Don't know why some shitbag bartender is protecting a serial killer," Stepp mumbled as he traversed the street toward his parked car. "Must be in cahoots together. I'll fix that." He turned to face the restaurant's exterior, while standing on the double-yellow solid traffic lines. "You hear me? I'll fix you up good, Fain!"

A horn honked as a car had to swerve to miss hitting him and startled Stepp into reality. He flipped off the driver and continued toward Salem Commons. When he slid into his IROC, he removed a baggie from his glove box and dabbed some white powdery substance on the length of his index finger.

He snorted the cocaine in a straight line and closed his eyes, letting his head loll on the headrest.

He snapped awake and violently shook the cobwebs from his brain. He reached under his passenger seat and let his fingers search for the item. He felt the cold steel and smiled. He removed a crowbar from among discarded cigarette butts and littered Wendy's wrappers. He let the crowbar fall into both opened palms, and then he gripped the long metal weapon.

I'll fix you right now, asshole.

Stepp flung open the car door and charged across the commons, tapping his weapon into an open palm like a metronome, and headed for Gardenia's front entrance again.

Straight back to the bar. Don't stop to talk or to look at anyone. One swing and he'll drop. Then get the fuck out of Dodge.

He wiped dripping snot from his upper lip and snorted the mixture of cocaine and mucus threatening to seep out. His unfaltering focus on the restaurant's front doors inhibited his ability to notice the large figure barreling across the commons or to hear the footfalls crunching the slush under each step.

Stepp didn't have time to react with the crowbar when the closed fist connected with his right ear. A loud yet faraway buzzing replaced the night sounds of the city as his body fell limp into a gray-colored snowbank, the crowbar landing …

Smith slapped Tony's arm to get his attention. "You hear that?"

Tony darted his gaze in all directions, like a child looking for an approaching ice cream truck.

"You hear me? I'll fix you up good, Fain!"

"That's Stepp!" Smith said and exited the Pinto, so he could get a better fix on the detective's location. He spotted Stepp standing in the middle of traffic, yelling at the restaurant. "C'mon. He's left and is acting erratic."

Tony fumbled with the door handle, manhandling it like the device was foreign to him, until Smith quickly circled the car and opened the door for his bantling. Once Tony had exited the car unscathed, Smith escorted him across the street and into the shadows of the commons.

"That's him there."

Smith stopped and extended his arm sideway across Tony's chest, like a boom gate.

"Wait," he whispered. "Looks like he's coming back."

Tony and Smith stood motionless in the shadow of the gazebo and watched Stepp cross the commons, tapping something long and shiny in his hands. Tony frantically tugged on the fabric of Smith's coat at the elbow, like a toddler trying to get their parents' attention. Tony squeaked with nervous excitement and pointed.

Smith swatted the ghoul's hand from his coat sleeve and followed the invisible trajectory of Tony's pointing.

"Blasted," Smith muttered and dragged Tony to the ground so their backs were against the gazebo lattices. Smith peeked over the banister to watch.

Smith and Tony watched the large albino man not even slow his sprint when he reached Stepp from behind and smashed his fist into the detective's head. Tony stood when Stepp hit the snowbank, but Smith yanked the ghoul to the slushy earth. Smith placed his index finger against his closed lips to shush Tony.

By the time Smith could settle Tony and had an opportunity to glance at the short-lived melee across the commons, Stepp had regained consciousness and was standing squared-off with the monster of a man.

Rhino grabbed a fistful of Stepp's blazer and yanked him to his feet.

Stepp took a step backward and got into a boxer's stance, knowing full well that, if it came to blows, he would be dead.

"You think I want to fight you?" Rhino chuckled. Plumes of white steam escaped his mouth and rolled into the cold air. "I want to fucking kill you, so put down your scrawny-ass arms and take the beating you deserve like a man."

Stepp squatted, trying to find his discarded weapon, and grabbed a handful of slush instead. He stood to meet Rhino's gaze again.

"What're you gonna do? Snowball me to death? *Cream puff.*"

Stepp dropped the snow and extended his hand in a Stop gesture. "Can we talk about this?"

"Sure. Let's talk about how you've cost me my number one golden goose. You didn't steal from me once, Stepp Ahead. You take from my purse strings every single night Amber is not on the streets. That means you owe me for every single night she—"

Stepp giggled. "You said *purse.* Don't you mean, *fanny pack?*"

Rhino punched him straight in the nose.

"What the shit was that for?"

"You need to learn some respect. You need to know who owns you."

"You don't own—"

"Until you've paid back your debt to me for Amber, I most certainly do." Rhino picked up Stepp's crowbar. "I'm gonna start with your legs."

Rhino wound up like a batter—*swing, batter, batter, batter, batter, swing!*—and drove the crowbar into Stepp's knee.

The detective crumpled to the snow.

"Too easy," Rhino muttered and pulled back the crowbar like a golfer.

Stepp used one hand to prop himself up and used the other hand to shield the oncoming blow. "Okay! Okay! What do you want from me? How can I make this right?"

Rhino did not relax his golfer stance. "I want to put your expertise to work for me."

"Well, can you lower the crowbar while we talk?"

"Nope."

"Fine. Can I at least get up?"

"Nope. You can sit there and get your fake-ass Armani pants wet."

Stepp shook his head and brought his knees to his chest so less of his pants were absorbing the melting slush underneath him.

"You're gonna work off your debt."

"I don't have a debt with—"

Rhino flexed the crowbar farther back and gritted his teeth. "Every fucking night that I don't have that whore redhead on the streets collecting money for me is on *your* tab. *Capiche?*" Rhino tossed the crowbar into the hedges, and powdered snow rustled from the small twigs to the ground. "Since you're so good at flipping my girls, you'll be my personal bookkeeper."

"I'm not following."

"Did I tell you that you could motherfucking speak?"

Stepp shook his head and reached inside his blazer for a Smolens. "Goddammit!" he said, remembering he had smoked the last one, and his fist had clenched the pack of terrible-tasting Brandts instead.

Rhino kicked Stepp's overly polished shoes. "You have a listenin' problem. I'll tell you when you can speak." Rhino squatted so he was nose to nose with the detective. "I'll even tell you when you can breathe." Without permission, he reached into Stepp's pack of cigarettes and removed one. "Bookkeeping. Or, maybe it's something closer to spring-cleaning—in wintertime. I dunno. *Bookkeeping* sounds less abrasive. I have a few girls who, for lack of a better word, have gone rogue. Owe me a shit ton of money for jobs they worked under my management. I have a list in the Buick. Some real names, mostly just street names. I need their tabs closed. You close their tabs, and I'll close yours."

Stepp took a puff off the Brandt, and the nicotine made his body feel sick but helped his mind relax. "So you want me to take this list and get these girls to pay up?"

Rhino bent to Stepp's eye level again. "Yeah, they're gonna pay up all right. You're gonna make sure they don't work for anyone else ever again. They're gonna settle their debt with their lives."

"Oh, you gotta be kidding me, man. How long have we known each other? How long have we been doing business together? How long have we been *friends*? And now you want me to start killing hookers who haven't paid their pimp?"

"This isn't business, Stepp. When you talked Amber into going straight, you made it personal. You stole directly from me and my enterprise. You *will* take care of these girls, or I'll take care of you. Think of yourself as a customer in a restaurant who forgot their wallet but still ate. You gotta wash those dishes to work off your check. Well, homeboy, you gotta work off your debt."

Stepp stood, this time without asking permission. "C'mon. Isn't there any other way I can make it up to you? I'll bring in ten new customers. Repeat customers."

"You scared of killing some skanks?"

Stepp looked at his scuffed shoes and moved some slush around. "Nah, man. I ain't scared. I could kill, if I had to."

"One other payment I would accept. Wouldn't involve any killin'."

Stepp didn't reply but gave Rhino his full attention.

"That little number who works for you. Get her to moonlight out here for me, as a side job and all that."

"Vicki? Shit, bro. I'm pretty much convinced Vicki is a virgin."

Rhino clapped in glee. "Perfect! You get her on my payroll, and you're scot-free. Virgins get me *paid!*"

Stepp smoked the last puff of the Brandt and tossed the butt into the bushes. "Nah, man. I'll take the list."

"They're on the move. Try to keep quiet," Smith begged his ghoul.

He and Tony tactically moved within the shadows, following Stepp and the large albino man as they walked side by side toward a blue Buick parked a block from Stepp's IROC. When the man and Stepp stopped at the Buick, Smith forced Tony down into a crouching position by pushing on his shoulders.

"Wait. Any closer and they could spot us."

Smith watched the albino man lean into his car, and the Buick's interior dome light shone on him retrieving a large folder–like binder. Smith recognized the binder as something close to what his grandchildren use for school.

Smith shushed Tony when he heard Stepp and the man speak, even though Tony had been silent.

"Are you fucking kidding me?" Smith heard Stepp say. "A fucking Trapper Keeper? What are we, in middle school?"

"*That's* what it's called," Smith said to Tony, who just cocked his head in confusion, then Smith chuckled. "Wish I could tell Wynn about this. She'd get a kick out of seeing a man of that stature whip out a Trapper Keeper during what looks like a drug deal."

Smith watched Stepp take the binder and open it. Smith turned one ear toward the two men, so he could hear them more clearly.

"All of these?" he heard Stepp say.

"That's my list," he heard the albino man reply. "Underneath each name is the best date of birth I could find for each of them. That's all I got. Some of these girls are ghosts, man. You do what we talked about, and consider my business with you closed."

Smith squinted to see the details of the transaction better and saw Stepp rip a single page from the binder and shove it into his blazer pocket.

"It'll be done. Then I never want to see your fucking face again, you albino freak."

Smith was surprised when the insult didn't faze the large man, and he just nodded and replied, "You have six weeks. Then I come after you."

Smith watched Stepp approach his IROC without acknowledging the large man's threat.

"This just got interesting," he said to Tony. "We need to find out what's on that page. I have a feeling it has nothing to do with a little cocaine."

Tony played with a frozen berry he had found in the slush and ignored Smith's dialogue.

"You'll get there," Smith said with confidence. "Soon I'll have you practically running the show, like how Anya has Pum'kin and Candy and the rest of her so-called generals running the Mushroom Cult." He patted the bantling's hand. "But now, c'mon. We gotta follow Stepp and see if he does anything with the information on that that sheet of paper tonight."

Tony grunted as the pair rushed across the commons and into the Pinto. Smith pulled onto Essex Street and caught up to the IROC after two traffic lights. Smith sighed in disappointment when he realized they had tailed their mark to the most mundane of places: his home.

Smith watched the IROC navigate into the long driveway off Lowell Street in Peabody, and he continued driving past the mini-mansion, Tony looking out the passenger window, like he were a tourist on a safari.

"Don't be disappointed. Tonight was not a bust." He patted Tony's knee in reassurance. "At least Stepp has given us a reason to investigate something again. We'll pick this up again tomorrow at Stepp's office. A good ol'-fashioned stakeout is what this'll be. It's like I can just taste those early years again."

Smith turned to Tony to see if his ghoul was listening, and the passenger seat was empty.

"Well, it's good to know he's at least mastered the ability to appear and vanish at will," Smith said to the empty vehicle and tuned the radio to a classical station.

Wynn had Smith's TOP GUN FOR HIRE mug filled with hot chocolate and topped with whipped cream waiting for him, when Smith walked through the front door.

"How's Fain?" she asked as he removed his jacket and shook off some residual snowflakes from the shoulders.

"Same. Met the chief tonight."

"Of police?"

"Yeah. Drank with me at the bar. Nice-enough fella. Loves his football."

"Did he say if there was any progress in the Wharf Killer case?"

Smith took his first sip of the hot chocolate, a clump of whipped cream clinging to his top lip when he pulled the mug from his mouth. "Said they have their eyes on someone."

Wynn giggled.

"What?"

She motioned for him to approach. "C'mere, you big lug."

Smith took a step toward his wife, and she wiped the cream from his lip.

"I don't know what kind of life I would've had if you hadn't wooed me back the second time, Detective. But I'm sure it wouldn't have been as rich and as full as the one you gave me."

Smith took another sip from his almost fifty-year-old mug and raised an eyebrow. "Are you trying to sweet-talk me, little lady?"

She giggled again. "Maybe. You're supposed to be the big bad detective. You tell me."

Smith set the mug on the counter and scooped up his wife.

He carried her over the threshold of their bedroom entrance as if it were their wedding night all over again.

Rhino had continued to watch the IROC until he could no longer see the taillights in the distance. Plus a jalopy pulled behind Stepp farther down the road, blocking Rhino's direct line of sight.

Rhino slipped into his Buick and headed toward Pickering Wharf. It was cold but not too cold for his girls to turn a few tricks tonight. He steered the vehicle onto Derby Street and became worried when he saw no traces of anyone around. The road curved, and, when he spotted one of the girls on the corner, he rolled down his window. He slowed the Buick to a crawl and motioned for her to approach the car.

"Where is everyone? Don't tell me it's another slow night."

"Tonight has been totally bitchin', Rhino. The girls have been so busy. There's no one around because they're all out with their johns."

"Then why are you out here?"

"Man, I've already had three paying. I'm out here on my fourth rotation."

"That's my good girl."

"Something about them holidays," she said. "Dudes get sick of the wife yappin' about making sure they get little Billy that toy he wants and come out here for some tension relief. Christmastime changes good men."

"That's very insightful. Didn't know you were a philosopher."

"Fuck you, Rhino," she retorted with a smirk. "You so

bad!"

"Alright, *gurl*. Stay safe. I'm expecting a chunk of moolah tomorrow morning, if what you're saying is true."

"The city is alive tonight, boy!"

"And God is good," Rhino replied and let his foot off the brake, and the Buick idled forward from the corner.

"Hey, Rhino!"

He pressed the brake.

"Do you think, because it's Christmastime and all, maybe us girls could, like, keep some extra income from tonight's jobs? You know? To have some extra cash for gifts and shit?"

Rhino rolled up his window and stepped on the gas, leaving her reflection in the rearview mirror to shrink smaller and smaller.

"God is good."

6: COMMUNION

"Mel, you almost ready for school? You're gonna be late," Travis called through the door after knocking three times. "You don't want another detention, do you?"

"Be out in a sec," Melissa answered with a mouthful of toothpaste.

She spat into the sink and grabbed her hairbrush. Looking at her reflection while dragging the bristles along her shoulder-length hair, she thought about meeting with Graham after school. She smiled about how she had faked receiving detentions so her parents wouldn't expect her home for at least an hour to ninety minutes after school had ended, using that time to rendezvous with her twentysomething-year-old boyfriend.

Sometimes being scolded at home for a "fake" detention was worth the stolen time she spent with Graham.

Daydreaming about her beau and the repetitive, almost hypnotic–like motion of her hairbrush distracted her from noticing the witch's reflection in the mirror, standing behind Melissa.

Anya cleared her throat to get Melissa's attention.

Melissa's gaze refocused from her faraway fantasy and onto the pale ghoul's reflection in her bathroom mirror. Melissa turned to face Anya, but she was alone in the bathroom. She turned back to the mirror, and Anya stood there again.

"Keep looking forward and continue getting ready. We only have a few minutes before your dad bangs down the door to get you to school."

Melissa placed her hairbrush on the sink counter and wrapped a red ribbon around her ponytail.

"You look all dolled up," Anya said.

"Seeing Graham after school today."

"And what fictitious trouble did you get into now?"

Melissa chuckled. "Parents think I fell asleep in English class and got two detentions this week."

"For just falling asleep? You need to be careful with your excuses. Your parents aren't stupid. If your 'detentions' get too far-fetched, they'll be onto you. Then you can kiss Graham good bye because you'll probably be grounded until you're twenty-one."

"I told them that I talked in my sleep, so I got one detention for falling asleep and the second for disrupting the class with my outburst."

"Brilliant. I knew there was a reason we would make a good team. But I'm not here to chitchat. I wanted to know if you've thought about my offer."

Melissa's gaze met Anya's dead eyes in the mirror. "I found the spell you left me from the book. I wish I knew when I was supposed to use it."

"You'll know. And, if you help me, you can be my apprentice, and I'll hand the entire book over to you—all its spells, all its power, all its control over the Mushroom Cult and the vultures."

Melissa swallowed hard and leaned closer to the mirror as she applied mascara. "I guess I'm still not 100 percent sure why though."

"If you can get close to Stepp's secretary, then I can use you as a catalyst. If she truly is the Chosen One—the virgin I've been anticipating for hundreds of years now—then I'll have no need for such earthly artifacts, like that book. I'll become divine and *be* the book. And you can carry on the Witch's Purpose, for as many centuries as you wish."

"Would there be a Chosen One for me to find too? Could I eventually become immortal, like you?"

"I don't see why not, child. But … baby steps. First, get me close to Vicki, and let's hope I'm not wrong again this time."

"Why don't you just do your *poof* magic and appear in her house and do what you need to do? You already have the power to appear wherever you want. For instance"—Melissa turned both hands' palms up and swiveled her body—"you're in my fucking bathroom."

"The Chosen One is special. She is protected by … well, *them*. The Chosen One is immune to spells and witchery."

"*Them?*"

"Let's just call them *the antivultures*. They think they're so smug, trying to keep the universe balanced, keeping power contained and out of the hands of who *they* deem dangerous. *Them*. They protect the Chosen One, so people like me—and you—can't supersede their own dominance. Selfish pricks are what they are. Scared that a woman might do a better job at controlling all the imps who infest this planet."

Melissa leaned away from the mirror, replacing her mascara with a tube of Covergirl's Love Me Later lipstick, and applied the pink gloss to her lips. "You said you thought you had found the Chosen One before. How were you able to get close to her?"

"She had stolen the book. The book granted me access to her. Plus, if you were fucking following the story, you'd remember it turned out she *wasn't* the Chosen One, so I would've been able to get to her regardless."

Melissa took her gaze from her Love Me Later application and met Anya's reflection. "Then just give Vicki the book and use it to get close to her."

"And how, Einstein, do you think that'll work?"

"I dunno. Hide it in her desk drawer at her office or something."

"You know what? When you say stupid shit like that, I reconsider this friendship."

"Well, I overheard Vicki's best friend's brother, who's a senior at my school, talking about Grandpapa."

Anya wrung her hands in delight. "How confident are you with turning on the charm?"

Melissa returned her gaze to applying the pink lipstick. "You think I'm putting on this shitty color lipstick for Graham? This is for the brother. He'll be eating out of my hands by final bell today."

Anya placed her bony hand on Melissa's shoulder. "That's my good girl."

Branch–like fingers squeezed her shirt, but Melissa knew, if she turned around, the witch would not be visible.

"Plus Graham wouldn't notice if I was wearing lipstick or not. He'd be too busy putting his mouth in other places."

"You do know he could go to jail, right? There's at least a ten-year difference."

"*Aww*, look at you! Caring about something other than yourself."

Anya cackled. "Don't tell your grandfather that. It'll ruin

my street creds."

Melissa rolled her eyes at the three-hundred-year-old witch trying to sound hip in her bathroom. "Get outta here, Anya. I need to get going before my dad wigs out."

"Good luck with loverboy today."

"Which one? The dweeb-o-rama brother or Graham?"

"You think I give two shits about your real boyfriend?"

"There ya go again, only caring about *numero uno.*"

"Would you expect anything less from your surrogate aunt?"

Melissa stuck out her tongue. "And I don't need luck when I turn on the charm."

She blew the mirror a kiss, noticing her reflection was the only figure in the mirror again.

Melissa spied Benji from the end of the hallway. The copious amount of mousse in his ridiculously feathered hair disgusted her. But ... she had a job to do.

She blotted her lips together to evenly distribute the fresh layer of Love Me Later lipstick and headed toward the cafeteria. She navigated around classmates, picking up speed to pass students in front of her as well as slowing her pace when she had overtaken Benji to get to the lunch line. She readjusted her trajectory so she "coincidentally" found herself directly behind him in line for food.

She reached for a red plastic tray first, so he was forced to bump into her hand as he reached for one, and then he apologized.

"No biggie," she replied.

He grabbed his tray and faced forward, waiting his turn to be served his Tuesday taco.

Melissa quickly ruminated all the believable reasons for her to continue engaging with him. She knew she had mere seconds before the space of time would have grown to where anything further said would feel forced and contrived.

"Taco Tuesday!" she said loudly.

Benji turned to face Melissa.

"My favorite," she murmured.

"These aren't nearly as good as Hank's Taco Shed. Now those tacos are dank," Benji replied.

"That's the new place in Lynn, right?" she asked, knowing exactly what place he was talking about.

"Yeah, downtown. I guess it's huge out in the Midwest. It just took this long to get to us over here."

She knew this too. Then she kicked herself for not using the fact that Hank Steel—the retired news reporter who had founded and still owned the Hank's Taco Shed food chain—was one of her grandfather's best friends as a conversational piece.

Man, he opened the door on that one, and I FUBAR-ed it all up.

"I've heard good things about it" was all she could muster. How could she tell him now that she had been there when Hank had flown in to personally attend the location's grand opening? And that she had then spent all weekend of the extended Thanksgiving school break with her grandparents and Hank?

Well, that ship has sailed.

She cursed herself again for letting slip through her hands such an easy way to continue engaging Benji. Not to mention that, based on his enthusiasm for Hank's tacos, her relationship with the owner could have given her bragging rights.

Stupid! Stupid!

Melissa could feel Anya shaking her head in disapproval, watching from the netherworld—or wherever it is she hides when she's not here.

"If you ever get a chance, check it out. You won't be disappointed," Benji added.

"Maybe I will."

Benji thanked the lunch lady after she placed a plate of processed-looking ground beef trapped inside a stale hard taco shell onto his tray.

Melissa shook her head and let him walk toward his desired table. She traipsed to her empty table with her head hung.

She spent the period eating alone—again—while stealing glances at Benji's table where he entertained the same two much-younger schoolmates. Their forced giggling nauseated her. She took a gulp of her Tab and scowled at them.

Enjoy him while you still can, hussies. He'll be mine soon enough.

Stepp strutted into the reception area to find Vicki. "Heading out for a bite to eat. You want me to bring you back anything?"

Vicki looked up from painting her nails. "So, you're being nice to me today?"

Stepp looked perplexed. "Had I been mean to you?"

Vicki flung her hair over her shoulder in disgust. *He doesn't even know how he was treating me. Maybe ... Maybe it was all in my head. Maybe it was my problem and not his.* "Sorry. I must have misread you. My bad," she answered.

"You know what? Let's close the office for an hour and go

get lunch together."

Vicki's eyes lit up. "For reals? Give me two minutes."

Stepp watched her trot down the hallway toward the unisex bathroom, his gaze lowering to rest on her sashaying buttocks as she ran. He clenched his lips and made a sound as if he were famished and a hamburger had just been placed in front of him.

After a few moments, Vicki exited the bathroom and approached him with a wide smile. He noticed her hair had been teased more than when she had gone into the bathroom, and she had applied a fresh layer of rouge.

"Ready?" he asked.

Vicki nodded, taking deep, silent breaths to curb her enthusiasm as he held the door open for her.

"We'll take the IROC."

She skipped down the single flight of stairs to Combs Avenue at street level, and they headed toward his parked IROC.

"What is this happy horseshit?" he asked as he navigated around the front of the sports car. He ripped off a pink slip of paper adhered to the windshield by the wiper blade. "A fucking parking ticket?" He glowered at the meter next to the vehicle. "I fed this motherfucker to get me to at least two o'clock! Well, I ain't paying this shit." He crumpled the paper and tossed it into the storm drain below the IROC.

Vicki had taken a step backward, caught off guard by his explosive anger. Again.

Stepp looked at her and noticed the trepidation on her face.

"Let me get that for you." He walked to the passenger side and opened the car door for her. "*Madame ...*"

Just like a real gentleman, she thought. *Who said chivalry is dead?*

"Why, thank you, kind sir," she replied and curtsied before

getting into the car.

Stepp got into the driver's seat and looked at her. "Top down?"

Vicki giggled. "That would be wicked."

Stepp unlatched the glasses of the T-top and tossed them into the back seat, creating a T-shaped open roof.

"Chinese sound good?"

"Sounds perfect."

Stepp placed his right hand on the automatic gear shift and moved the lever to Drive. The car squealed as he fishtailed into traffic, sending Vicki into wild shrieks of excitement and glee.

The driver of the Pinto who had been casing Stepp's office all morning had a hard time getting his jalopy to surge forward into traffic behind the IROC. The driver thought he had even heard his reanimated passenger deliberately snicker for the first time.

"Tony, did you just laugh at me?" Smith darted his gaze from the roadway to his undead passenger. "I know this car is a tin lizzie, but at least I don't look like a goober in that eyesore of a machine."

Tony remained silent as he kept his focus on the IROC ahead in traffic.

"I doubt he's going anywhere with his secretary to conduct any *real* business that we'd be interested in, but a good private eye facilitating a solid stakeout doesn't assume anything when their mark goes on the move."

Tony grunted and hissed.

"You're right. They could just be picking up his dry cleaning. But that's not the point. We leave no errand left unturned. The one time we decide not to tail him because we assume something wrong will be the one time we miss discovering what he's up to."

When the IROC pulled into the Fortune Cookie's parking lot, Smith continued driving past the Chinese restaurant and found on-street parking farther down Main Street, where he and Tony could observe when Stepp and his secretary were finished with lunch and continued on to their next destination.

Stepp raised a small white porcelain cup filled with hot Chinese tea. "Cheers, to my *favoritist* secretary."

Vicki blushed and enjoyed the *clink* sound when her cup touched his. "I don't even think *favoritist* is a word."

"It is now."

"Oh, yeah? Since when?"

"Since I said it out loud."

"You have that much power, do ya?" she said and squinted, trying to look seductive and flirtatious but then stopped when she realized he'd just think she had something in her eye or had a weird tic or something. She was well aware that *Smooth* was not her middle name.

"Oh, girl, you don't know how much power I can unleash unto the world."

"I'd like to see that sometime."

Stepp spooned a ladleful of chow mein onto his plate. "If you play your cards right, maybe one day you will." He finished the statement with a wink that sent Vicki's stomach into flutterbies.

"Any development on the Wharf Killer case?"

He shook his head and raised a finger in a *wait a minute* gesture while he swallowed his mouthful of food. "I got a new ... client last night, trying to track down some runaway family members from a list he gave me. Thought I'd work on that first before I really dive into the Wharf Killer."

"Oh? But isn't hunting down someone who is killing more pressing than some runaways?"

"I can probably bang out this list in a week. Plus the pay was something I couldn't say no to. Needs it done pronto."

"Well, I won't question you. You are the genius one here, after all."

Stepp tossed a crab rangoon into his opened mouth. "You can help me with the list tomorrow morning when I get into the office."

"Why not this afternoon?"

Stepp stopped chewing. "Are you questioning my process?"

Vicki swallowed hard, afraid she had overstepped her bounds.

"Are you questioning this mastermind of a detective? This brain, this marvel of science?" He tossed a boneless sparerib at her and smiled.

Vicki picked the sparerib off her pants—the teriyaki glaze leaving a small oily stain—and tossed it back at him.

Stepp ducked and laughed, the sparerib landing on the threadbare carpet. "See? I can be fun sometimes."

"Yeah, sometimes," she replied and adjusted her jelly bracelets.

"In all seriousness, I have a date."

Vicki stopped playing with her bracelets. "Oh?"

"Some gal I met at aerobics."

"You go to aerobics?"

"Yeah, every Tuesday night at the YMCA. She looked

totally bitchin' in her leotards and—You probably don't want to hear this stuff, huh?"

Instead of answering, Vicki dabbed her cloth napkin into her complimentary glass of water and scrubbed the oily stain on her pants, trying to distract her attention and her gaze from anything but the words coming out of his mouth.

"Do you mind hanging at the office for a bit in case any clients need to leave me a message?"

Vicki didn't answer but focused her gaze on the large dragon mural on the Fortune Cookie's far wall.

"You can cut out early. I'll pay you for the whole day."

Vicki composed herself and finally met his gaze and spoke in a monotone and without emotion. "That's very kind of you."

"Finish up, Mouse. I gotta get you back to the office, so I can go home and freshen up. I scored me and my date tickets to a sneak preview of that new break-dancing movie in Boston."

Vicki folded her soaking-wet napkin. "*Electric Boogaloo*," she muttered.

"No, I don't think that's it. It's a part two of something."

She pursed her lips and held her breath before releasing a long-drawn-out exhale. "Can we go, please?"

"Sure."

Stepp waved down the waiter and asked for the bill.

He still had not noticed the beat-up Pinto that merged with traffic behind him as he left the Fortune Cookie's parking lot and headed toward his office to drop off his secretary.

Melissa whistled as she passed the graveyard on her way to Pickering Wharf. She tugged at her shirt's hem for the umpteenth time, self-conscious someone would see the residual traces of Graham's fingers when he had rumpled her shirt during their necking session.

She turned onto Derby Street and glanced at her watch. She had maybe thirty minutes to spend on the wharf before she headed home, before her parents would get suspicious of the length of her so-called detention.

Melissa could close her eyes and still navigate to Madam Hapney's storefront. Sometimes she thought she knew the psychic's modest office better than she knew her own bedroom.

The small chime above the door rang when Melissa entered the hardwood-floored space. The tiny psychic, hunched over a large book at her desk, did not look up.

"Knew you were coming," Madam Hapney said.

Melissa approached the psychic and sat on the opposite side of the desk.

Hapney looked up. "Knew you were coming, child, but the reason why is a little fuzzy. What are you hiding?"

Melissa played with the plastic ring Graham had won for her at Salem Willows in the Captain Claw toy-grabber machine.

Madam Hapney cocked her head. "I don't think what's troubling you has anything to do with Graham, even if your nervous fidgeting with that ring he gave you is trying to throw me off the scent."

"How do you know he gave this to me?"

"Because I'm a psychic. And because that hickey looks new, and I don't think you would've bought that ring for yourself. It's called *adult intuition*. There's nothing mystical about being able to put two and two together."

Melissa touched her neck where the broken capillaries were already pooling and bruising her skin. "I kinda have to cheat on him but not really."

"Oh?"

"I have to fulfill a promise I made to a kind-of family member, and it involves me getting close to a boy at school, so I can get close to one of his friends."

"Sounds like a dangerous tryst."

"I don't know what that word means, but I'm more afraid of what'll happen to me if I *don't* do it. Plus I was promised a pretty radical reward."

"It's nothing illegal, is it?"

"Nah. But I don't want Graham to find out because I don't want to have to explain the situation to him, and he might not even understand. It's only gonna—hopefully—take a week or so to do it, and then I can go back to being with Graham again."

Madam Hapney leaned back in her wicker chair and pressed her palms together in a praying position. "So, are you more troubled by committing this favor for your family member or by Graham finding out you had to do it?"

"Graham. I *want* to help out my aunt—well, she's not really my aunt, just a close family friend—but I don't want to be unfaithful to my boyfriend."

"A boyfriend who is almost ten years your senior."

"Yes."

"Senior to a girl who is a freshman in high school."

"Alright! Jeez, I get it. What're you, my mom, for Christ's sakes?"

"I dunno. Does your mom even know about Graham?"

Melissa glared at Hapney. "You should know that, with your psychic-ness or whatever."

Hapney chortled. "In fact, you're right. I do. And you better make sure they never find out. I think your dad might finally have a reason to use that gun he keeps in his sock drawer."

"Wait. Dad has a gun in the house?"

She smiled a crooked grin. "Don't you know you're talking to the one-and-only Madam Hapney, child?"

A chill ran down Melissa's spine, and she glanced at the large celestial-decorated clock on the wall. "Sometimes that's what I'm afraid of."

"I see you have somewhere to be. Faking detention again to see Graham, are we?"

Melissa didn't answer. She was sure the psychic already knew.

"Okay, then. Let's see what the big ball can tell us about your conundrum."

Hapney removed a large cloth napkin that had been covering an opaque-colored glass ball. Before the napkin hit the floorboards, swirls and storm–like clouds appeared inside the ball. The psychic directed her unwavering attention into the images and shapes that Melissa could not see. "*Hmm ... Hmm ... I see. I see ... You don't say?*" And finally said, "Well, isn't that peculiar?"

"What? What do you see?"

Madam Hapney pushed the large glass ball toward Melissa. "Nothing."

"'Scuse me?"

"I see nothing. A black void. Whatever this favor is that you're doing for your 'aunt' is being protected by dark forces. Very, *very* dark forces. You're playing with fire, child, and I don't think you'd recover if you got burned. Whatever dark force is behind this favor has gone to great lengths to keep prying eyes, like mine, from seeing its intent."

"Not surprising."

Hapney glanced at the clock on the wall as well. "I have a client in ten minutes, so I'll finish up with this sage advice. *Use due care, child.* I'm not comfortable with the fact that I can't see what it is you've gotten yourself into, unless you want to come out and tell me."

"Not quite yet."

"Have you been practicing what we went over last weekend?"

"Whenever my parents aren't home."

"I agree that's best. I don't think they'd approve of my training."

"I feel like it's taking too long."

"You'll get there. All witches need to practice patience. Great witches know *how* to be patient with their studies."

"And you still promise I can work here, at your shop?"

Hapney cackled. "Child, I told you. When you reach a certain level of expertise in witchcraft, we will discuss the possibility of you being an understudy on location."

"I made a knickknack on my dresser move."

Madam Hapney's eyebrows furrowed. "That's not a lesson we have reviewed yet, not one I have sent you home to practice. Are you jumping ahead in our studies?"

Melissa spun the plastic ring on her finger. "I went to the library."

Hapney stood and pointed a finger at Melissa. "I've told you before, child. Those are for second-rate, wannabe, Salem-loving … phonies! You want to learn the true arts? You stick to *my* curriculum."

"Yes, Madam."

"You have something special in you girl. Something I haven't seen in anyone since … well, since I saw it in myself as a young girl. Don't go muddying your training with tainted advice from a book published by a pedestrian self-proclaimed expert."

Melissa looked out the window to the right of Madam Hapney's desk, and neither of them spoke. Hapney folded her hands as Melissa's gaze darted from the tourists walking the wharf toward the marina.

"Show me."

Melissa snapped from her trance and looked at the psychic. "Show you what?"

"Make something move. I don't believe you."

Melissa didn't acknowledge the request.

"Make something move, and I'll skip ahead in our studies and let you pick one spell from my book for me to teach you at our next lesson."

"The love spell?" Melissa kneaded her hands together and thought how delectable it would be to make Graham hers forever and ever, until death do them part and then some.

"If your heart so desires," Hapney replied and placed a silver thimble in the center of the desk. "Make that fall off the edge, and the love spell is yours."

Melissa cleared her throat and pushed back her shoulder blades, cracking her back. She placed both elbows on their respective chair arms and focused her gaze onto the small Monopoly playing piece. She clenched her teeth and squeezed her eyelids so she could only see a slit of light and the thimble. Then the same feeling she'd had a few days ago consumed her.

Golden sparkles danced around her lower back and climbed to the nape of her neck. Then, as if she had been displaced into a fifties-style robot sci-fi movie, she saw two laser beams shoot from her pupils and push the thimble across the desk and over the edge.

Madam Hapney grabbed the thimble from the floor. She gasped and dropped the metal item.

"Is everything okay?" Melissa asked, standing from the

chair.

Hapney stuck two fingers into her mouth. "Yes, child. Everything is right as rain. It's just the thimble is hot as coals. Burned my skin a bit. What did you use to move it?"

"Laser beams. Didn't you see them? They shoot right out of my eyes, and I can use them like a broom to sweep whatever I want."

"I didn't see any laser beams, child. I just felt your concentration, and then the thimble slid and jumped."

The chime adorning the front door jangled, and Madam Hapney peered over Melissa's shoulder to greet her next appointment. "Come in. Come in."

"Should I wait outside?" the client asked Hapney but looked at Melissa.

"That won't be necessary. We were just finishing up. I'll see you in a few days, Melissa? At our normally scheduled session?"

Melissa nodded. "Is that when you'll give me—"

"Yes. Don't worry about a thing," Hapney answered without taking her gaze from the new client in the doorway. "And keep practicing with your knickknacks. And be leery of those dark forces."

Melissa approached the exit, and, before the door closed behind her and left her in the cold wintery Salem waterfront air, she heard Madam Hapney's voice speaking to the touristy-looking twentysomething.

"Is this your first psychic reading?"

Smith fiddled with the Pinto's thermostat, when Tony nudged him and squawked. Smith followed Tony's pointing finger and saw Stepp bounding down his front stoop toward his IROC parked in front of his house.

"Here we go, my good friend," Smith said, more to Stepp than to his passenger. "And he's dressed to the nines! Must have a big date."

Tony and Smith watched Stepp veer the IROC onto the roadway as they merged into traffic a few car lengths behind him. They followed Stepp—unnoticed, they hoped—through Salem and into Marblehead. Smith made sure to stay far behind when Stepp steered his IROC down a side street without any traffic.

"This is far enough," Smith muttered as they watched Stepp stop in front of an apartment complex and ring the intercom bell.

Tony gurgled and hiccupped some guttural noises.

"I hope so too," Smith answered. "It certainly would make our life easier if this errand has something to do with that list. The way he's decked out leads me to believe it—"

Tony squealed in what sounded like an explosion of either fright or excitement.

"Well, well. What have we here, Mr. Detective?" Smith squinted, focusing on the well-groomed female who accompanied Stepp to his car from the front entrance of the apartment complex. "A hot date? The next victim? An entry on that to-do list you were given?"

The IROC made a U-turn and headed back toward the Pinto.

"Tony, get down!"

Smith grabbed Tony's head and guided his ghoul to duck underneath the visibility of the windows. When Smith heard the IROC's obnoxious-sounding engine pass, he lifted his head just enough for his gaze to crest the back window.

"Okay, he didn't see us."

Smith flipped around the car and mashed the gas pedal to catch up to the red IROC.

"You know, I'm not even sure, at this point, that he would even recognize me anymore if he did spot us."

Tony clapped and gurgled.

"Oh, don't flatter yourself," Smith replied to Tony's ridiculousness.

Smith caught up to the IROC as they entered Lynn, and he noticed the female passenger trying to keep her manicured hair in place from the wind blowing through the opened T-top's roof.

Tony reached for the radio dials, and Smith smacked his hand. "Unless you're putting on something I listen to, you are not to touch that dial. Do you understand me?"

Tony tilted his head like a puppy hearing a loud whistle.

"None of you kids' new-wave crap in my car, thank you very much."

Tony hissed and pushed the On button. He spun the dial until the chorus of the *Xanadu* movie theme song played through the speakers, then he stopped and reclined in the passenger chair.

"You have got to be kidding me. You expect me to listen to *this*? I thought new wave was bad, but a disco song about roller skating? I should make you walk."

Smith pressed a protruding tab, switching the dial to a preprogrammed station—smooth jazz, all day and all night.

"Looks like he's taking his gal pal into the city," Smith said as the top of the Tobin Bridge—the entranceway into Boston— came into view.

The Pinto followed the IROC through the Boston one-way streets and traversed tunnels and bridges.

"I think he's taking her to the movies," Smith said to Tony when the IROC entered the Cinemark parking garage. "Drat. I don't want to sit through something I don't want to see just so I don't lose him."

Tony gurgled and chirped.

"See? Now that's why I'm the top gun, and you are not. Okay, so let's say we go with your plan. What if he kills her while we're sitting and watching his car, waiting for them to come out? We'd miss the whole thing. That's such a rookie mistake, Tony Baloney. No, we need to stick to them like glue *until* they get back in the car."

Smith parked the Pinto a row from the IROC and exited the car.

"I think it best for you to vanish for a bit, stay hidden. I'll meet you back here. Don't need to send the lovely Bostonians into a full-on panic."

Tony had disappeared before Smith even had time to close his car door.

Stepp secured his sunglasses over the car's visor and exited the IROC.

His date paused to see if her suitor would be gentlemanly and open the car door for her. She noticed he seemed too preoccupied with fixing his hair in the sideview mirror to realize she hadn't exited his sports car yet. She smoothed out her dress to stall, giving him extra time to catch the hint that she wanted to be pampered a bit. Just one night. For once, she wanted to feel ... *wanted*.

She touched the left side of her face where her ex had

shattered her jaw a few months ago in a fit of rage over a dropped piece of pizza. It hadn't even been the last piece in the box; yet it was *his* piece. And she'd had to pay …

But she had freed herself from that maniac and finally, at the coaxing of her book club friends, had agreed to "get herself out there again." When she had expressed her reluctance to agree to a date with a guy from her aerobics class, her book club friends had assured her, "He's a detective! At least he can be trusted!"

Trusted maybe, chivalrous doubtful.

She shook her head and realized she would have to open her own car door when she saw Stepp standing at the back of the IROC, picking food from his teeth in the trunk's reflection.

"Ready?" Stepp asked when the passenger door opened.

She didn't reply, but she did let him place his hand on the small of her back as they headed toward the front of the movie theater.

"How did you score tickets to this again?" she asked.

"Radio contest. I was the fourteenth caller."

"Did you like the first movie?"

"I didn't see it. Not a big fan of movies where they dance-fight."

She chuckled. "So, no *West Side Story* for you then. Huh?"

"God, no! Give me a good Errol Flynn movie, and I'm happier than a pig in shit."

"I don't even know who that is," she replied and felt his hand leave her back, as if she had personally offended him. "Why did you want to take me to this then if you've never seen *Breakin'* and you hate dancing movies?"

"Because you looked so delicious in that leotard, and I wanted to impress you with having special tickets to something."

Stepp's date pursed her lips and cringed when he placed his whole arm around her shoulders. Her skin crawled at just the thought of spending two hours in a darkened theater with this man.

She would kill her book club friends on Thursday night when they met again.

Smith paused and redirected his gaze from Stepp wrapping his arm around his date's shoulder to the marquee above the theater's entrance.

"Special screening?" he muttered.

The sign boasted tonight's featured showing of *Electric Boogaloo* was sold out.

Smith approached the ticket counter. "Excuse me. I misplaced my ticket for tonight's picture. How do I go about getting a replacement?"

The teenage girl smacked her gum. "Not replaced if lost or stolen. Says so right on the ticket, mister."

Smith thanked the teenage girl as Stepp's voice got closer behind him, and he moved backward into the safety of the crowd.

"I'm *sure!*" a young man behind him said. "Mickey said he was grounded. His pops found that porn magazine and his doobie. So let's just go in and get a good seat."

"You should try to sell his ticket," another voice said.

"I ain't splitting the money with you, if that's what you're thinking."

Smith spun to face the two older teens, still arguing. "I'll buy Mickey's ticket."

A look of disgust and mistrust crossed the teens' faces. "You want to buy a ticket, to see *Breakin' Two*? Are you sure you're not lost? I think *Citizen Kane* is playing next week."

"Or maybe *Wizard of Oz!*" the not-Mickey teen said, and they both laughed, high-fiving each other.

"Do you want my doggone money or not?"

"It's fucking creepy, Gramps, but whatevs. I'll take your doggone money. Fifty smackers."

"Fifty?" Smith asked, raising his voice.

"I would've charged ten, but the rest is a pedophile tax."

Smith contemplated smashing not-Mickey's head into the bricks of the theater's wall and walking away. Instead, he handed not-Mickey a fifty-dollar bill in exchange for the ticket.

Not-Mickey giggled and skipped once in place as they walked away from Smith.

"What a sucker," Smith heard not-Mickey say.

Smith couldn't help but think how not-Mickey's demeanor and reaction eerily resembled Tony's when he got excited.

Kids these days are like the literal living dead.

"Popcorn okay?" Stepp asked his date.

She took a moment before answering, wishing she were anywhere else with anybody else. "Fine."

"One large popcorn," Stepp said to the concession attendant.

His date chuckled. "You think I can eat a whole tub of popcorn?"

"Who said it was just for you? Haven't you ever heard of sharing?"

She did all she could to stop herself from stomping on his foot and storming from the theater.

Stepp paid for the large popcorn and two sodas and forged ahead toward the screening room's entrance without saying anything to his date.

Guess I'm just supposed to follow, she thought. *Like a good, obedient puppy.*

Stepp maneuvered the crowded aisle toward the front of the cinema. "Two empty seats are up there on the end. I don't like to sit in the middle of the row."

"Of course you don't," she mumbled and flopped herself into the second-from-the-end empty chair.

Smith slithered into an empty seat at the back row of the cinema, between a teenager who looked like a walking billboard for Puma and a dual-cassette ghetto blaster someone had thought needed its own seat for the screening. From here Smith felt inconspicuous and had a direct line of sight on his mark. He also noticed that he was the oldest member of the audience, with Stepp and his date being a certified second.

When the lights dimmed, and the screen popped, the irony was not lost on Smith that this investigation was forcing him to sit through the exact movie he had pretty much told his grandson he wouldn't be caught dead seeing—ever. And here he was, at a premiere showing of the one movie his grandson wanted to see most.

The screen turned pitch-black until red lettering appeared, announcing Tri-Star Pictures as the company who had produced this addition to film history. Then a shot of a graffiti-laden boom box filled the screen as a red-gloved hand pressed Play, and a rap beat—at least that's what Smith thinks the kids call it—pumped from the speakers. The shot flipped to a hand adorned with spiked bracelets, snapping and moving to the beat. The electric boogaloo beat, Smith assumed.

He sighed loud enough for the nearby attendees to become fully aware of his suffering and returned his gaze to Stepp and his date. If he had to listen to the god-awful music in the movie, at least he didn't have to watch the actors making fools of themselves too. The back of Stepp's head would be a worthy distraction.

Smith made the mistake of glancing at the screen one more time during the opening credits. "What self-respecting actor refers to himself as Boogaloo Shrimp?"

"*Shh!*" Puma Man next to him shushed.

Smith slunk into the seat and folded his arms. He almost wished Stepp would try something crazy, just so the next ninety minutes could be a little more bearable.

According to his internal clock, the real show started approximately sixteen minutes into the film.

"You sure you don't want any orange Crush?" Stepp shook the half-empty cup of soda in her face.

"I'm totally sure," she replied, revolted that he would assume she would be okay with sharing not only the same cup but the same straw on a first date.

Stepp shrugged and took another gulp, slurping through the chewed end of the straw. He placed the cup into the designated armrest holder and scooped a handful of popcorn from the tub that his date hadn't even looked at once yet.

"Popcorn?"

"Please, just stop asking," she whispered. "I don't want anything, and you're talking really loud."

"Don't want anything? When I asked if you wanted popcorn, you were the one who said yes! I got this for you!"

She clenched her teeth to trap the words she really wanted to say until she felt confident they would not spew out ... not yet, at least. "To be honest, I said, 'Fine,' not yes. And, if you had picked up on my tone of voice, you would've heard that I was only agreeing so you'd shut up."

"Feisty! I knew your attitude matched those buns of yours. Hot as hell!"

"Hey, pal, either get a room or shut up," a voice said from the row behind them.

Stepp's date slunk farther into her seat. As she closed her eyes, she imagined being anywhere else. Any. Where. Else.

"Take me home, please," she whispered.

Stepp didn't respond. His body language and unbroken stare at the cinema screen led her to believe maybe he hadn't heard her. Flashbacks of Vinny exploding into a rain of fists and kicks over something as small as her asking the same question twice in a row prevented her from repeating herself. It was safer if she just endured the rest of the movie and tolerated this creepo's company until she could get home. Anything to bring her to the safety of her apartment.

I'm never dating again. I'd rather die a spinster than deal with this bullshit.

From her peripheral, she saw Stepp place the tub o' popcorn onto the floor between their feet and sit back. She decided to just focus on the movie and stop worrying about his every move. She would worry about his intentions after the movie had—

When his fingers hiked up her dress just enough so he could rest his hand on the bare skin of her knee, her eyes grew wide, and she became paralyzed. He cupped her entire knee and the fringes of her thigh with the palm of his hand, never once looking at her for a reaction, and continued to watch the screen.

Grit and take it. Grit and take it. Tonight will all be over soon.

She felt Stepp flex his hand, squeezing her exposed skin, then sliding off the bone of her knee and into the full softness of her thigh. Then she felt her hair brush back behind her ear as his breath fell upon her neck.

She blinked, and, when she opened her eyes, a red hue had filtered the images of the inner-city kids break dancing on the screen, and a loud buzzing had muffled the film's soundtrack. She reached for the popcorn tub and stood, her nostrils flaring. Towering over him, she now saw how weak and pathetic he really was. How *small* he was, sitting in the chair and looking up at her. It was about time a man looked up to her. It was about time someone else cowed away.

She tossed the remaining popcorn into his face, covering his prized suit in semipopped kernels and buttery puffs.

"You stupid bitch," he snarled and stood, popcorn falling off his clothes like snowflakes. Stepp snatched the empty tub from her hands and flung it to the floor behind him.

"Hey, buddy. Sit down and chill the fuck out," the street punk next to him said.

Stepp, ignoring that anyone had spoken to him, took an aggressive move forward toward his date, and she stepped backward into the aisle.

"You can walk the fuck home!" he spat. "Do you have any idea how expensive this suit is, you dumb whore?" He took another step forward and jabbed his finger into her breastbone.

A large bald man stood from the front row, obstructing everyone's view of the screen, and faced the fiasco happening behind him. "Holy Christ on a cracker! I swear to Jesus, Stepp, I will break your face if you don't shut the fuck up and let that girl get out of here."

Stepp swallowed hard and slunk into his seat; he knew better than to argue. He flapped the lapel on his suit jacket to rid the final few kernels from the fabric, trying to ignore the glares from the street punk next to him. He slid into his date's empty seat, to put some distance between him and the judging eyes.

The husky albino man in the front row sat down, allowing the audience to see the film again over his round head.

"Illin'!" Puma Man muttered when the crazy lady down front flung her popcorn at the obnoxiously dressed man.

Smith had already been homed in on the couple since the beginning of the movie, yet not too surprised to see the albino man here. Smith already knew of the connection between the albino and Stepp. So Smith focused on his mark instead, scrutinizing every move Stepp had made, never suspecting it would be Stepp's date who would give Smith—and everyone else in the theater—a show. Smith studied the woman's expression as she passed the last row and pushed through the doors into the lobby.

Smith took a gander at Stepp, and, when Smith was sure the hack of a detective wouldn't chase after his date—and now that the date seemed to be free from whatever sinister activities could have befallen her if she *had* stuck around—Smith excused himself through the row and followed the girl.

"Miss!" he called when entered the incandescent glow of the lobby.

She stopped but didn't turn around. "I'm sorry you have to clean up that mess, but I just couldn't take it any—"

"I don't work here."

She turned and faced the elderly man. "I'm sorry. I assumed I was being scolded by management."

"No, ma'am. My name's Smith. I was going to offer you a ride home. I know my offer may sound inappropriate, but I know the man you were on your date with, and he's not one of my favorite people."

She bit her lower lip and tapped one foot on the theater's carpet.

"I'm a private eye, and ironically I've been hired to investigate"—he used his thumb to point over his shoulder toward the cinema door—"him."

"I've had enough of private eyes tonight, Mr. Smith. If you don't mind, I think I'll call a cab."

"Suit yourself, miss."

"Plus I don't want to make you miss any of the movie."

Smith laughed. "This gives me the perfect excuse *to* miss the movie. I was only in there because I'm tailing him."

"Is he ..." She leaned in closer. "... dangerous?"

"I don't think to you. If you were in any real danger, I don't think you'd be standing out here chatting with me. It would be in your best interests to sever all ties and communication with Mr. Stepp."

"Stepp? He said his name was Arbuckle."

Smith startled aback at the sound of the woman speaking the same last name Smith himself had used as an alias when he had met George Covington's family back in Nevada in 1947. Before he had become curator to the Mushroom Cult. Before Anya had been convinced that sweet little Rose needed to be sacrificed. Before everything had changed.

"That lying scumbag," she muttered, oblivious to the stunned look across Smith's face. "Well, I thank you, Mr. Smith, for checking on me and for offering me a ride. I'm sure I'll catch a cab pretty easily at this time of night."

Smith nodded, still shaken by the alias coincidence.

Stepp's date trotted to the curb and flagged down a cab as it approached the theater.

"Where to, toots?" the cab driver asked.

She gave him her Marblehead address and closed her eyes, resting her head on the seat cushion.

Looks like I'll have to find another aerobics class to join. Again.

7: RAT ON A SINKING SHIP

"Righteous shirt," Melissa said as she approached Benji.

He glanced up from the dead grass where he sat before he took another bite of his sandwich, half of it still wrapped in the Ziploc bag. "Oh, hey ..." He snapped his fingers trying to remember. "The taco girl!"

"Yep, that's me. Brown bagging it today?"

"Sometimes you just gotta slow down and enjoy the finer things in life. Like PB&J."

Melissa forced a giggle.

"You like Depeche Mode?" he asked.

"*Hmm*? Oh, your shirt. Totally. Love all their albums. Mind if I join you?"

Benji nodded.

"Where are your other friends? The two girls?" Melissa asked as she sat Indian style diagonal from him.

"Wanted to eat inside."

"I don't blame 'em. Aren't you cold out here?"

"Nope." Another bite of peanut butter and jelly entered his

mouth. "Why are you out here?"

"I dunno. Saw you out here and thought you looked lonely."

Benji almost choked on his sandwich when he laughed. "What're you? A freshman?"

She nodded. "All year long."

"That's the cruel joke of it, isn't it? Most of us change age during the school year, but we're stuck in the same grade until we prove our worth to people who made these curriculums before we were even born. How old are you, Freshman?"

"Fifteen," she replied, diverting her gaze to cover up her guilt of adding a year to her age.

Benji raised an eyebrow in suspicion and crammed the rest of the sandwich in his mouth. "So, what's your angle, Freshman? Yesterday we chitchatted about food products, and today you use my T-shirt as your in."

"My name isn't *Freshman*. It's Melissa. And, like I said, I saw you sitting out here and thought I'd keep you company."

"Don't you ever like to just be alone?" he asked.

She knew perfectly well his statement was more of a cue for her to scram and less of an actual question, but she would not surrender that easily. She had a favor to fulfill, and this … boy stood between her and obtaining the powers within Anya's book.

"Sometimes. Until someone joins me, and then I realize that being alone isn't all it's cracked up to be," she said with the best conviction she could, cringing at her own words.

"Touché, Freshman. I like what you did there."

Dammit! Call me by my real name, you dweeb.

Melissa poked him in the rib cage. "See? Us freshmen aren't always annoying."

Benji rubbed his chest where he had been struck,

exaggerating his annoyance. "*Riiiiiight.*"

Melissa cursed herself for making such a rookie mistake in flirting.

"What should I call you? Sophomore? Junior? You sure don't look like a senior," she asked, trying to be cute and giving him a taste of his own medicine.

"Benji. And I'm a senior."

Melissa banged her forehead with the heel of her opened palm. "No way!"

Benji snickered. "I have the feeling I'm being played right now."

"Sheesh, all I did was compliment your Depeche Mode shirt and try to hang with you. Send me to the gallows, why don't you?"

"Know what I like about you?" he asked and waved a raw baby carrot at her. "You have spunk."

"And I'm adorable?"

"Jury's out on that," he replied and laughed when she pouted like a toddler. "Aren't you going to eat?"

"Ate inside. I'm not stupid. It's warm in there."

He waved another baby carrot at her and smirked.

Melissa refused to admit that she thought his smirk was a little endearing. Thankfully the bell announcing the end of lunch snapped her from her faltering thoughts about the dweeb.

"Well, gotta head toward history. Yuck," Benji said and packed his leftovers.

"Don't like history?"

"I would, if I weren't failing it."

"Ouch."

"It was nice chatting with you, Freshman."

It'll be so much easier if you use my name!

"You too, Senior."

"*Aah*, I see what you did there. Good one, Melissa."

A wide smile birthed across her face. "Thank you, Benji," she said and finished with a curtsey.

"Well, take care, and don't let the man grind you down."

A perplexed look adorned her face. "What man?"

Benji laughed so hard he had to stop collecting his lunch to double over. "Oh, never mind," he said between snorts. "It's just a saying. Oh, man, that made my day."

Melissa's blood drained from her face. *I said something stupid, and he's laughing at me. The fucking dweeb is laughing at me!*

"Catch ya around."

"Wait!" she called out.

Benji turned and faced her.

"Remember when you told me about Hank's Taco Shed yesterday? And you were saying how much you liked it?"

Benji nodded.

"And you told me how I should try it?"

"Yeah?"

"I was wondering if you'd like to take me there. You know? Friday night or something."

Benji became silent and used the tip of his sneaker to play with the dead grass.

Panic rose in Melissa's throat. *Too soon, Mel. You were too forward and asked him out too fucking soon. You jacked everything up, and now Anya will never give you that book. You'll never be the witch you deserve to be. Stupid, stupid girl!*

"Everything okay?" she asked. "I didn't mean to put you on the spot."

"Like, as a date?"

"*Um*, only if you want it to be. It doesn't have to be. I just thought I'd … To be honest, I don't know what I was thinking.

You know what? Just forget about it."

Melissa balled her fists and walked away from Benji. If she could manifest her thoughts and regrets into physical broods, they would be tearing her limb from limb right now as penance for ruining her best opportunity to get close to Vicki.

"Melissa, hold up."

She turned to face him as the second bell rang. "We're officially late."

"Look. I'm flattered. Really, I am. But I don't know you, and, before yesterday, I didn't even know you existed."

"Such a clichéd thing to say."

Benji laughed. "I can't tell if you're being sarcastic or flirty."

She put all her weight on one foot and placed her hands on her hips. "Does it look like I'm flirting?"

"Trying too hard to, I might add."

Melissa giggled. *No! I won't be smitten by the dweeb! The dweeb is just collateral damage for the bigger prize! Stay focused, Mel!*

"I have my sights set on someone else," he added.

"Oh, yeah? Who is he?"

Benji wagged his finger at her; the only thing missing was the baby carrot. "I'll let that one go this time, Freshman!"

"So, who is your Juliet?"

"Does that mean you're referring to me as Romeo?"

"You? *Eww!* Barf me out! More like Quasimodo."

"I don't know who that is."

Melissa couldn't reply. The silence became heavier with each ticking second that she didn't respond. *Well, good job, dweeb. You certainly wiped out any fears I had about my feelings toward you, all in one admission.*

"I take it I should know who he is?" he asked.

"My heart hurts," she said, reaching deep down inside her to turn on the charm again, when all she wanted to do was punch this stupid dweeb in his ignorant and illiterate face. "I'll get over it though."

There ya go, Mel. Swallow your disgust and stay the course.

"It's just a friend of my sister's. Had a crush on her since I was little. She's my sister's age and still looks at me like I'm the annoying kid who tags along because our parents make Caitlin take me with her. I just wish she'd stop seeing me as Cait's little brother and start seeing me as an adult."

Melissa looked behind her at the school campus. "I think we're in deep shit without a paddle. Everyone's gone and already in their next class."

"Shit! I can't be late again," he said and sprinted toward the doors.

"So, that's still a no for Friday-night tacos?" she called after him.

"Meet me out here again tomorrow," he yelled as he disappeared into the school's south campus.

Smith kept his driver's side window rolled down, so he could spit his sunflower seed shells onto the sidewalk of Combs Avenue.

Tony reached across the console and stuck his decayed hand into the bag. Smith balled the top of the bag with his fist, and a look of disgust crossed his face. "Don't touch my food."

Tony chirped and pouted.

"Not only is it rude and unsanitary, I'm not even sure what effect real food would have on you."

When Smith felt confident Tony wouldn't make another attempt at stealing his sunflower seeds, he relaxed his grip on the bag and tossed a handful into his mouth.

"Keep your eyes peeled on that building. I don't know where Stepp parked this morning, and I don't want to lose him if he leaves."

Smith let the salt from the shells absorb into his tongue.

"*Hmm*, his secretary is coming to work late this morning," Smith said as his gaze fell on Vicki, opening the office's front door and disappearing inside.

"Mouse, that you?" Stepp called from his office.

"Yeah. Sorry I'm late," Vicki answered and headed for her desk.

"No worries. I didn't even notice, to be honest."

Vicki stopped midstride and cringed. She sighed and looked at her high heels she had spent half her morning debating about, wrestling with which footwear might meet Stepp's fancy the most. *Why do I even bother to try so hard? He didn't even notice I wasn't here yet. Probably too busy fantasizing about his hot date last night.*

She bit her bottom lip and flipped her wrist to adjust her jelly bracelets, then touched her bare skin where the bracelets would have hung on any other day. *Even left my favorite jellies at home so I'd look more mature for him. I'm such a stupid head. He just wants bimbos in leotards.*

"Can you come in here when you're settled? I need some help."

Vicki flung her Scooby-Doo lunch pail and her chain-handle purse behind her desk and headed down the short hallway to his office and knocked on the opened door.

Stepp looked up from his computer. "That was quick. I wanted to get situated first. What'd you do? Throw your shit behind the desk and run down the hallway?"

Vicki's cheeks grew red as she flicked her empty wrist again. *Dammit. Why did I leave those at home? And ... is he gonna say something about my pumps?*

"How was your hot date last night?" she asked, lowering her voice as if the words could physically harm her.

"I don't wanna talk about that. Turned out to be a real airhead, she did. Just couldn't handle the twelve Stepp program." Stepp stood from his desk chair. "Here. Sit. You're better at this stuff than I am. I don't even know what I'm looking at."

Vicki moped to his desk and gulped. She had never been invited to sit at his workspace before. She lowered herself into the chair as if it might bite her.

"Remember how I told you that I had acquired a new client over the weekend and—"

"Right. Outside the office?"

"Yeah. An old friend. Ran into him in the commons. He runs a halfway house and gave me a list of troubled girls who he wants me to check on, to make sure they're doing okay."

"*Aww.* Sounds like a really nice guy."

Stepp chortled. "Yep, he's an all-around Good Samaritan, all right. Mr. Nice Guy in the flesh."

Vicki raised an eyebrow. "I can't tell if you're being sarcastic or making fun of him."

"Neither. Don't worry about it. But remember how I told you that I'd need your help on that this morning?" He waited for her to nod. "So here is the list he gave me. All he has are the girls' names and dates of birth. I have this floppy disk from the post office that—"

Vicki released the disk from the Apple IIe tower and looked at the handwriting on the label. "North Shore Residents and Census, 1984. How did you even get something like this? Isn't this federal government property?"

Stepp scratched the back of his neck. "I know high people in low places."

Vicki wagged her foot, trying to direct his attention to how good her shoes made her legs look.

"Do you think you can help me track down the addresses for these girls, so I can confirm they're safe and doing okay?"

Vicki slipped the disk into the slot and waited for the whirring to stop. She typed a command, and a scrolling list of yellow-highlighted names and addresses illuminated the screen.

"Let me see the first name on your list."

Stepp inched the paper toward her.

Vicki touched the name at the top of the page with her forefinger. "Are these even real names? They sound like hooker names."

Stepp's eyes grew wide, and he wiped the budding perspiration from the nape of his neck. "Both. And they're street names, not hooker names. Golly, Mouse. Sheesh!" He chuckled and cleared his throat.

"Well, let's try it and see."

Vicki typed the first name on the census list. "Looks like Adrielle Fugate is registered at 127 Western Avenue in Lynn."

Stepp leaned over her shoulder, his chest pressing against her shoulder blade, as he scribbled *127 Western Ave., Lynn* on the paper next to Adrielle's name. Then he placed both palms on his desk so his arms became pillars, confining Vicki's body, and leaned forward to look closer at the screen. He placed his face next to her left ear as he further reviewed the list.

Vicki felt his breath upon her neck, and her arms sprung goose bumps. She wiggled her feet with more exaggerated gusto, hoping the movement would catch his eye, and he'd steal a look at how great her legs looked in the red pumps and flesh-colored pantyhose.

She pointed at a name she recognized on the screen.

"Where are your rainbow bracelets?" Stepp asked before Vicki could comment on the familiar name.

Vicki slapped her hand to her chest and covered her bare wrist but couldn't help smirking that he had noticed *something* about her today. "I didn't think they were professional attire."

"Nonsense! I love that you wear them. They might look ridiculous, but they totally complete your style."

"So, you're saying my fashion style is ridiculous?"

"I think you wear ridiculous well."

His breath tickled her earlobe, and she thought she felt him press a little harder against her.

"I don't know if that makes it even worse."

He stood upright, his body moving away from her. "Would you like a drink?"

"Sure. I'll start the coffee." Vicki stood from the chair. Recognizing a name on the list was now a distant memory.

"No, I meant a real drink. A *man's* drink," Stepp said and approached his wet bar.

"Isn't it a little early for liquor?"

"I don't know. Is it? Time is all relative anyway."

He removed two glasses from the cabinet and dropped ice cubes into both. He filled them two-thirds of the way and handed one to Vicki. "A toast! To my secretary, who today acted as my partner in crime!"

Vicki jiggled her bare wrist and cursed herself for looking

stupid.

Stepp laughed. "You keep doing that, Vic, but nothing's there."

"Nervous habit. I keep forgetting I didn't wear them today."

Stepp clinked his glass against Vicki's and emptied the contents in one gulp. He grabbed the bottle and filled his cup again. "C'mon, kid. You're already falling behind. You gotta keep up if you're gonna play with the big boys."

Vicki put the glass to her lips; the smell of bourbon made her grimace. "Bottoms up," she whispered and let the brown liquid slide down her throat. She coughed and placed a hand over her mouth.

Stepp laughed and poured more into her cup without waiting for permission.

"Are you trying to get me drunk, Mr. Stepp? Because I think you're already halfway succeeding."

"Don't tell me that you're such a lightweight that one drink makes you tipsy?"

Vicki burped. The smell of recycled bourbon-filled vapors turned her stomach.

Stepp took a step toward her and placed a hand on her hip.

A tingle exploded through her body. She didn't know if she should close her eyes when he went in for the first kiss or if she should make the first move and put her hand on his—

"Okay, back to work. Thanks for the help, Vic," he said and moved toward his desk, looking at the Apple IIe monitor. "I saw how you did that search, so I should be good from here."

The phone at Vicki's desk rang.

"Chop, chop. Might be a new client. God knows, I could use the business. Off you go."

Vicki swallowed hard, smacking the alcoholic residue in her

mouth with her tongue. She set the half-full glass on his desk with more force than she had intended, sending bourbon splashing over the rim and onto the mahogany wood. She about-faced and stormed through his office door into the hallway.

"Hey, Vic!"

She stopped in the hallway but didn't give him the satisfaction of facing him.

"Those shoes look bitchin' on you. Red is your color. You should wear them more often!"

She balled her fists in randy frustration and but couldn't help let a smirk of delight and gratification cross her face.

He did notice!

"It's showtime!" Smith said to Tony, rousing the ghoul.

Smith watched Stepp exit his office with his secretary in tow and disappear around the back of the building. Moments later, the IROC emerged and headed west on Combs Avenue.

Smith maneuvered the Pinto into traffic, leaving behind a small mound of empty and discarded sunflower seed shells on the sidewalk.

Stepp crossed Buchanan Bridge on Western Avenue after entering Lynn from Salem.

"One-twenty-seven should be up here on the right," Vicki said, her hair blowing from the wind blustering through the open T-roof.

"I see it." Stepp pulled in front of the two-story white house. "Looks like someone's home. C'mon."

They exited the IROC and approached the front door. Stepp, ringing the bell, prompted what sounded like two large dogs to bark and to scamper to the door. Vicki flinched when both dogs' bodies collided with the wooden door.

"Coming!" they heard from inside. Then "Oh, stop it! Sit! Sasha! Noah! Sit! Down! … Good dogs."

The ruckus from inside stopped as the door opened.

"Good afternoon, sir. I'm Detective J. Stepp, and this is my assistant, Victoria."

Vicki furrowed her brows and darted her head in his direction. She didn't even realize Stepp *knew* her full name.

"Is everything okay, Detective?"

"I hope so. I'm looking for your … daughter? Adrielle?"

The man shifted his weight onto one foot and clenched his lips. "What has she done now?"

Stepp noticed Vicki shot him a glance from his peripheral eyesight. "She hasn't done anything. She's a witness and could help put someone away for a very long time. I need to get an official statement from her, so we can bag the perp."

Vicki covered her mouth to stifle a chuckle at Stepp trying too hard to sound like someone on *Miami Vice*. However, it seemed the charade had fooled Adrielle's father.

"Oh, yeah? How bad are we talkin'?"

Stepp leaned in closer and whispered, "Wharf Killer big."

Sasha cocked her head at Stepp and placed her snout underneath her large paw, as if she could understand Human Speak.

"Well, who am I to obstruct justice?" the man said. "Haven't seen Adrielle in a few weeks though. Not since I kicked her out. Broke her mom's heart when we read in the

Lynn Item's police blotter that she'd been arrested for hooking."

Vicki looked at Stepp again and watched his nod, as if this was exactly the answer he had been expecting.

"Any idea where I could find her?"

Adrielle's father used his thumb and forefinger against his chin to recreate the Thinking Man pose. "I assume Union Street. More specifically the corner of Union and Chatham. That's where they all congregate for their business."

"I thank you for your time, Mr. Fugate."

"Anytime. Glad to do my civic duty to help the police."

Stepp spun to head toward his IROC, and Vicki followed, understanding the urgency to leave before Adrielle's father realized he had mistakenly identified the private eye as a police detective.

"I didn't think Lynn PD had IROCs in their fleet," the father called from the porch.

Stepp stopped walking and closed his eyes and answered without turning around. "The undercover division does."

Adrielle's father grunted in acceptance of that explanation.

Stepp quickened his pace and did not exhale until he had driven four property lots from 127 Western Avenue. Feeling more relaxed, he mashed the gas pedal and covered Vicki's panty-hosed inner thigh with his right hand.

Vicki closed her eyes and smiled, feeling the power of the engine and the tingling sensation emanating from his touch.

At home, Stepp filled his workout duffel bag with rope, a hunting knife, chloroform, and a handful of rags. He had already placed a neatly folded change of clothes into the IROC's trunk. He checked his Rolex and felt confident the time had come.

He backed the red sports car out of the driveway and headed toward downtown Lynn, alone, without noticing the Pinto falling in line behind him.

Stepp idled in front of the bar on Union Street, scanning the sidewalk and waiting for any girl to solicit him. He drummed his index fingers on the steering wheel and hummed along to the band on the radio, singing about their affection of fat-bottomed girls on bicycles.

Stepp closely watched as a female exited the bar arm in arm with her boyfriend/husband/lover/john/brother … Stepp couldn't guess and didn't care. His gaze traveled to her buttocks and watched as each cheek sashayed with each step. "They certainly do make the rockin' world go 'round. I'll give cheers to that!"

"Hey, baby. You lookin' to party?"

"Oh, jeez!" Stepp placed a hand over his chest. "You scared the devil out of me."

The lady leaned through the IROC's opened passenger window, making sure he had a direct line on her overexaggerated cleavage.

"You trying to suffocate me with those pillows?" he asked.

"If that's what you're into. Everything you see here is for rent."

"I'm looking for someone specific."

She straightened her posture, withdrawing her torso from the interior of the car. "Figures. You lookin' for Jade? Every motherfucker wants Jade. Well, I'll tell you something. Those puppy-dog eyes are poison. She might be somethin'-somethin' to look at, but she gives shit blows. Now me, on the other hand? We can party all night long."

"I'm not looking for Jade. You know a girl named Adrielle?"

"El? Fuck yeah. She my homegirl. She'll treat you good too. Do you all up and down and shit. Sometimes we get gangbanged together, if you want me to join in."

Stepp lowered the radio's volume when some sappy ballad played and flashed a toothy grin at the girl. "Not tonight, doll. Just want El."

"Alright, suit yourself. You're robbing your dick of the time of its life but whatevs. His loss. I'll go get her."

Stepp waited with the IROC idling and watched patrons enter and exit the bar with almost airport–like foot traffic. His new friend emerged a few moments later accompanied by a girl with crimped rainbow-dyed hair, who looked no more than seventeen.

"You requestin' me, mister?" Adrielle asked and peered into the car. "You lucked out. I don't have a date tonight yet."

"Get in," he said.

Adrielle giggled and slid into the passenger seat.

Stepp steered hard left and swung the car across the double solid lines and into the opposite lane.

"Where we headed?" she asked.

"King's Beach."

"*Ooh*, I'm not used to my dates being all romantic–like. What should I call you?"

"Daddy."

"Really? You like being my big, strong daddy?" She slid her hand into his crotch.

He grabbed her wrist and studied her fingers. "Cute tattoo."

"Octopuses are boss. They're my spirit animal. See? His tentacles wrap around this finger."

Stepp examined the eight tentacles circling Adrielle's middle finger and then returned her hand to her lap. "Not yet."

After a few city blocks, the ocean sprawled in front of them. Stepp found a parking spot next to Red Rock Park and retrieved the duffel bag from the back seat, stuffing a rag coated in chloroform into his back pocket.

Adrielle used the side mirror to apply another layer of ruby-colored lipstick, matching one of the many hues in her crimped hair.

"What's in the bag?" she asked as they headed toward the cement stairs that would lead them away from view of the nighttime beachgoers and into the crevices and small caves of Red Rock.

"Some drinks and rope."

"So, we're doin' the kinky thing tonight. Alright, I can dig it."

Stepp helped her navigate over the uneven rocks and small pools of ocean water and around the corner where no one could see them from the beach or the esplanade.

"Here should be fine," he said and wrapped his arm around her waist, pulling her into him.

"We haven't discussed payment yet." She trailed a fingernail down his white undershirt and stopped at his belt. "Fifty, and I'm yours for the hour. And I do it all."

"Sounds good to me," he said and let her unbuckle his belt. "You freelance or is there a pimp I need to pay?"

Adrielle lowered herself to her knees in front of his zipper as the spray from the crashing waves on the rocks dotted her face with mist. "I'm my own boss now. Used to let some fucktard control me but no more. I really stuck it to that albino shitbag too."

Stepp placed his fingers under her chin and lifted her face to meet his gaze. He was surprised how soft her skin felt and how the moonlight and the sheen on her face made her look so young and innocent.

"Your hour has already started," she said. "I mean, we can just gawk stupidly into each other's eyes, if that's what you're into. In fact, that's less work for me, at the same price."

"Let's do a line first," he said and stepped around the girl on her knees.

"Now you're talkin'."

He rummaged through the front pouch of his duffel bag and removed a bag of cocaine.

"Here. Let me do the honors," she said and took the baggie from Stepp. She licked her finger and dipped the end into the bag, then rubbed her fingertip along her bottom gums like a toothbrush. She finished by sticking her finger into her mouth and gliding it out while never breaking her gaze on Stepp, then cupped the sprouting bulge in his pants. "You like the way that looked?"

Stepp let her dance her fingers into his unzipped waistband as he took the bag from her. After he had taken his hit, he closed his eyes and focused on the repetitive yet tranquil sound of the crashing waves on the rocks as he felt the warmth of her mouth envelop him. The world disappeared for a few moments as her rocking became more eager and hungrier.

Right as he felt the familiar buildup in his loins and before he crossed the point of no return, he placed his hand on her forehead and pushed her from him.

She looked up and pouted.

"Too soon. I'm paying for a full hour. You're gonna give me a full hour."

She stood and placed her palms against a large jetty of rock, bending at the waist. "Wanna do me from behind?"

"I want to tie you up first," he answered and retrieved the rope from the duffel bag.

Adrielle spun around, pressed her back against the rock, and held her hands high in the air, pressing her wrists together. "You're not some creep who I have to worry about, right?"

"Does a creep share his coke with a stranger?"

She nodded and closed her eyes. "Bind me and ravish me, you mad dog!"

Stepp flung the rag from his pocket and shoved it into her face with such force that her head bounced off the rock. She opened her eyes wide and screamed a muffled cry through the rag. She clawed at the skin on his arms and brought her knee to his groin.

Stepp scuttled backward to avoid the low blow, which gave him better leverage to push harder on her face.

Adrielle's eyelids fluttered, and her eyeballs rolled backward into her head.

Stepp felt her body relax, and he didn't release her until she was only being held up by the pressure of his hand pushing her head into the boulder-size rock. Adrielle crumpled to the rocky ground, and Stepp quickly hog-tied her. He returned to his duffel bag, glanced upward to better hear if anyone was in their vicinity, and, when he was confident no one would crash this party, he withdrew the hunting knife.

He was surprised how soft and buttery her flesh felt as the blade made one fatal slice through her neck. However, he did have to saw a few times to sever her middle finger from her hand.

He secured her finger into the duffel bag and climbed the stairs to King's Beach, leaving the chloroformed girl hog-tied and bleeding out on the rocks.

"Water washes everything clean," he whispered as a large wave crashed upon the rocks below and as he trooped to the IROC.

Smith lowered the binoculars and tried to hand them to Tony. When the binoculars were not taken, he turned to look at his bantling.

"What in tarnation are you doing?" Smith asked.

Tony glanced up at Smith from a kneeling position, drawing random patterns of lines in the sand with a large stick.

"What's next? You gonna start making doggone sandcastles now? Stand up!"

Tony stood and brushed the sand from his tattered clothes.

"He just killed the girl. He's messy and reckless. I cannot believe this is Anya's first pick." Smith brought the binoculars to his eyes again. "And he's just leaving her!"

Tony clapped and bounced as if the sand were a trampoline, pointing at the Pinto.

"No, my dim-witted friend. This time we are not following him. We're gonna check on the girl."

Tony swung his arms back and forth, like he was a gorilla rocking a baby to sleep.

"Jiminy Crickets, Tony. You're one step away from snapping your fingers and trying to dance-fight against the Sharks and Jets. Calm down!"

Tony whimpered and kicked the stick he had been using to

make his modern-art sand masterpiece.

Smith traveled across King's Beach toward Red Rock Park. Tony shambled behind him, his steps creating long dragging footprints in the soft sand. Smith kept glancing at Stepp, making sure tonight's murderer didn't change course and head back to the kill site. Smith watched the IROC's taillights glow red, and the car pulled onto Lynn Shore Drive.

Smith quickened his pace, grabbing Tony's arm, so the ghoul wouldn't fall behind.

Tony chirped and squawked at Smith.

"Nope. I don't care about that. All I care about is getting to her, hopefully before she completely expires, so I can find out who she is and maybe why Stepp wanted her and what's on the contents of that list. Then she can die a painful death for all I care. Just another bottom-feeder cleaned off the streets. And, this time, one not enlisted into Anya's ranks."

Tony ducked as a black-feathered bird of prey swooped down, headed for Red Rock.

"Blasted!" Smith yelled and looked upward, focusing on a multitude of black dots in the sky, all homing in on the large rocks in the distance.

Lightning flashed across the sky, illuminating the beachy landscape. Anya's silhouette flashed for a moment—surrounded by a small gaggle of her brood—and then disappeared from their sight.

"Candy, see if you can stop that bleeding," Anya instructed. "Nikki, help her out."

The two ghouls stepped from behind their leader and

approached the lifeless girl lying on the rocks. Candy covered the laceration with her hand, and the blood stopped pooling around them. Nikki grabbed Candy's other hand and convulsed, while babbling and gurgling.

Anya looked into the sky and smiled when she saw her vultures dotting the cloud covering.

"They haven't completely abandoned me," she whispered.

Two vultures landed on each of the dead girl's feet and swiveled their heads to Anya.

"Yes. She'll make a fine addition to my coven. The Mushroom Cult needs someone as vile and filthy as she was. It's always the most tainted who come back to me just as squeaky clean as clean can be. My best soldiers are the ones who had the most to repent. Isn't that right, Pum'kin?"

Pum'kin nodded and made a *Gah-huh! Gah-huh!* sound in excited agreement.

"Alright, girl. Flip her!" Anya took a step backward to let her ghouls and the vultures perform the rebirthing ritual.

"Wait! Stop!" Smith said, panting and out of breath, stepping from around the corner.

"Well, well. If it isn't the party pooper himself," Anya said and lifted her black veil to expose her pale face to the salty spray of the ocean waves. She extended her arm to stop the cult and the vultures from continuing. "No reason to stop, Smith. She's a goner. Dead as a doornail. Stick a fork in her, she's done! Stepp done good tonight. Gave me his first addition to the ranks, and what a doozy he gave me! She's a perfect specimen, not like those two-bit woe-is-me girls. No, this one is ripe with deviance and moral decay." Anya sniffed for as long as she could, rocking her body onto her tiptoes as if she were following a cartoon-drawn scent into the air.

"The devil you say? You mean to tell me that Stepp is

already killing for you? What kind of poppycock is this? What the heck do you need me for then anymore?" Smith's blood pressure rose, and he stepped closer to the witch. "If he's already working for you, then release me and let me live out the few remaining years I have left in peace! You at least owe me that much, especially if the torch has already been passed."

"He's not killing for me. Not yet anyway. This here"—Anya kicked Adrielle's thigh—"was personal for him. I'm just reaping the benefits."

"The list?"

Anya nodded. "He got himself into a pickle with someone who—"

"Tony!" Smith yelled, startling Anya. "Stop playing with the girls."

Tony whinnied and returned Cyana's nose to her.

"Sorry about that."

"Bantlings. Aren't they fun?" Anya snuggled herself to add a sarcastic exclamation to her statement. "Just like toddlers."

"So, the list …"

"The list is for Stepp to settle a tab he has with someone else."

"All street walkers?"

"Every single one. It's like shooting fish in a barrel. He'll deliver more girls to me because of this list over the next few days than you can manage in a few months. Can you please control your fool?"

Smith glanced at Tony again and rolled his eyes. "You know what, Tony? You're excused for the night. Time to go bye-bye."

Tony removed the starfish from his mouth and vanished.

"Regretting him yet?" Anya asked.

"He has his moments."

Anya laughed. "They all do. Some more than others."

"So, what are we doing with her? I see you summoned the vultures in almost record-breaking time."

"We're gonna flip her. Bring her back cleaned and reborn."

"I'm sure she'll be a great asset to your cult, Anya. Good luck with her."

Smith turned to use the stairs to get to street level, but swarms of Anya's ghouls stood in perfect rows, blocking his path. "I hope this isn't a show of intimidation," he said to the priestess without turning around. "Because it isn't working, and I don't appreciate it."

"You haven't seen even a glimpse of how I could intimidate you, if I wanted to, you foolish imp." Anya materialized in front of Smith. "I could haunt every corner of every dream. I could rot every pleasant thought your pathetic brain has. I would turn your rice into maggots and your noodles into worms. You would never have a peaceful moment. So, Smith. *Don't. Fuck. With. Me.*"

"Then stop toying with me, and let's get Stepp on board, so I can be done with all this."

"He's not ready yet. He hasn't had that big awakening, that big moment. You remember yours, right? That moment when something inside you just felt—no, you knew—that Covington was doing right by society."

Smith glanced at Candy. "Yeah, I remember."

"Good. And you remember when that moment felt life-changing, like your entire course had been changed? Well, Stepp hasn't had his moment yet. Until then, he can't be trusted to completely commit to the cause."

Smith hung his chin against his chest. "Fine. Can you tell them to move so I can go home?"

Anya flicked her hand, and the ghouls made a perfect

divide for Smith to travel.

"Like parting the doggone Red Sea," he said and stepped into the hallway made of the undead. When he reached the end of the parted pathway, he heard the vultures' unmistakable hissing and the sound of the ghouls' gnashing teeth.

He knew the rebirthing process had begun.

Rhino navigated his Buick toward Pickering Wharf to check on his girls. He yanked down the rearview mirror, so he could check his teeth for any trapped dinner food, and noticed the glare of headlights heading straight for him. He spun the steering wheel toward the curb to maneuver away from the oncoming car, and the Buick came to a stop on someone's front lawn, spilling the extra-large cup of orange Fanta all over his white suit.

The oncoming vehicle fishtailed and sideswiped the opposite curb.

"Fucking drunk driver is gonna pay the cleaning bill with his teeth!" Rhino said and reached into the back seat for his snub-nosed revolver.

The driver of the other vehicle flung open their driver's side door, and Rhino jumped out of the Buick, pointing the gun in the driver's direction. Then he took a moment to look at the other vehicle.

"Oh, for fuck's sake," he yelled, looking at the red IROC. "Stepp, this better be good—dry-cleaning-bill level good."

Stepp didn't reply, and the two men met on the single dotted line in the middle of the road. Stepp reached into his pocket and removed an item, holding out his hand.

"What's this?"

"A souvenir," Stepp answered. "Take it."

Rhino opened his hand, and Stepp placed an octopus-decorated finger into his palm.

"Figured you'd want proof beyond just my word," Stepp said.

Rhino pinched the finger with his other hand and raised the severed digit to eyelevel. "Well done, if I do say so myself. And fast! You didn't waste any time. I'm glad you took my deal seriously."

"I'll have another for you tomorrow."

"Don't make promises you can't keep."

"I don't."

Rhino laughed, dropped the finger, and clamped his hand on Stepp's shoulder. "God is good. And He most certainly is good tonight!"

8: A CORPSE IS A CORPSE

"Hey, Senior." Melissa sat down next to Benji in the cafeteria, squeezing her tray into the smaller-than-a-tray-size space separating the girls and him.

His two groupies exchanged a look of contempt and disgust as Melissa's body and tray forced them to slide over.

"Hey, Freshman. What's shaking?"

"*Freshman?*" one of the girls spat. "*Eww!* Gag me with a spoon!"

The other stood with her tray. "Have fun babysitting."

The two girls walked away from the table, and Melissa watched them dispose of their uneaten lunch and head toward the exit.

"Well, they're pleasant."

"Snobs," he corrected. "The whole lot of 'em!"

Melissa giggled and punched him in the bicep. "So, tomorrow's Friday."

"Yep, sure is," he replied and took a bite from his hot dog—extra mustard, no bun.

"Hank's Taco Shed really sounds amazing."

Benji almost choked on his laughter. He slapped his hand over his mouth to catch any projectile food. "Jeez Louise, Freshman, you are persistent."

"What can I say? I'm a sucker for an older man who's obsessed with Depeche Mode shirts. Although that hot dog has lost you megapoints. Gross to the max."

Benji glanced at his shirt. "Didn't even realize I wore another one today. I promise I have non Depeche Mode shirts in my wardrobe."

"Uh-huh. *Suuuuure* you do. Prove it." She took a sip from her chocolate milk through a white straw. "Wear something different when you take me out tomorrow night. Or, better yet, wear something different but bring me a Depeche Mode shirt to wear."

"Look, Freshman—"

"Mel."

"—Mel. Not to sound like a prude, but I don't know you. I didn't even know who you were a few days ago. And now you want to wear my clothes? What's next? You wanna wear my skin or some creepy shit like that? Plus I already told you. I have my eyes set on only one—"

"That's why you should go out with me! I figured it out last night."

"You were thinking about me last night?" he asked and scooted his chair a few inches away from her.

"We should all hang out tomorrow night. You, me, your sister, and the friend you are crushing on. Introduce me as your girlfriend. You know? To make her jealous. Has she ever seen you with another girl?"

"Nope. I've only ever wanted her. Turned down a lot of girls though."

"I'm sure you have." Melissa rolled her eyes. "Maybe that's why she's never given you the time of day. Because she knows you'll just be a puppy behind her the entire time. There's no threat."

"She doesn't even know I like her."

Melissa placed her hand on his. "She knows. She's known for a while. Trust me. I'm a girl."

"Sorry, Freshman. I gotta stay true to the course. I can't risk losing any ground I may have gained by years of flirting on just one fake date. It might backfire. She could be happy for me, while secretly I'm dying inside and resenting you. Sorry, can't risk it."

Melissa hoisted her backpack onto the table with a *thwump!* She unzipped it and rummaged through the contents. She removed a white notebook adorned with a hand-drawn Twisted Sister logo; underneath in stencil was *Stay Hungry*.

"You draw that yourself?"

Melissa nodded, her hands shaking as she fumbled to open the notebook's cover.

"Looks great. You a big Twisted Sister fan?"

"Second-favorite band," she replied, trying to control the tremor in her voice.

"*Second* favorite? I'm scared to ask who's your first favorite. Don't tell me. Depeche Mode?"

"Wham!"

"*Wham!*" Benji yelled, tossing his hands into the air as if he had just forfeited on a winless poker game. "And to think I was starting to respect you, Freshman. Then you have to go throw those pansies into the mix. I can get behind some Twisted Sister. Quiet Riot and the Scorpions and Mötley Crüe are pretty boss too, but you just cashed in all your rad credits with admitting ..."

Melissa knew Benji was still speaking, but her intense concentration on removing the folded parchment without raising his suspicions had muffled his babbling, and eventually she couldn't hear him at all—even though she saw his mouth moving. She unfolded the parchment once so she could read the first line of the spell. She closed her eyes and prayed to Anya that something would happen when she said the spell out loud. She figured, if nothing happened, she would be dead in the water, looking like a freako who just spit some gibberish for no apparent reason in the middle of a conversation about music.

Gosh, this could go so bad so fast if I'm wrong about when to use this.

Melissa opened her eyes just enough to see the old-time calligraphy and tried her best to pronounce the words. The sounds escaping her mouth sounded foreign and intrusive. When she reached the end of the first line, she glanced over the top of the parchment at Benji.

He had stopped talking midword; his mouth hung open, stationary, and his body was as rigid as a mannequin's.

"Well, I'll be damned."

She returned her focus to the parchment and skimmed the remaining lines, afraid a teacher or passerby would notice her catatonic lunchmate. The pronunciation of the foreign words rolled off her tongue with ease, as if someone else who lived deep inside her mouth were saying them.

She finished and directed her gaze to Benji.

Benji's eyes lit up. "Date. You ... instead. Make ... her. Jealous." A small spittle of drool left the corner of his mouth as he spoke like he had been tranquilized. Then, like watching a Betamax video-cassette tape in fast-forward mode, he regained normality in both demeanor and speech. "Maybe you're on to something, Freshman."

"I'm fucking Mel!"

Benji laughed and shushed her. "Okay, okay. And what do you get out of it, if you're just helping me make my dream girl jealous?"

"A free Depeche Mode shirt."

Benji snorted and waved his hot dog at her. "You're like a fungus, Mel. You're beginning to grow on me."

Melissa shoved the folded-up parchment into her back pocket and smiled, batting her eyelashes as flirtatiously as she could. "It's a date then!"

Smith kept the IROC in sight ahead of him as they traversed the unkempt streets of Revere. "You sweet on Cyana or what?" Smith asked Tony.

Tony cocked his head in a gesture of confusion.

"In my experience, the best way to let the ladyfolk know you're interested in them is *not* to literally steal their nose from their face."

Tony whinnied and looked at his feet, embarrassed.

"But, then again, I've never tried to woo someone of the undead. Maybe that's what she's into. To each his own, I guess." Smith took his eyes off the road and glanced at his passenger.

Tony groaned and touched his own nose.

"I'm just yanking your chain, you knucklehead. Look. He's pulling over."

They watched Stepp slow down just before the Wonderland train station parking lot to talk with three girls standing on the corner. Smith reached under the driver's seat and retrieved his binoculars. He reached into his trench coat pocket and touched the flask of whiskey to his lips as he brought the binoculars to his eyes. His knuckles scraped against the fabric of his fedora, and he grunted, flinging the annoying obstruction into the back seat.

"It's the one in the red. He's not even pretending to look at the other two. Here." He handed the binoculars to Tony and took another swig from the silver flask and popped a handful of sunflower seeds into his mouth.

Tony leaned forward in the seat, as if those few inches would help him see better.

"Yep. That's the mark," Smith said as the red-dressed woman got into the IROC's passenger side. "It's showtime!"

Smith merged with the traffic right behind Stepp and followed a few blocks to a motel not marked with any identifiable signage. Smith veered into the parking lot and counted only three other vehicles. Every single floodlight was either missing or burned out.

"This should be fun," he said to Tony and caught a glimpse of his ghoul from his peripheral vision still holding the binoculars to his eyes. "Give me those, you stupid devilkin! Gosh dang, you are worse than my grandkids sometimes."

Smith backed the Pinto into a spot underneath the shadow of a willow tree and reached into the back seat. His fingers grazed the faux-suede fedora, and he batted away the hat, continuing to search for his ... "Gotch'ya."

He maneuvered the Polaroid camera into the front seat and turned to Tony. "This, my friend, has seen more action than you can only dream of."

Tony chirped and clapped. When he tried to reach across the console to touch it, Smith slapped his hand.

"Not so fast, Tony Baloney. Don't want your grimy little hands all over this beauty. Me and her go way back together, to the beginning of all this mess. I used this here ditty to take all the photographs of one George Covington."

Smith caressed the extended viewfinder like a delicate flower and took another swig of his whiskey. He brought the flask away from his lips and shook it, the cap swinging back and forth on its silver chain.

"Figures," he said and tossed the empty container into the back seat where it hit his fedora and bounced to the floorboard.

Smith raised the Polaroid and looked through the viewfinder.

Snap!

Stepp exited the IROC and stretched—

Snap!

—not making any overt action to escort his passenger from the car.

Snap! Snap!

The female used one hand to struggle with her hoop earrings as—

Snap!

—she closed her door with the other. Stepp waited for her to walk around the car and join him before—

Snap!

—they headed toward the unnamed motel's entrance.

Snap! Snap!

The Polaroid's whirring motor stopped when the camera had spat the last undeveloped picture from its exit slot.

Smith looked at Tony. "You ready to do some good old-fashioned spying?"

Tony bounced in the seat and clapped.

"Thought so, you brainless fool." Smith stowed the Polaroid in the back seat and grabbed his fedora. "Maybe it's time I name that camera. What do you think?"

Tony nodded, and some spittle flung from his opened maw onto the window.

"People name their boats and their cars, right? I think she deserves a proper name after all these years." Smith pursed his lips in thought. "I think I'll name her Rose. You know, as an homage."

Tony pointed to the entrance and jittered in his seat.

"Ah, yes, old chap. Looks like we've lost them already into the doldrums of this fine motel."

The detective and his bantling used the burned-out floodlights as sign posts to navigate across the parking lot shrouded in almost complete darkness. They reached the front door, and Tony vanished as Smith entered the small vestibule that acted as the lobby.

He approached a counter encased by bulletproof glass and waved to the large hairy man wearing a stained wifebeater behind the glass.

"Need a room?" the greasy-haired clerk asked, his Mom-with-a-heart tattoo flinching on his upper arm with each twitch of his face. "We only charge by the hour."

"Of course you do," Smith mumbled and glanced behind the clerk to scan the room keys still remaining on the row of hooks. Smith deduced that guests occupied Rooms 13, 17, and 25, based on the absence of keys on those hooks. "I'll take whatever you got available, partner." Smith stuck the first cigarette from a fresh pack of Smolens between his lips. "I assume smoking is allowed in your rooms?"

The clerk turned around to grab a key from the wall. "Pal, there ain't much of nothin' that's not allowed here at the Vertigo."

Smith's lips separated just enough for the cigarette to dangle from his bottom lip. "What did you say the name of this place was?"

The man handed Smith the key through a makeshift trapdoor in the bulletproof glass. "Pay when you leave."

"That's very trusting."

"Oh, we have installed what we like to call our guarantee that you'll pay before you leave."

"And again, what's the name of this motel?" Smith asked, waiting with bated breath.

"Well, it ain't the fucking Hotel California, Mr. Asking Too Many Questions. Get the fuck outta here."

Smith walked away from the counter and glanced at his key—Room 11. Faded and worn from countless fingers handling the large key, Smith could only decipher a *V* and the letter *T* as part of the motel's name.

He passed Room 11 without stopping and headed straight for the first of the three occupied rooms to track down Stepp and the girl whose name was obviously next on the hack-of-a-detective's list.

"Tony!" Smith whispered as he stood outside Room 13, listening to two guests caught in the throes of passion. "Come on out."

Smith's bantling appeared next to him in the hallway.

"Go in there and see if that's Stepp's and the dame's room."

Tony chirped and clapped and disappeared from Smith's sight.

Smith placed his ear to the door but kept his gaze down the hallway as a lookout. The male and female voices on the other side of the door swelled louder in fervor—the sounds coming from the female led Smith to believe that she had started her rise to a climax—and then she screamed. Smith grinned, feeling a rustling in his loins those sounds awoke in him, then realized the woman wasn't screaming in pleasure any longer. Her wails sounded of terror and fright.

"Blasted! Stepp's killing her!" he muttered to the closed door. "Tony! Let me in! Now!"

The door flung open, and a naked older teenage male, covered in sweat, fled past Smith into the hallway. Smith diverted his attention to the young female laying on the bed and screaming bloody murder, pointing to the ghoul standing at the end of the mattress. She covered herself with the blanket when she saw Smith standing there. Smith darted his eyes from the girl to Tony and back again.

"Dammit, Tony! Did you materialize inside the room?"

Tony hung his head and whimpered.

"I'm so sorry for the fright, miss," Smith said to the high-school-aged female. "He wasn't supposed to show himself to you." Smith pushed the last four words through gritted teeth to punctuate his discontent and glared at the ghoul.

She screeched something that sounded closer to a burp and a choking sound and leaped from the bed, the blanket still draped around her, and followed her gentleman caller out the door.

Smith stole a peek at her naked behind as she scurried, screaming and flailing her arms down the hallway as the blanket flapped around her frontside like a sail.

"Holy cow, Tony," Smith said and paced the now-unoccupied room. "I wanted you to just see who was in the room, from that netherworld place you guys go to. I didn't mean for you to appear at the foot of their bed, like some morbid Houdini. Gosh, I really hope they were on something, so they won't think any of this was real. They were just kids! You really could've jeopardized everything by doing that, you know?"

Smith sat on the blanket-less bed.

"Hey!" the clerk yelled from the front vestibule. "You guys haven't paid yet!"

Smith waved his hand at Tony to signal him to disappear when the sound of heavy footfalls approached from the front desk. Smith stood from the bed and inched toward the door.

"Fucking high-schoolers," the clerk said as he entered the room. "And what in the hell are you doing in here?"

"I was unlocking my door and heard a scream. Thought I'd make sure everyone was hunky-dory."

"Probably just high as a kite. That dude is a regular here. Hot-shot quarterback. Always bringing his dates here. I should call his parents for the welched bill." He looked from Smith to the bed. "And I'm gonna charge him for that blanket."

Smith squeezed past the large man in the doorway. "Well, I'm gonna head to my room."

The man nodded and turned toward his bulletproof counter area.

Smith entered Room 11 and summoned Tony. "We have two more rooms to check. Could you *please* just check on the occupants without revealing yourself? Can I trust you to do that much?"

Tony stared at the floor and nodded.

"I can't hear you."

Tony gurgled a response.

"That's better. I'll stay in here, and you go check out who's in Room 17. If it's *not* Stepp and the girl, continue to Room 25. Do you think you can handle those instructions? This is a big responsibility—your first mission on your own."

Tony chirped and clapped.

"If you don't disappoint me, I'll talk to Anya and see if we can get you and Cyana some alone time."

Tony squealed and jumped, looking like a toddler learning how to skip when raising only one foot off the ground.

"I'm only kidding. That's just gross."

Tony's gleam turned upside down into a frown, and he grunted.

"Go. Off with you. Do my bidding!" Smith said and chuckled at his own ridiculousness.

Tony turned and vanished into thin air—or into the netherworld or into wherever it is the vulture-turned ghouls go when they aren't on this plane.

The cement-gray coloring of the netherworld rippled, allowing colors from this world to penetrate through as Tony peeked into Room 17's interior. Like trying to focus on something through the backside of a waterfall, he squinted to decipher the features on the two guests. Any farther through the distorted waterfall and he'd be at risk of materializing inside the room. And his new daddy wouldn't like that. Oh, no. He certainly would yell at Tony, and Tony didn't like being yelled at, no siree.

Maybe just a tad closer, he thought.

He advanced forward, the topography of his face bisecting the waterfall of colors, acting as a barrier between the two dimensions. The tip of Tony's nose and surface of his cheeks materialized in the room—a free-floating nose suspended in midair. The Invisible Man would be rolling over in his grave if he could see the carelessness of exposing any appendages.

As the details of the world he used to belong to sharpened, Tony observed two men embraced with each other—all bed linens discarded onto the floor. He withdrew his face from the waterfall gate, his Invisible Man–like levitating nose disappearing without the lovers noticing.

Tony navigated through the netherworld, spatially mirroring our dimension, and found Room 25. He didn't even need to conjure the gate to know he had found the correct room. Stepp's high-pitched babble was undeniable.

Tony chirped in excitement and zoomed toward Room 11.

The air popped behind Smith as Tony materialized in the room. "Please tell me that you found them and didn't get distracted by something shiny instead."

Tony nodded and giggled. He gurgled and groaned his findings.

"Room 25. Good work, compadre. There's a cookie here for you yet!"

Tony cocked his head and frowned.

"Oh, that's right. You can't *have* cookies. You're dead! How silly of me. C'mon."

Tony obediently followed Smith from the room and down the corridor.

Counting the room numbers aloud as he walked, Smith pointed to the next door in line ahead of him. "Twenty-five."

Smith looked at his watch—9:29 p.m.

"What're you doing down there?" the clerk asked, spotting Smith and Tony loitering in front of a room that was not theirs.

"And who's that with you?"

Smith turned and heard the popping sound as Tony vanished. "I'm not with anyone."

"Bullshit." He increased his walking speed toward Smith. "Another dude was standing next to you."

Smith exaggeratedly looked around—he even looked at the ceiling for good measure. "Nope. Just me, an elderly man traipsing the hallways."

The clerk slowed his pace and pointed a finger at Smith's chest. "I don't like you. I don't know why yet, but you give me the heebie-jeebies."

"I'll be on my way," Smith said and headed toward Room 11.

"What's your business here anyway? You waiting for an escort or something? People only come here for one thing."

Smith stopped. "And where is *here*?"

"Oh, jeez, pal. Don't go all New Age on me."

Smith turned to face the clerk. "I'm being serious. What's the name of this establishment? I thought you called it the Vertigo earlier, and my key has all the letters worn off except the *V* and the *T*."

The clerk tightened his lips and rubbed his chin. "*Hmm*, the Vertigo Motel. Has a nice ring to it. Why didn't I think of that?"

Smith exhaled in relief, his question satisfied without getting an actual answer. "You know what? It doesn't matter. I'm turning in for the night."

Smith once again traversed the hallway to his room.

"Vito's. This is Vito's Motel. And I'm Vito."

Smith stopped without turning around and nodded.

"And you've come to the wrong place if you were looking for a room just to sleep. This is a fuck palace."

"Then I'm at the right place," Smith replied and moved forward down the hallway.

Vito glanced at Room 25's door, heard the screams from the female inside, shrugged, and returned to his bulletproof capsule.

"We gotta give him a few minutes to get settled back at the front desk," Smith said to Tony in their room. "But not enough time where we miss Stepp dispatching tonight's girl."

Tony gurgled and groaned.

"Cinnamon? You heard him call her Cinnamon?"

Tony nodded.

"Jeez, streetwalkers these days have lost all creativity. I mean, isn't there *any* respect anymore for the art of creating a solid working name? Jade, Cinnamon ... All recycled porn names from the seventies. Addie could come up with better names, and she's three!"

Tony squawked and clapped.

"Not the same thing," Smith answered. "Pum'kin and Candy are *not* generic names. They're sexy and classy and were original back in the forties."

Tony rolled his eyes and stuck out his tongue.

"Alright, I think our window of opportunity is closing. That's if he hasn't killed Cinnamon yet."

Smith opened the door and stepped into the hallway. A body, traveling at an almost sprint, collided into him. The force flung Smith into the wall, and he ricocheted onto the floor. Hiding his eyes with his upper arm and keeping his chin pressed against the carpet, he glanced at the figure who had barreled into him.

"I'm sorry, mister. I didn't see you there."

Smith buried more of his face into his arm and the carpet. "It's okay, son. I'm fine."

"You sure, Pops?" Stepp asked. "'Cause I gotta go, but I wanna make sure you're all right."

"I'm fine."

"Can I help you up?"

"No!" Smith barked.

Tony stepped into the doorway and hissed, showing all three rows of baby fangs.

Stepp stumbled away from the ghoul until the far-side wall stopped his backpedaling.

"What the fuck are you?" he yelled.

"You better go"—Smith embedded as much of his face and profile into the protection of his arms and the floor—"if you don't want him to eat your heart!"

Tony lunged at Stepp, using Smith's hyperbole as a cue to build on Stepp's rising terror.

"What in God's green toilet bowl is going on down there?" Vito called out from behind the desk. "I'm about to start whooping asses and faces, and not necessarily in that order, if you don't shut the fuck up!"

Stepp turned to flee but tripped on his ankles in his haste. He crumpled to the floor and scooted backward on his hands and feet, his frontside facing upward with his back to the carpet, looking like a scampering upside-down tarantula. He repeated a string of "No-no-no-no," while shaking his head.

Smith rotated so he could sit up, and his back would face Stepp. Once in a seated position, Smith made eye contact with Tony and winked.

Tony smirked, then lowered his body and powered toward

Stepp.

The panicked detective flipped over and lunged to his feet, pushing Vito out of the way to clear the front entrance.

"Is it a fucking full moon tonight or something?" Vito yelled, his sawed-off shotgun hanging by his right leg. "And is that you *again*, old man? Holy shit snacks! I'm starting to think it's not a *co-inky-dink* that you've been out of your room every time something fucked-up has happened tonight around—"

Tony, remaining in his hunched-over posture, hissed at Vito. Spittle flung from his decayed lips and pointy teeth as his gaze darted from the shotgun to Vito's eyes.

Smith stood and turned to face Vito. "Don't do anything stupid. My little friend here hasn't eaten yet today, and he gets pretty cranky when he's hungry. And I just know he's looking at that gut of yours as a gourmet meal."

"What the fuck *is* that?" Vito mumbled and rolled a bulge from his bottom lip and spit a wad of chewing tobacco onto the hallway floor at Smith's feet. "Is that a fucking Halloween costume or something, fella? He looks like a cross between *The Exorcist* and them zombie creatures from *Dawn of the Dead*."

"Yeah, it's a Halloween costume. Just go back to your little cubicle and—"

Vito arched his back, and his body stiffened.

Smith tiptoed backward and looked at Tony, making sure his bantling hadn't done something stupid—again. Tony had the same shocked look on his face and then cowered when Anya stepped from behind Vito.

She removed her elongated fingernail from Vito's back and let him crumple to the hallway floor. She wiped the blood from her long opaque finger onto her black robe and retracted her weapon-nail to a less ghastly length.

She stepped over Vito's body and peered behind her. "Go

get her, girls."

A swarm of ghouls—shoulder to shoulder, wall to wall—pushed past Smith and Tony like a tsunami. The two men pressed their backs against the wall, trying to flatten themselves as much as possible while Anya's coven rushed by and swarmed into Room 25.

Smith glared at Anya when the last ghoul navigated through the doorway. "Two for two, huh? That's two new girls in two nights."

Anya pulled the black veil from her face and let the fabric rest on top of her head. "No contest. He's embarrassing you. And he isn't even trying!"

"Neither am I, Anya. I'm done trying. You know what? I've been hoping this Stepp character blunders in the worst way, so you won't suck him into your sick little world. But he's so moronic, and you're such a wonderful lady, now I hope you two have a harmonious partnership. You both deserve each other. Heck, if I'm lucky, maybe Stepp's stupidity will finally be your downfall."

"You're pathetic. Get out of my face. Go call your sex hotline and drink yourself to death."

Smith pursed his lips and darted his gaze at Tony, ready to collect his ghoul and leave.

"You may have disappointed me beyond refute, Smith, but at least Melissa isn't a lost cause yet. She's proving to be quite the obedient apprentice."

He jabbed a finger at the witch. "I've already warned you about going near her again. … Tony, stop ogling the girls, and let's go. We're leaving."

Tony stood motionless in the opened doorway to Room 25, staring at the gaggle of Mushroom Cult ghouls as they prepared Cinnamon's body.

"Tony!" Smith yelled again.

His bantling stepped into the room, leaving Smith's sight.

"Oh, for Pete's sake. Tony!"

Anya smirked and shook her head. "Wow, you really have control over your cult-of-one. Does *anyone* take what you say seriously anymore? *Tsk, tsk.* Must be so sad for Smithy-Poo."

Smith refused to acknowledge her taunts and entered the room. He grabbed Tony by his tattered shirt and yanked him from the room and into the hallway. He dragged him past Anya and toward the front entrance, like a parent dragging a noncompliant toddler from a toy store.

Smith released his grip when they reached the cold winter air. "What's with you?"

Tony chirped and squealed.

"Really? Cyana again? Did you not see the back-and-forth Anya and I were engaged in? Could you not tell that it was getting heated and that I needed us to go? And yet all you were worried about was getting a quick peek at your zombie girlfriend. Give it up, pal."

Tony whinnied and looked at his threadbare sneakers.

Smith motioned for his sidekick to get into the Pinto as a black cloud of flapping wings descended on the parking lot. Smith could no longer see Tony nor his car nor Vito's Motel as feathers and beaks enveloped them. The front glass doors shattered as the lead rank of birds infiltrated the hallway.

Smith sighed. "Predictable."

He waited for the gale of vultures to pass before moving. He repeated the same gesture to Tony, silently instructing him to get in the car. He glanced at the front entrance of the motel and saw the final bird of prey coast through the shattered opening of the glass doors and land on the carpeted hallway.

"And Anya wins again," he spat as he turned the key in the

ignition, then looked at Tony. "What are you smiling about?"

Tony clapped and gurgled.

"Is that all you think about?" Smith asked and retrieved his silver flask. "Scram, kid. I'm going home to forget about—well—everything."

Tony was gone into thin air with a *poof* as Smith shifted the Pinto into Drive and headed home to his wife and whatever semblance might be left of a normal life.

Stepp noticed the familiar Buick traveling along Derby Street and flagged the driver. The vehicle pulled to the road's shoulder, and the large albino man exited the driver's side.

"You got another one for me?"

Stepp nodded. "Couldn't bring you proof though. I was interrupted right after I had cut her."

"I hope you weren't identified. That'd be *your* ass doin' twenty-five ta life, not mine."

Stepp crammed his hands into his pants pockets and refused to make eye contact.

"You good, bro? You lookin' like you just saw a ghost or somethin'."

"I guess you could say, *or somethin'*."

Rhino leaned into his car and retrieved a copy of the hit list. "Who was it tonight?"

"Cinnamon."

"Going in order. I like your meticulous approach." Rhino crossed her name off the paper. "But I'll need some sort of proof."

"I left her at Vito's. You can go check for yourself. I'm not going back there."

Rhino folded his arms, the movement crumpling the paper now pinned to his chest. "See? Here's the problem. The burden rests on *you* to bring me proof, or I'll assume it never really happened. Figure it out."

Rhino slid behind the Buick's steering wheel, revved the engine to punctuate his threat, and disappeared into the Salem night.

Stepp huffed and removed a Smolens from the pack. He lit the cigarette and tapped his foot, contemplating his next move. He exhaled a rolling mixture of nicotine smoke and steam.

"Goddammit!" he yelled, his voice ricocheting off the surrounding buildings.

After sitting in the IROC's driver seat for more than half his cigarette, he grabbed the steering wheel and bucked his body back and forth, rocking the car. Panting, he rubbed his face and scratched the stubble covering his cheeks and chin. He shifted the car into Drive and headed toward the one place on Earth he never wanted to return to.

Melissa heard a knock on her bedroom door. "It's unlocked."

The door creaked open, and Travis poked his head through the crack. "Lights out, okay, Mel? It's almost midnight."

She swiveled in her desk chair to face her father. "Ten more minutes? Please, Daddy?"

"Ten minutes." He pointed at her to show his seriousness. "I'll check on you before I turn in myself."

"Good night, Daddy."

Travis smiled at his daughter and closed the door.

"He's nice," Anya said, standing next to Melissa's desk. "Hard to believe he's Smith's son."

Melissa stood and crossed the room to retrieve her book bag. "I wish you'd stop getting down on Grandpapa."

Anya shook her head. "Cut from the same cloth, you two are."

Melissa turned around. "But I'm better. I'll be way better than him, if you give me the chance." She slid onto her bed, sitting crisscrossed. "Teach me what you know, and I'll do whatever you need. Let me replace my grandfather. Bring me into your world, and I won't disappoint you."

Anya crawled onto the bed next to Melissa and patted the girl's knee. "You're stronger than any of my contingents so far, that's for sure, but I don't know if you have the stomach for it yet."

Melissa broke her gaze at the witch and stared at her Wham! poster on the back of her door.

"What is it, child? I can sense your trepidation."

"What happens to the Chosen One after you have your way with her?" she asked, not taking her attention from Andrew Ridgeley's dreamy eyes.

"The book is ambiguous about that, but I don't see why I can't do whatever I want with them."

"And, once you sacrifice her, you then become immortal?" Melissa asked, confirming what she had already been told, while returning her gaze to Anya's pale face.

"That's how I've interpreted it. There's nothing that would lead me to believe otherwise. The book is fairly descriptive about the path to immortality."

"So you could, theoretically, bring the Chosen One back, as anything?"

Anya tilted her chin upward and stared down at the girl.

"What're you getting at, child? I have an inkling, but I want to hear you say it."

"I'm still a virgin."

"Oh, Mel. I knew that's what you were getting—"

"Just listen." Mel scooched her body to face the witch sitting on her bed. "I'll give myself to you, so you can attain this … higher power, and then you can bring me back as, like, your sidekick. Or let me lead the Mushroom Cult. Wouldn't you have that ability?"

Anya sighed. "The Chosen One needs to be sacrificed. No coming back. Given as an offering to the book. Plus I don't choose the virgin. The book does. And I would've known if it was you or not the moment I first visited you in the hospital when you were born. I sensed something great in you, but it certainly wasn't the stigma of being the Chosen One. And I've told you how the Chosen One is protected—and noxious—and that's why I need you to help me get close to her. Remember?"

Melissa nodded and fiddled with the plastic ring Graham had given her.

"And I need her to stay a virgin until you can get me to her."

"I used the spell you gave me."

"I know. I could feel it when you did. I hope it was worth it. You only get to use it once."

Melissa proceeded to review her plan with Anya, detailing how she sold Benji on hanging out with her by using the potential of Vicki's jealousy as an angle.

"And we both know it won't really work. Vicki is an adult. She's not gonna look twice at a high-school kid who she's known since he was an annoying little brat. But the spell convinced him that it would work, and we're seeing each other tomorrow night." Melissa leaned to one side to straighten her legs. "I do have a question. What exactly do you need me to do to get you close to Vicki?"

Anya stood and slid the black veil over her face. "The Chosen One's protectors are very powerful. More powerful than I am now, but that'd change if I succeeded in the sacrifice. When the time comes, I'll need you to read a special spell from the book, which will make her vulnerable for a very short period of time."

"How short is short?"

"A second? Two tops."

"Holy smokes."

Anya chuckled. "The influence the protectors have over the dark arts prevents me from reading the spell."

"What would happen if you just ... tried to read it?"

"An infinity of brimstone and gnashing teeth, I presume. I wouldn't dare tempt it."

"So Anya the Great *is* afraid of something."

"Not for long, child. If you come through for me, not for long."

Melissa peeled back her comforter and slid underneath the cool sheets. "What's stopping me from showing up at her office tomorrow morning and reading the spell? You know? Like guerilla warfare or a surprise telegram. Why do I need to get close to her?"

Anya reached into her robe and removed the maroon-bound book adorned with the shining eye situated inside the golden pyramid and flipped toward the end of the entries. "And I quote."

"Good night, Mel!" her mother called out as she passed Melissa's closed door.

"Good night, Mom!"

Anya cleared her throat. "*An ally shall be the sole infiltrator*

*of the shroud protecting the Chosen One, unless said Chosen
One holds voluntary possession of this Mushroom Cult Book."*
Anya glanced over the top binding of the book at Melissa. "How
would you interpret that?"

"I guess it doesn't leave a lot of room for misunderstanding.
I just hope we've targeted the right person."

"I was wrong last time. That's why I was able to get to Rose
with such ease. I won't make that mistake again."

Melissa turned on her side, feeling the softness of her
feather down pillow, and reached for Anya's hand. "And what
makes you so certain this time?"

Anya took the girl's hand and caressed it. "She smelled of
decay and sweets. It's a pungent odor but very specific and
unique—one I can't describe unless you've experienced it
yourself."

"Who are the protectors you keep talking about anyway?"
Melissa asked, feeling herself falling into slumber with long
blinks.

Anya traced the etched eye inside the pyramid with her
fingertip. "I will not give them the satisfaction of speaking their
name aloud."

Melissa didn't reply, and Anya noticed the teenager's
breathing had deepened.

"Sleep tight, child." Anya brushed a clump of hair from the
sleeping girl's forehead. "Soon everything will be in its right
place."

Stepp poked his head through the shattered glass of the front
doors to Vito's Motel. "Hello?"

When he didn't get an answer, he swallowed hard and maneuvered his body through the opening, careful to not cut himself on the hanging shards of glass that resembled shark's teeth.

The overhead lights flickered, and he saw a figure laying on the ground farther up the hallway. He squinted, focusing between flashes from the malfunctioning light fixtures. He stepped against one side of the corridor and used the wall to guide him toward Room 25.

"Hey, pal. You okay? Too much to drink?" Then he muttered, "I hope."

The lights flickered in stages, from off to on and back again, as if they struggled to maintain power, like a car with a dead battery trying to start. The flashes threw moving shadows against the walls.

"Oh, fuck," Stepp whispered when he got close enough to recognize Vito's unmistakable girth and greasy hair. Stepp covered his mouth and concentrated on his increased breathing. "Just calm down and walk past him. Whatever the fuck mutant that was here is probably gone now."

Stepp closed his eyes and counted to three, taking a breath and building his courage between each number. He opened his eyes and raised his leg to step over the body. He noticed the gaping hole where Vito's spine should be and gagged. "Oh, God."

"Hey!" a voice yelled from behind him.

Stepp squealed and jumped backward.

"Scaredy-cat," Rhino said, laughing.

"What are you doing here?"

"Just checking on you," he said and approached Stepp. "Poor sucker. What happened to him?"

"That *thing* got him."

Rhino raised an eyebrow. "What thing?"

"I dunno man. It was something out of a horror flick. It just appeared in the room while I was taking care of the girl and chased me out. Like a zombie or something."

"You need to lay off the dust, man." Rhino strode over Vito's body. "Now which room were you guys in?"

"Right there. Twenty-five."

Rhino entered the room as Stepp composed himself. He stole another look at Vito's desecrated body, then laughed from inside the motel room.

"What's so funny?" Stepp asked.

"It's like you want me to go on some wild-goose chase, or you want me to hurt you."

Stepp furrowed his brows and turned the corner into the room. "What in the hell?"

"Cut to the quick, man." Rhino spun around and poked a finger into Stepp's forehead. "What gives?"

"I-I don't know. I don't get it." Stepp glanced around Rhino's large body at the immaculately clean and unoccupied room. "I left her right here, bleeding all over the floor."

"I'm no cleaning expert, but I'm gonna tell you anyway. No bloody body is here. Are you sure we're in the right room?"

Stepp returned to the hallway and looked at the number on the door. "This is it."

"Well, until I see a body, or you bring me proof, I'm considering this as incomplete."

A black feather on the hallway floor beyond the door caught Stepp's attention. He picked it up and rolled it between his thumb and forefinger. "I betch'ya that thing took her."

"And then flew away on Pegasus or some shit like that, right? Get real, man."

"Pegasus was white, not black. And not real."

"Like your zombie spook was real?"

Stepp looked from the vulture feather to Rhino. "It was. I saw it. It hissed at me."

"Sure, then it magically became a janitor and cleaned the place?"

Stepp remained silent, his hands shaking for a smoke.

"But leaves the body in the hallway? C'mon, fool. Don't play me."

"Fuck you. And fuck your list. I'm out." Stepp turned for the entrance. "I've taken care of two of your piss-ants in two nights, and this is the thanks I get?"

Rhino chuckled and shook his head. "You just bought yourself a ticket to the dance."

Stepp removed his pack of Smolens from his pocket. "Fuck you and the whores you rode in on."

Rhino charged down the hallway at Stepp, his boot catching on Vito's spread legs and sending the large albino headfirst into the door of Room 22, knocking him out cold.

"The bigger they are, the harder they fall." Stepp ducked and turned sideways to make sure none of the shark-teeth glass slices touched him as he exited the motel and walked past the Buick toward his IROC.

9: VERNAL EQUINOX

Smith awoke in a sweaty panic, wiping the bloody images of his first wife's murder from his vision as the sanctity of his bedroom came into focus. As the dream-state replay of Wendy's final minutes faded, the sound of a ringing telephone became louder. He glanced at Wynn; the noise had not yet stirred her.

He swung his rickety legs from the side of the bed and traipsed into the kitchen.

"This better be good," he said into the receiver and cleared the phlegm trapped in his throat.

"Smith, love! Did I wake you?"

"Hank, it's"—Smith glanced at the large yellow clock in the shape of the sun hanging over the kitchen table—"not even six o'clock here yet. The real question is, why aren't *you* sleeping?"

"HBO had a marathon tonight. First *Grease Two*, *Rocky Horror Picture Show*, then topped off with a little *Xanadu*. You think I would miss that trifecta of cinema?"

Smith laughed and hit the Brew button on his coffeemaker.

"Don't ever change, Hank."

"You bet your britches I won't. I'm fabulous as is."

"I'll drink to that. Now I know you didn't call at this godforsaken hour to just chat about crappy flamboyant musicals."

"Hey! I resemble that remark."

"You said it, not me."

Hank had a bout of coughing. Smith heard him pull the phone away from his face as Hank's fit turned into wheezing and a whistling sound with each deep inhale.

"You okay, Hank?"

"Yeah, love. Give me a sec." Hank cleared his throat; the sound of loose sputum rattled in the receiver. "Sorry about that, chap. This emphysema is for the birds. I wouldn't wish this on my worst enemy."

"At least it's not Alzheimer's."

"Not yet, at least. You still smoking?"

Smith looked at the freshly lit cigarette between his two fingers and snubbed it out in the sink. "Nope. Quit a while ago."

"That's *mah* boy. I wish someone had made me quit three decades ago."

"Olli tried, if I remember correctly."

"Olli got what was comin' to him. That's all I'm gonna say about him."

"Fair enough, but the Devil's in the details, Hank. We both know that."

Hank exploded into another round of hacking and fighting for breath. When the coughing subsided, he said, "Look here, love. I need a favor."

Smith took his TOP GUN FOR HIRE mug from the cabinet and poured himself a cup of coffee. "Anything."

"I think my manager, Roxanne, is using the Taco Shed to deal after-hours. I can't afford to have the fuzz bust the place. With the shop so new, that'd be signing its death certificate. The bad publicity would keep the families away, especially with downtown Lynn starting to nosedive, and I couldn't recover financially from that. And it's just too much for me to make that flight from Vegas to Boston again. Not with my emphysema. Too taxing on these pretty lungs of mine. It almost killed me last month."

Smith lit another cigarette, holding the lighter from the receiver so Hank wouldn't hear the spark of the flint. "I can do that. What tipped you off?"

"The owner of Poof and Snoofin's Boutique lives in an apartment that overlooks the rear of the shop. A real gentleman, that one. He attended the grand opening and offered to keep an eye on the place, with me being so far away and—"

"Old?" Smith finished, laughing. "You want me to try to buy from her, as proof?" He blew a puff of smoke from the corner of his mouth farthest from the phone. "She won't be suspicious of a senior citizen. It's not like there are eighty-year-old cops working undercover."

"Don't you mean *elderly*?" Hank laughed. "*Senior citizen*? Please! You stopped being a senior citizen twenty years ago. You are borderline decrepit, love."

Smith chortled. "Remind me again why we're still friends?"

"Because you can't resist the steel in 'Hank Steel.'"

Smith shook his head and chuckled. "Welp, that's when I know it's time to bid you adieu."

"So, you'll help me out? I wouldn't drag you into it, but you still are the bulletproof detective."

"Flattery can only get you so far."

"How about a year of free tacos? All you can eat?"

"You've stooped that low, Hank? You should be ashamed!"

"Have you tasted those tacos? It's like winning the lottery."

"Have *you* tasted your tacos? I don't know if that's a lottery worth winning."

"That's how I know you love me. You only know how to express your affection through sarcasm and insults."

"See? This is why we're friends. You get me. In another life, Hank, maybe we would've been an item."

Hank laughed so hard his glee quickly transformed into another outburst of rattling coughs and wheezing. "Are you *trying* to kill me?"

"I don't know. I think those marathons of musicals are doing a fine job of that themselves."

"Good night, love."

"Good night? I know you're three hours behind me, but I don't think *good night* is the appropriate salutation."

Another bout of coughing consumed Hank, and Smith heard Hank struggle to hang up the phone. After a few moments of rustling and wheezing, the line disconnected.

In a rare state of emotional weakness, Smith let himself acknowledge that Hank's time was running short. But Smith wasn't ready to grieve his friend just yet. He would only cross that bridge when Hank's death forced him to.

"You're up early," Wynn said, entering the kitchen.

"Hank called and woke me."

"Oh?" she said, pouring herself a cup of coffee. "Everything okay?"

"Thinks there might be an issue with the manager he hired for the Taco Shed."

"That nice girl? Roxanne? What kind of issue? Is she stealing?"

"Worse. Dealing. Hank's afraid it'll give the place a bad rap if she gets busted."

Wynn covered her mouth and gasped. "Oh my! Why doesn't he just fire her?"

"Under false pretenses? I'm sure Hank wants a lawsuit as much as wants his place to be associated with drug dealers. He needs solid proof first."

"Please don't tell me that you're getting involved."

Smith remained silent and rubbed the rim of his coffee mug.

"Babe! Leave the detecting to the younger folks. I don't want to see you get hurt."

Smith turned to face his wife. "Hank's my friend, and it might be the last favor he ever asks of me. How will I feel if I can't do this one small thing for him? He's not doing well, Wynn."

Wynn clasped her husband's hands. "You're a good man, Detective Smith. You do what you feel is right. Just please be safe."

She planted a kiss on his cheek and excused herself to take a shower.

He sipped his coffee and took another pull from the cigarette and watched the sun crest above the roofs of the sardined houses, signaling the start to yet another glorious day of walking among the fine and upstanding citizens of this wretched city.

Stepp locked the IROC's door and again didn't notice the Pinto with two male passengers parked a few spots down Combs Avenue. Stepp shoved the car keys into his pocket and rubbed his forehead, groaning. The morning sunlight stung his eyes, and he used the topside of his opened hand as a shield while he climbed the few steps to his office's entrance. He tugged on the locked door, and something popped in his elbow when it didn't give way.

Stepp grumbled and cupped his hands to the glass to minimize the glare from the sun as he pressed his face to the door to see if Vicki had already arrived. He saw her fiddling with her stationary at her desk and beat on the window.

Vicki looked up and smiled before maneuvering through the waiting area to open the front door for him. "Good morning. You're a little worse for the wear."

Stepp entered the warmth of the office, stumbled, and caught his balance on the gaudy fake Christmas tree. He shook his head and scratched at the two-day stubble growing from his face.

"You okay?" Vicki grabbed him by his upper arms, guiding him into an upright standing position.

"Is there coffee?"

"Not yet. I can put some on right now."

"Please, Vic. That would be great."

She turned toward the complimentary coffee bar and began the percolating process.

"It's been a rough few days."

Vicki glanced over her shoulder and took in his appearance again. She returned her attention to brewing the morning's first—and certainly not last, by the looks of it—pot of coffee. "Is it the list?"

"I think I've slept a total of two hours since Tuesday, and I still haven't been home yet. Do you know if I have a change of clothes here? Or at least clean underwear? And deodorant?"

Vicki touched her reddening cheeks without turning to face

him. "Why haven't you gone home?"

"That fucking list, Vic. It's taking a lot out of me. Lots of leads to follow up on. Every door I close, two more seem to open."

She collected a disposable cup from the tower of cups next to the Mr. Coffee and waited for the pot to fill. "Sounds like it's one for the ages."

"What is? My ripe body odor?" he said, laughing.

"The case, silly!" she replied and wiggled her thick collection of jelly bracelets.

Stepp approached the table and stood beside her. "See? Now that's more like it! Something just feels off when you're not wearing those gooey bracelets, or whatever they're called."

Vicki chuckled and removed the fresh pot from the burner and poured the coffee into his cup.

"Only halfway, please. Need to leave room for the good stuff."

She stopped pouring at the halfway mark, and Stepp excused himself to his office, leaving her standing with his coffee still clutched in her hand. He returned down the hallway, holding a bottle of Amaretto. He unscrewed the cap and topped off the cup with a mixture of caffeinated liquor.

"Can you get some sleep tonight?" she asked, adding creamer to her cup.

"I wish. Have another lead to follow up tonight in Lynn. I'm hoping this'll be the last stop on this wild-goose chase, and I'll close out the list for my client. If the manager doesn't give me any issues, it shouldn't take too long." He brought his cup to his lips and paused before taking a sip. "You got any wild plans tonight? Last Friday you had that blind date that took a nosedive … into a Dumpster."

She glared at him.

"I'm sorry, Mouse," he said and snorted. "I didn't mean to make a joke. Humor is the only thing keeping me from losing my mind right now. Want some hair of the dog in your there java?"

Vicki looked into her cup. "I'll pass. But that doesn't mean I wouldn't be up for another night of sleuthing with you and maybe finishing it off with a nightcap."

"No bones tonight, babe. I should work alone. A little too dangerous for such a delicate flower."

Vicki scoffed and spoke in the best flirtatious Marilyn Monroe voice she could muster. "You think *I'm* delicate? I guess you haven't really gotten to know the real me yet, Mr. Detective. And don't flatter yourself. I already have plans for tonight."

She turned to seductively sashay to her desk but clipped the end of the coffee table, sending her and her coffee into the coat rack. She grabbed onto her jacket and toppled the stand, coffee waves like high tide spilling from the cup, and all fell in a heap on the floor.

Stepp scooted to the mess on the floor and grabbed Vicki from her nondrenched coffee hand and burst into hysterics. "You okay, kid?"

Vicki pushed the coat rack off her and stood. She bent to retrieve the now-empty coffee cup from the floor and inspected the large pools of stains on her pants and blouse.

"I'm fine. Just … don't look at me, please."

"Oh, don't be embarrassed. I'm a total klutz too." He grabbed a handful of napkins and dabbed the brown stains. "What are your plans for tonight?"

Vicki snatched the napkins from Stepp. "You're just asking me that to redirect my attention and make me feel better."

He raised both hands in front of him as if she had just

stuck a gun in his chest. "Whoa, whoa. Just because we are both having shitty mornings doesn't mean I'm not sincere."

Vicki huffed and sat in her desk chair. "I'm sorry." She fiddled with the edges of the napkins. "I have plans to go out with Caitlin and her brother for coffee and maybe something afterward. And I guess her brother is bringing a friend that he wants us to meet."

"A double date? With a minor? Scandalous!"

"The friend is a girl. And, I'm not dating Cait's brother. He's in high school. Plus … I'm kinda interested in someone."

Stepp scratched his crotch. "Oh, really? Who?"

Vicki tried not to let him notice that her gaze had followed his fingers to his groin. "Trust me. Someone older. An adult."

"Well, maybe you should focus less on wasting your time on blind dates that end in homicide or hanging out with kids on a Friday night and put your energies into the Mystery Man."

Vicki remained silent and flipped her jelly bracelets toward her elbow.

"What do I have for appointments today?"

She opened the daily ledger, her elbow knocking over the bronze horse paperweight, and used her fingertip to navigate to today's date. "Nothing until two o'clock. A woman from Marblehead who thinks her cleaning lady is slowly poisoning her."

"Why don't these whack jobs go to the actual police instead of wasting my time with these hare-brained cases?"

Vicki righted the paperweight and rubbed her elbow. "Says here that she did go to the police, and they suggested that she talk to a doctor. So you're her only hope."

"Great. I'm turning into the fucking Obi-Wan Kenobi of nutcases."

Vicki giggled and tossed her wad of napkins into the

wastebasket.

"I'm gonna head to the house and shit, shine, and shower. Why don't you take the morning off and get tidied up too? Just make sure you're back before Whack Job arrives for her consultation."

Vicki closed the daily ledger and slipped her jacket around her torso, tying the waistband strings taut around her hips and flipping the fur-lined hood over her head. She opened the front door and took a step into the bone-chilling winter wind.

"And, Vic? Just send me the bill for your getup's dry cleaning."

Vicki headed toward her car, not sure whether she felt elated about him worrying about the stains on her clothes or slighted that he thought of her well-thought-out ensemble as a "getup."

Melissa tried not to burn her fingers on the hair-crimping iron. She tilted her head so she could see the clump of brown hair better in the mirror's reflection. She put pressure on the viselike handles, squeezing her hair into wonderful chicane designs. Holding the crimping iron in place, she glanced at the clock sitting next to the sink. She still had about fifteen minutes before Benji would pick her up for their quasi-date. She released the pressure on that clump and inserted the next section of straight hair while inspecting her Quiet Riot T-shirt for lint and wrinkles—she wanted him to think of her as fun and a little rebellious. Her favorite Wham! shirt just wouldn't do.

Melissa tapped her foot to the beat of "We're Not Gonna Take It," coming from her cassette boom box resting on the closed toilet lid, and noticed movement behind her in the mirror's reflection. She spun around, vigilant not to rip her hair from the iron or to burn herself. Six female ghouls stood in a shoulder-to-shoulder line between Melissa and the bathroom door.

She dropped the crimping iron and tripped over her own sneakers before the sink counter stopped her backpedaling. The iron's cord had reached its max extension, and the crimping device swung like a swinging pendulum from the wall outlet. Melissa composed herself and willed her heart rate to slow when she identified her visitors as Mushroom Cult clanswomen.

"Didn't take you for being the jumpy kind," Anya said, sitting on the closed toilet seat with crimping iron in hand. The boom box had been relocated to the floor. She leaned down and pressed Stop, pausing Dee Snider's demonic crooning.

Melissa extended an open hand, motioning for the witch to return the crimping iron, hoping a nonchalant gesture would show Anya that Melissa could be stoic in the face of consternation and was not just a jumpy child. After Anya returned the iron, Melissa surveyed the ghouls shifting uneasily in her bathroom. She recognized four of them from the morgue episode, when she had witnessed the vultures recycle that Blind-Date Killer. The fifth and sixth visitors looked unfamiliar and appeared to be the ripest.

Melissa slowly reached for one of the new dead girls she didn't remember seeing at the morgue. The ghoul's face looked ashen and not quite as decayed as the veteran coven members.

The ghoul hissed and snapped pearly white teeth at Melissa's splayed fingers.

"Adrielle!" Anya scolded and then readdressed Melissa. "I don't think that's wise yet, child. She's still a bantling. Think of the new ones like confused and hungry lion cubs. They don't look as intimidating as the rest of the pride, but they're quicker to play rough."

Melissa turned toward Anya but locked her gaze on the two newest members. "What about them?"

"That one—the one who almost took off your finger—I turned a few nights ago on the beach. And that one"—Anya furrowed her brow in the other bantling's direction—"is the result of a motel-room offering last night. Goes by the name Cinnamon. Have no idea what her real name is."

Melissa huffed, trying to keep her best poker face so Anya wouldn't see the disappointment she felt on being excluded from the previous two resurrection extravaganzas. She placed the crimping iron on the counter and leaned toward the mirror, putting her back to the row of ghouls bouncing and vibrating in anxious excitement behind her.

"Do you ever know their real names?"

Anya snorted. "Hardly ever. I guess the names they were using when I got my clutches on them *are* their real names now."

"Why did you bring them here?"

"I wanted to show you what is at stake for you tonight. I figured a little visual firsthand reminder couldn't hurt."

Melissa unscrewed her red lipstick tube and froze her lips in a half pucker.

"Use this." Anya handed Melissa a tube of jet-black lipstick. "It's so much more sinister and commanding."

Melissa accepted the gift and turned over the tube in her hand, inspecting the label.

"Pull this off tonight, and I'll gift you with every member of my congregation. You're in control of your own destiny." Anya placed both hands on Melissa's shoulders and leaned in so both of their faces were flush with one another, and she made eye contact with the teenager through the mirror's reflection. "I believe in you, child. I know you won't fail me, won't fail us."

Melissa grinned and spun the bottom of the tube, watching the black cosmetic rise in a circular motion. She pressed the chilly makeup to her upper lip and held her breath as she applied it. When the color met where she had started—a pall of black now concealing her naturally pink lips—she stood upright, nudging the witch backward.

She took a deep breath and held it as a wide smile consumed her face. Her lips tingled and then went numb. She touched her bottom lip and felt as if a warm and safe blanket had been draped over her shoulders.

Anya placed her mouth next to Melissa's ear. "If you can get him to kiss you before that lipstick wears off—*woowee!* Watch out world! He'll forget the little bitch Vicki even exists."

Melissa sidestepped and peered into Anya's eyes. "But that's not the plan. The plan is to use him to get Vicki to trust me, so *you* can get close to her."

Anya clasped Melissa's hands. "I know that, child. I'm just saying, for an added *boom*, if the moment struck your fancy, he would be yours, at full attention—if you catch my drift—for as long as that lipstick is still on you."

"I don't want to scare off Vicki and Benji's sister. I mean, they're adults. Would they want to hang out with a high-school kid with black lipstick?"

"They both just recently turned twenty-one. They're hardly adults. You'll see."

Melissa glanced at the clock again. "He'll be here soon. I talked him into picking me up. Plus Dad wants to meet him."

"Auntie Anya wants to meet him too."

Melissa chuckled and slapped the witch's shoulder with the back of her hand. "Yep. Just one big happy family."

When the front doorbell rang, the six ghouls turned their heads in unison, as if all controlled by a single remote.

"C'mon, girls. We'll watch this from the comfort of home," Anya said, and Melissa found herself standing alone in her bathroom, fixated on her lips that looked like the entrance to a black hole.

Benji stopped at the red-colored front door and paused. He cleared his throat and tugged at the bottom of his polo shirt. He didn't know why he had felt the need to dress up beyond a T-shirt and jeans, but some tenacious force drove him to donning the most respectable item in his wardrobe. *This isn't even a real date, right?* He had continued to convince himself throughout the process. But that nagging voice seemed to think otherwise.

Why am I so nervous to press this button? I'm not even after her.

He stared at the orange-glowing doorbell, closed his eyes, and pressed. He heard the singsong ding-dong chimes from inside the residence and prayed Melissa would be the one to answer so he could evade the dreaded parental niceties that sometimes felt more like an interrogation. Plus he didn't know how well his acting skills would be, considering this whole "date" was a ruse in the first place.

He heard footsteps approach the front door—Please be Mel … Please be Mel … Please be Mel … Please be—and licked his fingertips and smoothed back the hair above his ears.

"Hello. You must be Benji."

"Yes. Nice to meet you, Mrs. Smith."

Gwen invited him inside and called for her daughter.

Benji glanced around the foyer, his gaze landing on the hanging chandelier above him, and saw Melissa's father come from the kitchen. "Good evening, sir."

"Sir?" Travis said and shook Benji's hand. "I think I like him already."

"How did you and Mel get to know each other?" Gwen asked, leading Benji into the living room to sit.

"Lunch line. Leave it to tacos to bring people together."

Travis chuckled and rolled his lips into each other and nodded. "Well, okay then. What are the big plans for tonight?"

Addie sprinted through the living room with an E.T. action figure clenched in her hand, her brother in hot pursuit and yelling a series of shrill, "*Mine! Give me that back!*"

Gwen intercepted the toy from Addie's grasp as she passed in front of her and handed it back to Shaun.

"Are you Melissa's boyfriend?" Addie asked, the alien toy now long forgotten with no way to phone home.

Benji shifted on the couch and darted his eyes between Melissa's parents. "*Um ...*"

"No, sweetie," Gwen answered. "This is just Mel's new friend, and they are going out for a few hours."

Addie turned and swiped the E.T. doll from Shaun's hands and bolted downstairs, a sound cloud mixed with screaming and pleading followed.

"I'm sorry about that, Benji."

"No worries, Mrs. Smith. I'm sure me and my sister were the same way."

"And Mel said you're a senior?" Travis asked.

"That's right, sir. Looking to go to Salem State next year for health education. Want to be a gym teacher."

Benji noticed both parents looking toward the living room doorway as Melissa entered the room.

"What in the world do you have on your face?" Travis stood from the couch. "Absolutely not. You are not leaving this house looking like some Halloween freak. Wash that off, or Benji can say goodnight."

Melissa swallowed hard and touched her lips. Benji looked at the floor, trying to make himself as invisible as possible if he was to witness a family teenage-makeup feud. She about-faced and stormed from the room, and Benji traced her path across the house by her heavy and stomping footfalls.

"I'm sorry, Benji," Gwen said.

Benji waved away her apology. "It's fine, ma'am. And we'll meet my sister and her friend at the new coffee shop at Redman's Place, and then all four of us might go to the arcade or something."

"I *love* Sweet Insani-Tea."

Travis snickered and shook his head and stood. "Well, Benji, it was a pleasure to meet you. Make sure Mel's home by ten."

"Will do, sir."

"You can wait here for her. I'm sure she'll only be a sec," Travis added, shooting his wife a look of discontent.

The Smiths' vinyl collection caught Benji's eye. He focused his attention on the bins full of Benny Goodman and Frank Sinatra and Louis Armstrong records while he waited for his non-date to remove her black lipstick.

Melissa flicked on her bathroom light and slammed the door. "Think they can tell me what to do forever? They got another think coming."

She grabbed a hanging washcloth from the wall with such force that the clear plastic holder ring ripped from the wall and fell to the tiled floor. She doused the washcloth under the faucet and didn't bother to wring out the excess water. She pressed the soaking wet towel to her lips and scrubbed the black from her face with her right hand. She placed her left hand on the counter for support, and her fingers landed on something plastic. She glanced at the counter, gray water staining the sink's bowl and dripping on the faucet head.

The washcloth fell into the sink as she clasped the unused tube of secretly placed black lipstick. "Thank you, Auntie Anya," she whispered and slipped the lipstick into her back pocket.

Melissa retrieved the washcloth from the sink and continued to remove the black coloring from her lips, appeasing her parents' wishes. She just hoped Benji's car had a passenger-side mirror in its sun visor so she could reapply the makeup.

Melissa entered the living room and wasn't quite ready yet to make eye contact with Benji after that embarrassing scolding from her parents.

"See? Now isn't that better?" Gwen asked, when she saw Melissa without the lipstick.

"Yep, Mom. You're always right about fashion."

Gwen slapped her thighs in acceptance of her daughter's confession to conformity and stood. "Have a good time tonight. Do you need any money?"

Melissa shook her head. "Still have babysitting money."

Benji stood, the anticipation of escaping the tension in the room now in full force, and escorted Melissa to his car parked out front.

"I am so sorry about that," she said as she slid into the passenger seat.

"It's cool. I get it. Parents just don't understand sometimes."

"How about *all* of the times."

Benji eased the car from the driveway onto the street and headed toward Redman's Place Mall.

Melissa leaned forward, the shoulder seat belt strap catching and pinning her from moving any farther, and wiggled the black lipstick tube from her back pocket. She flipped down the sun visor and discovered his ride did not contain a built-in mirror. She reached over and grabbed his rearview mirror and titled it toward her face.

Benji glanced at her, puzzled.

"This'll just take a sec. Keep your eyes on the road."

She adjusted the reflection to her lips and spun the bottom of the tube. She puckered and slowly traced the silky cosmetic across her lips.

"You *are* a devious one, Freshman. I like your moxie."

Melissa finished applying Anya's lipstick and sat back in the seat. "How about some tunes?"

Benji smirked and turned on the radio.

"And you can have your mirror back," she said. "Sorry about my parents."

He readjusted the reflection so it pointed out the back window. "Don't even mention it. Plus I think that color looks wicked fresh on you."

Melissa grinned and stared at her hands. *Don't fall for him. That's not the reason why you're here. Stay focused on the mission.*

"We're meeting my sister and Vicki at Sweet Insani-Tea. I hope that's okay."

Melissa nodded and looked out the window at the passing Victorian-style houses, all with bushes adorning the front yards and covered with a frosting of snow. "What's your sister's name again?"

"Caitlin."

Melissa made a mental note and took her gaze from the landscape to look at Benji. "So you're not taking me out for the world's best tacos tonight?"

"I feel that Hank's Taco Shed is more second-date material."

"Keep dreaming, lover boy," she teased and bit her bottom lip, tasting the sweetness of Anya's lipstick.

"Hey, Freshman, it's your band." Benji turned up the volume on the radio's broadcast of Wham!'s newest single.

She chuckled, nestled her shoulders together in a comforting squeeze, and crossed her legs. She couldn't stop the dangling foot from shaking.

"So what's the plan?" he asked.

"The plan?"

"How're we gonna make Vicki the most jealous? That's why we're all going out tonight, remember? And since you just made it bogusly clear that there won't be a second date with the Mel-o-maniac."

"Mel-o-maniac? If that's your attempt at being clever, don't quit your day job. And I remember very well why we're going out tonight."

"Good. Because you have no idea how hard it was to score the Friday before Christmas off with my job and then talk Cait into hanging out with me."

"You really like this girl. I mean, like, pathetically."

Benji smiled. "She's pretty radical."

Melissa looked out the window again, trying to not allow the twinge of jealousy to distract her from the prize.

Benji held open the door for Melissa, and they entered Sweet Insani-Tea. She spotted two young women sitting at a table and assumed they were Benji's sister and her mark. Sure enough, the two females smiled and waved. When they reached the table, Benji slid out a chair for Melissa, and she sat, suddenly self-conscious of her blackened lips.

"Did you guys order yet?" Benji asked.

"Nah. We were waiting for you guys." Then to Melissa, she said, "Hi, I'm Benji's sister, Caitlin."

Melissa nodded and smiled to acknowledge the greeting, her first thought being, *So, the other chick is the Chosen One.*

"Nice to meet you. I'm Melissa," she said to both women.

"Ready to get some drinks?" Caitlin asked and stood.

"This place is hoppin'," Benji said, surveying the crowd. "Do you want to take them to go?"

"Totally," Vicki said. "I'm really not in the mood to deal with crowds today."

They got in line, and Benji asked, "Rough day at work?"

"My boss is in the middle of this big investigation, and it's really bringing down the vibe of the office."

"Did anything ever come of you talking to him about the killer?"

"What's this?" Melissa asked, wedging herself between their shoulders.

Benji gave Vicki an apologetic look and pretended to study

the drink menu.

"It's nothing. Boring work stuff," Vicki answered and wiggled her jelly bracelets toward her elbow.

Melissa noticed the plethora of rainbow-colored accessories worn by an adult with an adult career and now understood what Anya had meant about her black lipstick. She certainly did not feel foolish anymore.

"I like your bracelets."

"Aw, thanks. They make me feel powerful. And fun. Like Madonna."

This *is the Chosen One? And who Benji is infatuated with?*

"I think they are totally rad."

"Neato. Your crimped hair is wicked rad. And I love your lipstick. It's very The Cure."

Benji slipped his arm around Melissa's waist and squeezed her into him. "Yep, Vic. Funny you say that because it was music that brought me and Mel together."

Melissa shot him a confused look. "I thought it was cafeteria tacos."

Benji chuckled. "And here I was thinking it was Depeche Mode."

"Ah, because of your adorable T-shirt," Melissa replied and rubbed his chest.

"You know what's really adorable? You kids!" Vicki said and stepped forward to give the barista her order.

Melissa already hated Vicki's bubbly demeanor so much that she was ready to plant a big kiss on Benji's lips and let the lipstick change the course of the night right then and there. But she thought of Anya and the promise of controlling the Mushroom Cult once the witch attained immortality.

"It's like totally subzero temperatures out there tonight," Caitlin said. "Do you wanna just hang out at our place and watch HBO? *Raiders of the Lost Ark* is playing tonight."

"That's not too lame for you, right?" Benji whispered to Melissa.

"I don't care what we do," she whispered, and then her voice grew louder as she grabbed his hand. "As long as I'm with you."

Benji squeezed her hand to show his appreciation of her acting tactics.

"You owe me a Depeche Mode T-shirt for this, bucko," she whispered and laughed.

The line moved up, and Benji gave his and Melissa's coffee order as she studied the back of Vicki's head, not believing she was in the presence of the Chosen One—the virgin who would fulfill both her and Anya's destinies.

When they had returned to the house with their coffees and ice cream—from a pit stop at Baskin Robbins in the North Shore Mall—Melissa thought it would be a nice touch if she sat in Benji's lap. He wrapped his arms around her stomach, and she snuggled into his chest.

Caitlin pressed the buttons on the cable box so the television tuned to the Home Box Office channel and showed the movie's opening sequence.

"You know what, guys?" Vicki said. "It's been a rough week. I think I'll head home."

Benji jumped from the chair, catapulting Melissa onto the floor. "But it's a Friday night. And we all need decompression time."

Melissa caught a fleeting glimpse of Anya's robe fluttering

around the corner.

"Are you wearing Jovan Musk?" Melissa asked, derailing Vicki's need to leave. "That is my favorite perfume!"

Vicki touched her neck. "You have a good nose! You just might be my new best friend."

"And ... And she has a great ear too. Her taste in music is totally bodacious," Benji said.

Caitlin snickered. "Bodacious? What are we? Surfers in California? You're such a tool."

He sat down on the chair again, his cheeks pinking from embarrassment as he shot a glance at Vicki.

"That's okay, Benji," Vicki said, resting her hand on his knee. "Don't listen to her. You can say whatever ridiculous things you want. You'll always be Cait's annoying little brother to me."

Melissa shot a sympathetic look at Benji and snorted when her gaze fell upon Anya's reflection in the mirror just above Benji's head. The witch stood in the doorway behind them, unseen, and flashed a smile filled with sharpened teeth. She winked at Melissa as Anya touched a yellowed fingernail to her own lips in the reflection. Melissa spun to look at the doorway, but the witch was gone.

"Mel? Earth to Mel!" Vicki said.

"Huh? Sorry?"

"I was saying that Anne & Hope is having a big sale for Christmas on all Jovan Musk products. That's where Benji works. He lets me use his employee discount too."

"See? ... He's not just the annoying little brother," Melissa said.

Vicki looked at Benji and smirked. "He's all right, I guess. I've known him since he was a toddler. It's hard to see him as anything but."

"C'mon. Stay. I really like hanging out with you guys," Melissa said, making eye contact with both Caitlin and Vicki.

"Fine. I'll stay. But we gotta turn off *Indiana Jones*."

Caitlin stood to change the channel as Melissa asked, "So where do you work again?"

"I work for a private eye."

"*Ooh*, that must be juicy!" Melissa said and sat on the couch, leaning forward and propping up her chin with cupped hands as her elbows acted as pillars on her knees.

"Not as juicy as she'd like it to be," Caitlin said, punching the buttons on the cable box.

Melissa glanced at Caitlin and gasped when she saw both Pum'kin and Adrielle standing next to the television, hovering their decaying ghoulish hands over the cable box and pretending to mess with the channels. Melissa pursed her lips and shook her head with as little movement as she could to not draw attention to herself.

Pum'kin flashed a toothless grin, like a defiant child, pointing at a wall outlet after already being scolded not to touch it. Melissa clenched her teeth and glanced toward the doorway, hoping Anya still stood there. The witch's black veil entered the frame of the doorjamb, the rest of her body hidden around the corner. Melissa gestured with her head toward the two ghouls acting as if they would pull some *Poltergeist* tricks with the cable box.

Anya shook her head, smiled, and what little Melissa could see of the witch disappeared around the corner of the doorframe.

"Vicki's got a thing for her boss," Benji explained, furrowing his brows as he tried to follow Melissa's gaze to see what she was looking at.

Melissa smiled and nodded, directing her attention to

Caitlin switching channels. She sighed louder than she had anticipated when she saw both ghouls sitting on top of the television, arms folded, and mouthing exaggerated miming gestures as each person in the room spoke.

"Holy Scooby snacks! Cait, go back to the news!" Vicki said and approached the television set.

Caitlin flipped to the previous channel she had surfed past and stopped.

The two ghouls sitting atop the television lowered themselves and stood next to Caitlin and Vicki, watching the screen.

"Everything okay?" Benji asked.

"I know her!" Vicki pointed to the picture of the woman filling the screen as the news anchor spoke. "That's Shannon Peterson! She lived two doors down from me throughout elementary school, and we took some college classes together last year."

Shannon Peterson's name appeared underneath her picture on the screen as the news anchor reported how the police had found her body in the woods near Vito's Motel early this morning. Then the image on the screen split, and Vito's picture was placed next to Shannon's, along with the information on his death as well.

Melissa noticed Pum'kin and Adrielle glance behind them at the doorway. She followed their gaze and noticed a bantling standing just inside the room, with Anya standing behind the new ghoul, the witch's hands petting the undead girl's shoulders. Melissa's attention was drawn back to the two ghouls in front of the television when they began clapping and chirping and pointing from the bantling to the screen.

"Go ahead, Cinnamon. It's safe. They can't see you unless you want them to. Except that one." Anya motioned at Melissa.

"Remember her, Cinnamon? You met her earlier tonight in her bathroom." Anya now made eye contact with Melissa. "You really do have to speak to them like they're toddlers. Only they're not as squishy and delectable!" She laughed and addressed Cinnamon again. "Go check out what they are saying about your previous wretched self before I saved you, child."

Melissa watched as Cinnamon stepped farther into the room and passed in-between Caitlin and Benji already standing in front of the television.

The newly reborn ghoul reached out a hand and touched the glass screen, her rotting and decrepit splayed fingers covering the picture of her at a time before she had lost herself—a time before the partying and drugs and turning tricks had consumed her. Cinnamon swallowed hard and tilted her head, taking in the displayed picture of a happier and healthier time—a picture certainly her parents had made sure the news would use, not one of the more recent photos where she closely resembled the walking dead.

Pum'kin slapped Cinnamon's shoulder and pointed to the screen and then pointed at Cinnamon's chest. Cinnamon nodded and glanced back at Anya. The witch summoned the bantling with her finger, and Cinnamon squeezed between Benji and Caitlin again to exit the room.

Melissa noticed Benji glanced at his right sleeve just as Cinnamon grazed by it, then returned his attention to the broadcast.

"I hope they catch the Wharf Killer and hang him from his testicles," Vicki blurted out.

Melissa jumped to her feet. "You don't know if he did this."

Benji and the two girls looked at her.

"I mean, this could be a copycat. We don't even know if all

the murders are even by the same dude," Melissa said and took a step backward.

"Whoa there, spaz. Little defensive, are we?" Caitlin said.

"No. Of course not. It's just"—Melissa scratched the length of her right forearm with her left-hand fingernails—"It's just, everyone's so quick to jump to conclusions." She fluttered her eyelids to try to clear the image of her grandfather from her thoughts. "It's dangerous."

"Dangerous?" Vicki stepped toward Melissa and pointed an accusatory finger at her chest. "I'll tell you *dangerous*, missy. How about waiting outside for a blind date to show up to take you to dinner, when he was lying just yards from you in a Dumpster, ripped apart by the fucking Wharf Killer."

Anya sprung up from behind the television set like a Whack-A-Mole game, casting an ominous shadow on Melissa only, and glared at Melissa while wringing her hands in disapproval.

Melissa shrugged her shoulders and mouthed, *What?*

Anya pointed an accusatory finger in her direction and mouthed, *Knock it off!* Then she disappeared behind the television just as fast as she had appeared.

"Okay, okay. Let's just chill out," Benji said, extending his arms like a referee parting two wrestling contestants. "Cait, why don't you turn off the boob tube altogether, and we can listen to some tunes and play cards or something. We gotta have some booze hidden in here that Mom and Dad haven't inventoried for themselves."

"No. I wanna hear the rest of this, thank you very much," Vicki said and focused on the flickering screen. "Shannon was such a sweet girl. Loved jelly bracelets as much as I do."

Melissa caught a glimpse of Cinnamon standing in the doorway, watching the remainder of the news broadcast about her untimely death. Then a pale hand landed on the bantling's shoulder and guided her away from view.

"Hey, Freshman," Benji whispered. "What's wrong with you? Unless this is all part of the plan."

Melissa bit her bottom lip, feeling her teeth scrape a line in the magic cosmetic.

"Maybe this isn't a good idea. I should take you home. You're overacting and somehow have managed to embarrass me. You're gonna muck this all up for me. I knew hanging out with an underclassman was a bad—"

Melissa squished her lips against Benji's, keeping her eyes open to monitor his reaction. The soft skin of his lips pressed against the stickiness of the black lipstick as he closed his eyes and placed a hand behind her ear, cradling her neck with his open palm. He tilted his head to get a more comfortable angle and returned the kiss with a passion that surprised Melissa.

"Hey, cradle robber!" Caitlin yelled. "Get a room!"

At his sister's yell, he stumbled backward.

Melissa giggled and wiped the smear of black lipstick from his lips and chin.

Vicki turned back to the television to catch whatever else they might say about Shannon's death, but the screen now flickered with a commercial for the new break-dancing movie which Stepp had taken that woman to see on his date earlier in the week. With that reminder of Stepp wanting to date other women ringing in her ears, along with the music from the movie's trailer, Vicki turned to the other three people in the room and said, "Did somebody say drinks and cards?"

"Now we're talkin'!" Caitlin replied and headed toward her bedroom to retrieve a deck of cards and the bottle of vodka hidden in her duffel bag.

"Your sister is like twenty-one," Melissa said to Benji. "Yet she still has to hide booze from your parents?"

"You don't know our parents. Living here is so bad that Cait tried to get a job as a stripper just to make enough money to escape this prison," Benji replied and intertwined his fingers with Melissa's.

"A stripper?"

"Yeah," Vicki said and cleared the clutter from the coffee table. "Tried to go by the stage name Aurora."

"What happened?" Melissa asked, feeling Benji place his hand on the inside of her thigh. *I should market this shit*, she thought and touched her bottom lip.

"Let's just say I had an aversion to a certain pole," Caitlin said, entering the room with the liquor and a deck of playing cards. "Who's up for poker?"

"Strip poker maybe," Benji answered, winking at Melissa.

She stifled a chuckle, thinking how absurd even he would think of himself if he could see how he was acting under the spell of the lipstick's kiss.

Caitlin dropped the cards in the middle of the table and leaned toward the gramophone, placing the needle on the beginning grooves to side one of the record album.

"Finally picked it up, huh?" Benji asked as the opening beats to "Material Girl" began.

Vicki helped Caitlin distribute shot glasses and stopped when she got to Melissa. "Wait. How old are you again?"

"Sixteen," Melissa said and saw Benji glare at her. "What? I stayed back a few times."

Satisfied with the freshman's age, Vicki handed Melissa a shot glass and filled it with vodka. When she had filled all four glasses, they held them over the table and toasted them together with a *clink*, spilling some liquor onto the cards below. Benji grabbed the deck, dried the top cards with his pants, and dealt them out.

Melissa thought the shots coincided with the rounds of poker. After the third game—and the third shot—she felt as if the air in the room had become lighter, and the house had somehow found a way to slowly rotate.

The needle on the record player struck the center label after the final song on side two had ended, and Caitlin stood from the game to change the music.

Melissa took another shot and felt some vodka slip from the corner of her mouth. She chortled, dribbling more liquor from between her closed lips. Benji noticed the leaking vodka, leaned forward, and pressed his lips to hers. His tongue danced over the tastes of cheap distilled liquor and the satiny-smooth lipstick. He clutched her hips, and his off-balance weight sent them sprawling to the floor.

"Kids!" Caitlin said, using an old lady's voice to mock them. "Now, kids! Leave room for Jesus Christ! And get off my damn lawn!"

Benji laughed and helped Melissa to an upright sitting position again, touching the corners of his mouth to savor her taste as well as to wipe away any residual lipstick.

"Go fish!" Melissa yelled and revealed her poker hand, fanning the cards faceup on the table.

Benji and Caitlin burst into laughter as Vicki poured herself another shot and tilted the glass toward Melissa while she spoke. "You know what? When I tell Stepp that I did hang out with my best friend's *pukey* little brother and his freshman girlfriend on a Friday night—because he already made fun of me once for it—he's gonna be *sooooo* jealous that he wasn't here. Because, sister girl, *you* are funny!"

Caitlin slid the Madonna album into its slip sleeve and removed another vinyl from her collection. She placed the record on the turntable and focused on getting the needle right at the beginning of the first song as the room kept rocking like a boat. The needle caught the groove, and she turned toward the table.

"Oh, my God!" Melissa screeched and scrambled to her feet. She had to grasp a corner of the television to keep from toppling over. "This is my band!"

Benji placed his forehead in his right palm and shook his head as the intro to "Wake Me Up Before You Go-Go" filled the room.

Vicki stood and cranked the volume knob higher. "I love his voice!"

Melissa grabbed Vicki's hands, and they performed some kind of drunken and stumbling boogie that loosely resembled the Ring around the Rosy game from kindergarten times but to the beat of the song playing now. Benji leaned back on his elbows, glancing at the woman he had been in love with practically his whole life holding hands and awkwardly jitterbugging to Wham! with the girl he had unexpectedly fallen in love with just a few hours ago.

Melissa twirled Vicki like a ballroom dancer, losing her balance and falling over the couch into a bin of old magazines.

"I'm okay!" she yelled from her backside.

"She is so much fun!" Vicki said to Benji. "I think we'll keep her."

As Melissa's eyes crested the couch's armrest, she saw Anya standing in the doorway.

Good job, child. You got this, Anya mouthed and clapped. *I have other business to attend to now at some taco place.*

Melissa knew she was the only one in the room who could hear the witch's clap, but she would not be the only one to feel her wrath.

Smith looked at his watch as he stood in the shadows of the back parking lot for Hank's Taco Shed. Roxanne should be locking the doors for the night in a few minutes, and Smith would then spy from any number of the windows to see if Hank's manager was indeed dealing junk from the restaurant. Smith focused on the last family eating their combo meals and then diverted his gaze to the back room. He saw Roxanne excuse the only other employee still working.

Smith raised his camera and snapped the shutter, hoping to document for Hank any wrongdoings in his restaurant. The family of four finished their meal and tossed their trash into the garbage bin, waving at Roxanne as they exited the Taco Shed. Smith snapped shots of Roxanne returning the wave and then ambled, slouching, toward the rear of the building.

Smith took a few steps closer, pushing his back straight again. "This getting-old stuff is for the birds," he said to Tony— who followed him but was not visible. Smith ducked into the shadows, keeping a clear view on the rear door.

Tony emerged beside him and snapped a twig from a tree in his way.

"I know this isn't exciting, Tones. But friends are friends. And Hank is the only friend I have left. I can't say no to the guy. Plus the integrity of his business means a lot to him."

Tony grunted and used his finger to draw in the snow beneath his feet.

"Look alive," Smith said, slapping Tony's chest and pointing toward two headlights that had entered the rear parking lot. "This might be over sooner than we thought."

Smith raised his camera and clicked the shutter, capturing

an almost perfect picture of a red IROC parking in the closest slot next to the back door.

Stepp killed the engine and surveyed the back door to Hank's Taco Shed. He glanced at the final girl on Rhino's list and chuckled as he repeated her name. "*Roxanne. I'm about to turn off your red light.*"

He exited the IROC and banged on the back door. He whistled a familiar Police tune as he waited for the door to open, his exhaling breath causing rolling steam clouds to strike the Loading Zone Only sign attached to the building.

The door cracked open just enough for him to see a woman's prying eyes, and he kicked the door inward, sending her sprawling on her back.

"*Heeeeeeere's Stepp!*" he said as he entered the hallway and approached the woman on the floor. "I have a personal telegram from Rhino himself."

She gathered her feet underneath her and sprung forward. She turned and sprinted toward the kitchen.

Stepp gave chase, his sockless penny loafers slip-sliding around on the greasy floor. He turned the corner into an office space and met up with Roxanne, who brought down a large cleaver high into his chest, like trying to separate his arm from his body. He was again thankful for the recent hit of his favorite white powder, which seemed to be blocking his pain receptors now. He gripped the blade's handle, still embedded in his flesh, and kicked her in the groin. Roxanne stumbled but lunged at the protruding weapon—bringing her again closer to Stepp. He grabbed a fistful of her hair and guided her to the floor as he tried to dislodge the knife from his shoulder pit.

A building sense of agony shot through his arm into his chest, and then a pooling of blood on the faux-ceramic floor caught his attention. He explored his wound, his fingers sliding down the cleaver into a soft, gooey mixture. Black dots appeared in his vision, and a faraway ringing invaded his ears. He blinked hard and tried to focus on his mark, who had risen to her feet and reached for her handgun he now saw hidden underneath the counter.

There was two of her. He again touched the cleaver embedded in his shoulder, trying to orient himself. The barrel of her gun lined up with his forehead.

The world went feathery.

Tops became bottoms.

Colors spun.

Life drained from him.

So this is how it ends …

Tony whipped open the back door to Hank's Taco Shed and let Smith run through first. Following behind, the bantling navigated the hallway with the detective, using the sounds of the melee to guide them in the correct direction. Smith removed his revolver from his shoulder holster and turned the corner to the manager's office and stopped short, Tony colliding into his back.

"Who the fuck are you?" Roxanne spat, glancing at Smith and Tony but keeping her gun trained on Stepp's forehead.

Stepp, with one last ounce of energy, scooted backward until he struck a file cabinet and pointed at Tony. "Keep … that

... *thing* ... away from me!"

Smith leveled his revolver at Roxanne's chest. "Put down the gun, and we can all talk about this."

Stepp's eyes closed and did not open again as a wave of unconsciousness consumed him.

Roxanne moved her weapon from Stepp and pointed it at Smith. "I can't go back there. I can't work for Rhino again. He took so much from me."

Smith's finger moved into the trigger guard, preparing to shoot as Roxanne's voice filled with desperation. "Look. I don't know what you're talking about, and, if it makes you feel any better, I don't know this Rhino chap. I'm here because Hank asked me to make sure you weren't dealing drugs afterhours from his place."

Roxanne's gun-hand quivered, and her eyes filled with tears. "Rhino didn't send you to kill me?"

"No, doll. I'm here as a favor to Hank." Smith bounced his attention from her handgun to Stepp lying unconscious against the file cabinet.

Tony chirped and batted at Smith's elbow.

"I know. I see he's still breathing too."

"I promise, mister. I'm not selling drugs. I'm trying to get my life in order. I was working the streets for Rhino, but, after I got my face smashed in by an unhappy john, I just ... took off. I never turned in that night's cash to Rhino, and I crashed at a shelter for the next few weeks. After that, I went home and made up with my folks and then got this job. I've been waiting for the day when Rhino comes lookin' for me again."

"Today is not that day, Roxanne. Now put down the gun, so we can talk about the drugs, and we can call Hank together and sort this all out."

Roxanne's gaze darted at Stepp. "Then who the hell is he?

He barged in here, attacking me."

Smith swallowed and contemplated how to play this. "I ... I have no idea. It's a Friday night, so maybe he's a crackhead who knew there'd be a good amount of cash in your deposit? Robbing for a score?"

"That doesn't make sense. He said he had a message from Rhino for me."

Smith sighed, wishing he had known what Stepp had said beforehand. "I'm just speculating. I'm not with him. I'm here as Hank's friend. Look at me. Would this Rhino chap send an eighty-something-year-old man to do his dirty business? Or do I look like someone who might be friends with Hank—another eighty-year-old man?"

Roxanne nodded and lowered the gun, and Tony squealed and clapped.

"And *you*"—Roxanne looked past Smith at Tony— "should get checked out. You don't look so good."

Smith chuckled and holstered his revolver. "He's fine. Think of him as a child with measles. He's harmless, but I wouldn't get too close just the same."

Tony whinnied and slouched his shoulders.

"If I check on the status of Mr. Miami Vice over there, can you promise not to shoot me in the back?" Smith asked her.

Roxanne nodded and placed the gun on her desk.

Smith lumbered across the room and crouched beside Stepp's body. He tilted his head to inspect the cleaver's entry point. "Doesn't look like you hit anything major. But I'm afraid, if I pull it out, I'll make the bleeding worse."

"Should I call 9-1-1?"

"No!" Smith stood and glanced at Tony.

Roxanne shot Smith a dumbfounded look.

"I-I don't think Hank would want that kind of attention at

his place. I'll drive this guy to the ER myself."

Roxanne sized up Smith's elderly body. "Can you carry him?"

"Tony, can you drag him out to the car, please?"

Tony took a step forward, and Stepp's eyelids fluttered. Smith stood from his kneeling position and turned his back to the injured and unconscious detective.

"Maybe I should call Mr. Steel myself, while you're still here," Roxanne said. "He should hear this from me, so he knows I'm not trying to hide anything—especially since you said he already suspected me of doing shitty things here."

"That might be wise. And I'll make sure I tell him that we talked as well," Smith said, thinking how he'd have to pick another night to stake out the joint to confirm or deny her claim.

Tony bent over and secured his wrists underneath Stepp's armpits when Stepp's eyes flung open. With Tony's decaying face filling Stepp's field of vision, he elbowed the ghoul in the stomach—doing his best to ignore the searing pain shooting through his shoulder—and lunged for the butt of Smith's revolver. Tony stumbled backward from the blow and growled, showing three rows of tiny sharpened teeth.

Stepp struck Smith in the back and clamped on the revolver's handle as the old man fell forward, the gun easily sliding from the archaic shoulder holster. Tony crouched and set his sights on Stepp's injured shoulder, looking like a defensive lineman, and charged forward. Stepp heard the ghoul's guttural scream and swiveled, firing three shots into Tony's face and spraying bits of gray flesh and brain matter across the far wall.

Smith's head struck the corner of Roxanne's desk as he glanced behind him, startled by the abrupt bursts from his stolen revolver. He landed on the floor and used one hand to press on the impact site next to his left temple and used his other hand to prop himself up.

Roxanne grabbed her handgun from the top of her desk and pointed it at Stepp's chest as she put her body between the two men. She slipped an arm under Smith's stomach to help him to his feet, keeping the gun extended and aimed at Stepp.

"Bitch, get out of the way! That's the Wharf Killer!" Stepp yelled, matching Smith's face to the photo Eva had given him, and spun the chamber of Smith's gun to confirm it had more rounds.

Just as Stepp squeezed the trigger on the stolen revolver again—the muzzle aimed at the old man trying to get to his feet—Roxanne snatched the trigger of her gun, firing two rounds at the maniac with the cleaver protruding from his shoulder, then screeched.

When Anya's army of ghouls flooded the office through the open door, Smith covered his face and curled into the fetal position for protection.

The sounds of lips smacking and chomping flesh replaced Roxanne's terrified screaming.

Anya plucked both bullets from midair before they struck Stepp in the chest, and she signaled for the Mushroom Cult to storm the room—their only objective: neutralize the threat to Smith's hopeful replacement. Her coven of undead girls swarmed Roxanne like a dust devil and pounced, and Anya crushed the two lead bullets in her hand, letting them fall as a fine powdery dust to the floor.

Stepp pressed his backside as firmly as he could against the filing cabinet, his stolen firearm forgotten in his hand as he watched a brigade of humanoids—ones resembling the freak that the old man traveled with—dismember the girl he had been sent to kill. The squawks and excited grunts coming from their throats as they tore muscle from bone, tendon from joints, and veins from flesh made Stepp drop the gun and slide to the floor, the pain in his shoulder all but forgotten. His eyes grew wide, and he shook his head in hopes to repel the reality of the towering grotesque female figure approaching him as she sprinkled silvery powder from her clenched fingers.

Anya knelt in front of Stepp, her large body blocking the feeding frenzy happening on the other side of the room, and raised her black veil. She leaned forward, her pale nose inches from Stepp's face, and, in one swift motion, dislodged the meat cleaver from his shoulder.

He shrieked and then placed a hand over the gash.

Anya let the large knife fall to the floor with a *clink!* and knocked away his hand. Then she pressed against the incision. Blood trickled between her fingers at first and then dried up. She removed her hand and stood, casting a large shadow over his trembling body.

"Ladies!" Anya called. "That should be enough. You're all excused, except my two newest into the brood and my generals."

Smith sighed in relief upon hearing that—also about not getting shot here too—and unfurled himself from the fetal position as the bulk of the Mushroom Cult vanished to their netherworld, leaving just the witch and her six ghouls to deal with the fiasco still laying on the floor and bleeding out—hopefully.

Cinnamon and Adrielle stepped forward as Cyana shambled toward Tony, lying motionless against the far wall, pieces of his face nearby.

Smith watched as Stepp's hands shook as he scrambled to check his injured shoulder by fingering his suit coat's jacket and then frowned in confusion. He jetted his gaze from the approaching cluster of ghouls to his upper arm, still questioning. He held his attention on his jacket and shook his head. "My wound, the tears in my suit ... they're all gone." When he returned to look at the hubbub happening elsewhere in the room, he saw the large woman standing with some ashen-faced and decaying zombie-looking creatures.

"Oh, fuck. Oh, fuck. Oh, fuck," he repeated in a single breath. "I recognize you ... and you ... You're supposed to be ... I-I fucking killed both of you!"

Anya extended both arms outward as if she were crucified to an invisible relic. "And with much gratitude."

"Is this some kind of sick mindfuck?" Stepp yelled and scrambled to his feet. Then he saw Smith use Roxanne's desk to pull himself upright. "That's the fucker you want right there! That's the shitbag Wharf Killer!"

Anya brought a single finger to her colorless lips. "*Shh ...* You're too excitable for your own good. Now, hush."

Anya waved her hand over Stepp's body, and he fell silent.

He grasped his mouth and panicked.

"I'll let you speak again when you finally calm down." Anya glanced over her shoulder at Smith. "Is he always like this?"

Smith shrugged. "You're the one who picked him. You tell me."

"Is your bantling okay?"

Smith looked at Tony lying in a heap of chunks of decayed flesh and scattered dislodged teeth. Cyana knelt beside Tony with her forehead on the ghoul's chest, wailing and pounding the floor.

"Doesn't look like it," Smith answered.

"Tragic," Anya muttered and closed her eyes for a moment of silence. "Welp, that's enough boo-hooing."

Smith glanced at Cyana, now cramming displaced chunks of Tony's skull back into place.

Anya brushed Stepp's feathered hair behind his ear. "First, I'd like to thank you. You've been doing your civic duty. You're providing the area with a great service, while giving me new recruits at a rate I haven't seen in a very, very long time." Anya shot an accusatory look at Smith.

Smith made a rolling gesture with his hands for Anya to continue. "But you forgot 'recklessly' and 'with amateur skill.' Stop being so cryptic and just tell him what he needs to know, for goodness sake."

Anya waved her hand over Stepp's head, and the pressure released from his lips.

He opened his mouth and moved his jaw around to loosen his muscles.

"Oh, don't be so melodramatic, you pansy. It was only for a few minutes," Anya retorted.

"Again, he's your choice, not mine," Smith said and used the tip of his shoe to play with the few remnants of Roxanne's bones left on the floor, drawing circles in the small piles of powder.

"I just saved your life," Anya told Stepp. "I can take it away just as fast. You're indebted to me now."

"Always the altruistic," Smith mumbled. "Basically what the witch—and, yes, I say that with dual connotations—means is that you just jumped from Rhino's grasp into hers. But I think you'll find hers is probably less forgiving and will last a lot longer. So, good luck with that, pal. I'm sure you're gonna love what she's about to tell you. I'm heading home." Smith took a last peek at Tony lying on the floor and then returned his attention to Stepp. "And, oh, you owe me a bantling."

"A what?" Stepp asked, surveying the five ghouls standing at attention beside Anya. "Is that what these freakoids are called?"

"You have a lot to learn, my friend," Smith said and turned for the door. "One more thing, Mr. Stepp." Smith turned to face his replacement. "What made you tell that nice lady you took to the movies that your last name was Arbuckle?"

"Your granddaughter, who hired me to track you down, told me that you sometimes used that last name as an alias. When the bitch asked me my name at aerobics class, it just slipped out of my mouth. I wasn't even thinking about you. I didn't even know I wouldn't give her my real name until *Arbuckle* just … slipped out."

Smith sneered at Anya. "Puppets. That's what we are to you. Nothing more. And now I realize something else. I always thought the Mushroom Cult were your pawns, moving them around and controlling them to facilitate your growing power. But it's not them. It's us." Then Smith pointed a finger at Stepp. "Free will, as you know it, is gone."

As the office door closed behind Smith and as he stood alone in the corridor leading to the back parking lot, he heard Anya's voice addressing Stepp.

"This book here, this book is a wealth of wonder and

necromancy. It's a ticket to be vigilantic and pious and provides an opportunity for you to do something great and to be as powerful as you ..."

Smith slid into the driver's seat of his Pinto. A lump formed in his throat as he let his shoulders slump when he noticed the empty passenger seat.

"It's time Anya's reign comes to end." He rested a hand on the space where Tony should be sitting. "And it's long overdue."

Wynn turned the corner and stood in the bathroom doorway. "How did it go?"

Smith glanced at her reflection in the mirror and spit the toothpaste from his mouth. "I don't think Hank will have to worry about Roxanne again."

Wynn stepped into the room. "Oh, hun. What did you do? You didn't interfere, did you?"

Smith wiped his mouth on the face towel hanging next to the sink. "You know what? I'm too old to be getting my hands dirty anymore." He kissed the top of her head. "I overheard her telling a friend in the parking lot that she was running away and eloping tomorrow."

"Running away? A grown woman?"

Smith shrugged. "I'll call Hank before I turn in, to let him know he'll need to hire a new manager tomorrow."

"Do you want me to put on some tea?"

"Thanks, doll. That'd be great."

Smith heard Wynn traipse down the hallway to the kitchen and rummage through the mug cabinet as he headed for their bedside telephone.

Hank answered on the third ring.

10: PINK RIOTS

Stepp rubbed his eyes and yanked apart the bedroom curtains, so the morning sunlight could fill the room. Rays like fingers groped his unmade bed as he stretched.

"It's a good day," he muttered and then moaned as his body stretched to its capacity.

He relaxed and scratched his groin through his silk pajama bottoms and watched a melting icicle hanging from his gutter *drip, drip, drip* onto his driveway. He turned from the glorious new day and headed for the bathroom. Peering at his reflection in the mirror, he scratched at his stubble and splashed water from the faucet onto his face. He let the water trickle from his chin into the sink and smiled.

"Nothing can stop me now. I'll usher in a new dawn for this shit stain of a town." He winked at himself in the reflection. "Isn't that right, Anya?"

He felt the witch's hand rest on his shoulder from behind but could not see her in the mirror.

"That's right, my pet. Nothing's gonna stop us now. This

place won't know what hit it. And I'd like to give you a gift, as a token of goodwill for what I know will be a very bountiful friendship."

Stepp caught movement from the corner of his eye but couldn't see anything in the mirror.

"I'm gifting you Pum'kin for a few weeks, until you settle into your new position. She's my most trusted general and will help keep you focused during what might be a tumultuous transition for you."

Pum'kin revealed herself, standing in the tub.

"I'll be fine. I got this," he replied.

"Don't be so cocky. You don't wear it well."

Stepp turned to the open doorway and chortled. "Witch, I *am* perfection."

Pum'kin giggled and left Stepp alone in his bathroom.

He knew exactly how to celebrate his newfound importance and preponderance. He grabbed the wireless phone from his nightstand and extended the long silver antennae and dialed seven digits.

Vicki's see-through ConAir telephone rang, startling her from sleep. Keeping her head underneath her pillow, she fumbled for the phone—more to silence the piercing ring than to actually talk to anyone. She felt the curlicue cord and tugged the receiver to her ear. "Yello?"

"Vickster! What'cha doin'?"

"Mr. Stepp? What time is it?" Her eyelids flung open, and her heart pitter-pattered at the sound of her boss's voice. "Is everything all right? Is there an emergency?"

"Whoa, kiddo. Slow down. Just seeing how my favorite mouse is today and how last night's soiree went. And stop calling me Mr. Stepp. Just call me J."

Vicki adjusted her pillows and sat upright against them. "It went fine. Cait's little brother's girlfriend is so wicked cute."

"Hanging with the youths."

Vicki's cheeks blushed. "To be fair, J, I was hanging out with my *adult* best friend. It just so happened her little brother wanted us to meet his girlfriend. So put that in your pipe and smoke it."

"You crack me up, Vic. Have any plans for tonight, or are you babysitting again?"

Vicki reached for her jelly bracelets on her dresser and slid the stack over her wrist. "Nada."

"Want to meet for a drink? I got a new lease on life and want to celebrate with my favorite girl."

Vicki froze and darted her gaze to her wardrobe hanging behind the opened closet door, already scanning for the perfect outfit. "Absolutely. Name the place and time."

"Pale Horse. I'll pick you up at eight."

"Why are we celebrating again?"

"I finished that list of missing girls and was given a hefty bonus from another affiliate. That's really all I can say about it now."

Stepp's answer faded into the background as her focus now lay on her blue-jean miniskirt and pink halter top.

"Spot-on," she whispered.

Melissa slipped her Twisted Sister shirt over her head when she heard the familiar popping sound that accompanied a visit from the heretic priestess.

"You did good last night—better than I had anticipated—but I won't need you to help me with Vicki anymore."

The color drained from Melissa's face as she turned toward Anya. "What do you mean, *won't need me anymore*? What the fuck's that supposed to mean?"

"I didn't foresee Detective Stepp's initiation to happen as fast as it did, but all was revealed to him last night, and he got on board earlier than anticipated. He officially has become your grandfather's replacement and has been enlightened about everything—the book, the cult, me, the mission. Everything."

"I'm sorry, but I don't accept this. And how did he take being told that he now has to read from the book so you can kill his secretary? I'm sure that went over like hotcakes."

"That … I didn't get to. Yet. He has a soft spot for Vicki, and I need him to really buy into his new responsibilities before I ask him to sacrifice her to me."

"So you *do* need me," Melissa said and pulled a pair of socks from her drawer. "Because why wait? We can do it Monday morning as soon as she gets to work. I can show up, all crying with some bullshit story about some fake ex-boyfriend hitting me or something, after finding out about Benji, and tell her I didn't know who else to go to. And then *blammo!* I say the magic words, and you swoop in and do whatever sorcery stuff you need to do, and she'll never see it coming."

Anya pulled the veil from her face and rubbed her chin. "You *are* wickedly, child. I knew there was a reason I picked you."

"Plus you owe me this. I've been faithful to you since I can first remember you coming into my life." Melissa stuck out her bottom lip in a pout. "*Pahleeeeease*, Auntie Anya?"

"Good grief, child. It does not behoove you to beg. Only weak and despicable cowards beg."

Melissa chuckled and tied the laces of her Converse sneakers. "So I'll see you Monday morning? The earlier the better."

"Why wait for Monday? If tonight goes well, let's find a way to move forward tomorrow."

"Can't. Dad's taking me and Addie on a father-daughter bonding trip all weekend. We won't be back until Sunday night."

Anya nodded. "The sacrifice of the Chosen One is so close now. I can taste it."

"Just don't welsh on what you promised me," Melissa said and hit Play on her boom box, filling the room with George Michael's voice.

Anya produced the maroon-covered metal book from underneath her black robe. "Learn it. Love it. Memorize it better than the words to those dreadful Slam! songs."

Melissa shook her head. "*Wham!* not Slam!"

"I'm sure they are," Anya replied and handed Melissa a ripped-out page from the book. "I want you able to recite this in your sleep. Once you start saying these words to Vicki, you can't stop. If you stutter or need to begin again, the spell won't work from your lips, and I'll have to find a new helper, and you'll look stupid standing there, speaking gibberish."

Melissa scanned the old parchment and nodded. "I'm just glad these words are shorter, not like that influence spell—or whatever it was called—that I used on Benji in the cafeteria."

"A monkey could read this and not muck it up."

Melissa nodded.

"So don't muck it up!"

Stepp held open the Pale Horse's front door for Vicki and made an *After you* motion with his arm. She giggled, and he let his gaze fall to her behind, snugged tight in the fabric of her jean skirt. He smacked his lips and shook his head at the sight of her perfectly round bottom—a bottom he was quite sure he'd never get near with a ten-foot pole. He knew Vicki was not only proud that she was still a virgin but was as sealed shut as Fort Knox.

With an extra swagger in his strut, he took the lead and escorted Vicki around the tables and toward the bar. He slid a stool from underneath the counter for her before he chose his own seat.

Vicki smirked and nodded a thank-you.

"What'll it be, guys?" Baron set two napkins in front of them.

"Something special—out of this world. I feel like I have the world at my fingertips." Stepp looked at Vicki. "But tonight the lady goes first."

Baron rolled his eyes as Vicki jiggled her jelly bracelets to her elbow and surveyed the rows of spirits, resting one finger on her closed lips to help her think.

"What're your specials tonight?" Stepp asked, interrupting Vicki's contemplation.

Baron turned toward the bottles as he spoke. "I can make a nightrider. That's sake and orange juice."

"Yummy!" Vicki said.

Stepp gave his order of cranberry juice and vodka while Baron mixed Vicki's nightrider. After the drinks had been placed on the napkins adorned with the Pale Horse logo, Baron excused himself to assist a large group who had pushed together three tables to accommodate the size of their party.

Stepp placed a hand on Vicki's bare knee. "Aren't you cold, wearing a miniskirt in the tundra of December?"

She shrugged while taking a sip of her drink through the black straw. "Fashion over comfort, right?"

"You won't hear any complaints from me. I think your legs look scrumptious."

Vicki rested her hand over Stepp's fingers and took another sip. She could feel the sake shooting straight to her brain, making every inch of her exposed skin warm and fuzzy.

Stepp wiggled a finger at the bartender. "Hit me."

Vicki shot her boss a look. "Already?"

"What can I say, Mouse? I'm thirsty. And we're celebratin'!"

Baron filled the glass with the mixed drink and pointed at Vicki.

"Not quite yet," she replied and laughed. "I'm not trying to tie one on as fast as he is."

A round of cheers erupted from behind them, and they swiveled on their stools to see a man with an acoustic guitar and a keyboard standing in front of a microphone.

"Didn't know they had live music in here," Stepp mumbled and tapped his already-empty second glass.

"Open-mic night," Baron answered and filled Stepp's glass again.

The man touched a button on the Casio keyboard and played a juxtaposition of a 5/5 time signature on the guitar while a generic 4/4 beat played through a small speaker amp. He leaned into the microphone and sang the opening lines of "Rebel Yell."

"I'll take a refill," Vicki said, getting Baron's attention.

"That's my girl!" Stepp said, bobbing his head and drumming with his index fingers on the bar to the Billy Idol cover. "Glad to see your friends came with you too."

Vicki shot him a perplexed look as she waited for Baron to finish mixing the sake and juice.

"Your *friends* ..." Stepp used his fingertips to jiggle Vicki's bracelets. "Duh!"

She laughed and wiggled her wrist to maneuver them back to her elbow, then put the filled glass to her lips and sucked down a big gulp.

"I'm waiting for you to start naming them all," he said.

She slapped him with her free hand and spit a ball of alcoholic mist across the bar.

"Good thing you moved!" Stepp yelled down the bar at Baron. "That would've been a direct hit!"

Vicki's laugh turned into hysterics, and she nudged her forehead into his chest.

"I'll tell ya, Vic. I feel so good tonight. Invincible even," Stepp said and tested her tolerance by sliding his hand off her knee and stopping at the middle of her thigh. He smirked when her only response was to take another long sip of her nightrider.

"I gotta be honest with you, Mr. Detective." She pointed a finger at Stepp after the last of the alcohol had been ingested through the straw. "I've always thought you were invincible. Even before tonight. And I also think you are absolutely ..."

A large man pulling the empty stool from underneath the bar next to Stepp distracted Vicki and went unnoticed by Stepp.

"Vic, you okay?" Stepp asked her.

Vicki leaned close to Stepp's ear. "I don't think I've ever seen an albino person before. I mean, a *real* albino."

Stepp closed his eyes and removed his hand from Vicki's bare thigh.

"Just the person I was looking for," the familiar voice said. "I hope your missus doesn't mind that we have some *bidness* to take care of tonight."

"A client," Stepp said to Vicki, still not turning around.

"Oh, well, hi!" She extended her hand. "I'm Detective Stepp's secretary. I don't remember seeing you in the office."

"He's the one with the list you were helping me with this week," Stepp whispered.

"So this fine piece of work is the infamous Vicki?" Rhino took her hand and gently kissed the top. "I've heard a lot about you, sweetheart."

"All good, I hope."

"Depends if you consider still being a virgin at twenty-one 'good.'"

Vicki glared at Stepp and crossed her legs.

"I've got a bone to pick with you, J," Rhino said. "A lot of bones, in fact."

Stepp swiveled his stool to face Rhino. "This is between you and me. Leave her out of this."

Rhino leaned outward so he could see Vicki around Stepp's body. "I would tap that so hard that she'd go from virgin to a one-man girl forever. Or she could be the hottest meat on the market, if you'd let me turn her out."

"What the crap is he—"

Stepp surged to his feet, and the bar stool fell on its side. "You may have a beef with me, numb nuts, but she is off-limits. Take your eyes off her and cram your sleazy comments up your ass."

Vicki placed a hand on her chest just below her neck and smirked.

The commotion at the bar stopped the performer on stage from strumming his guitar and singing. The factory-programmed beat from his keyboard continued to play for another few bars until he could hit the Stop button. The patrons' gazes were now all transfixed on the three people at the bar.

Baron reached below the counter and retrieved the Peacekeeper. "I want all three of you out of here right now. I'm not in the mood tonight."

Rhino, ignoring the bartender, stood to tower over Stepp. "I'd rather cram something up *her*—"

Stepp slugged Rhino in the chin. The open-mic performer shrieked a shrill noise, the microphone picking up his startled reaction and sending it magnified through the speakers. The large party behind them froze and turned their attention to the growing and building melee.

Baron slammed the baseball bat onto the wood counter—the *clink* from the row of glasses resounding as they jumped. "I'm not kidding. Let's go."

Rhino touched his chin and moved his jaw back and forth like a pendulum. "Is that all you got, hoss?"

Stepp hunched forward and charged. His left shoulder struck Rhino's stomach dead center. Both men tumbled backward. They landed on a recently abandoned table and sent the uncollected plates of half-eaten popcorn chicken and glasses of Guinness shattering onto the floor, before their bodies tumbled there also.

Vicki squealed. She took a step forward to grab Stepp from the backside of his suit jacket. Baron shoved her aside and raised the Peacekeeper over his head like an ax. Vicki screamed something that sounded like *"No!"* and grabbed Baron's fingers clenched around the base of the bat.

The large party behind them had now all stood and taken refuge from the brawl against the far wall as the performer flung his keyboard and guitar into their cases.

Rhino had scissor-clamped his legs around Stepp's hips and then flipped him over in a graceful-looking wrestling maneuver. The albino straddled Stepp and brought down his fists against the detective's jaw and cheekbones. Stepp flapped his arms like a seal, trying to ward off the attack.

Baron pushed Vicki off him and swung the baseball bat across Rhino's shoulders. The large man glanced over his shoulder at the bartender winding up for another strike. Rhino got off Stepp, and, in one fluid motion, removed a snub-nosed pistol from his waistband and had it pointed at Baron's stomach. Vicki yelled something unintelligible. The microphone picked up the performer as he left the corner area, exclaiming, "Oh my!"

The Pale Horse emptied as the patrons pushed and scrambled to get through the doors and outside into safety.

"Hit me again, motherfucker. Go ahead," Rhino said, shaking the gun at the bat-wielding bartender. "I'll blow you to kingdom come."

Vicki placed a hand over her mouth to stifle any further sounds that might involuntarily escape.

"Take your business outside," Baron said—cool, calm, and collected. "This is my castle in here. So get the fuck out."

Stepp rolled over and climbed to his feet, wincing and grabbing his left shoulder.

Rhino took a step backward from Baron, his gaze transfixed on something visible behind the barkeeper's shoulder. "What in good God's grace is *that*?"

Baron pivoted his head so he could peek behind him but could keep the large man with the gun within his peripheral vision. Two ashen-faced and decaying figures stood behind the bar.

"What is what?" Vicki backpedaled, shaking her jelly bracelets to her elbow.

"Anya," Baron said in a whispered growl.

Stepp came to Vicki's side and held her elbow, his gaze landing on the two ghouls standing behind the bar at Baron's post.

"I thought you said you took care of them!" Rhino said, turning to Stepp. "You even brought me that one's finger!" He pointed to Adrielle, and she raised her rotting hand and wiggled all five fingers to show her intact octopus-tattooed digit, still attached. "You filthy liar. I *knew* you were a coward and couldn't go through with our deal."

"J, what the hell is going on?" Baron asked.

"What's he talking about?" Vicki added.

"It's okay, Mouse. More is going on here than you can ever handle. Just stay behind me."

Adrielle and Cinnamon leaped onto the bar counter in unison. Rhino stumbled backward and darted the muzzle of the gun between Baron and the two ghouls approaching him.

Stepp smoothed the front of his lapel. "I did take care of them, Rhino."

Rhino flicked the gun in the girls' direction. "Obviously not good enough."

Adrielle and Cinnamon continued side by side on their trajectory without slowing, bisecting Baron, like a running river did when encountering a stone, and then resumed their shoulder-to-shoulder march.

"Get her outta here, man. She doesn't need to see this," Baron said to Stepp, anticipating the ghouls' motives.

"Doesn't have to see what?" Vicki asked, her voice high-pitched and squeaking. "What is everyone looking at?"

Stepp hesitated, his eyebrows furrowing as he deciphered

the bartender's statement, and nudged Vicki toward the door as he looked at Baron. "You know about them?"

"Know about *what*?" Vicki pleaded and tripped as her ankles crisscrossed from Stepp yanking her backward faster than she had anticipated.

Rhino fired the first shot at Cinnamon's head, and Vicki screamed.

"C'mon, Mouse. We gotta get outta here," Stepp said and pulled her harder.

Vicki got her footing and spun around so she faced the exit. "What's he shooting at?"

"Um … nothing. He's just gone loco."

Vicki glanced behind her once more before turning the corner onto the sidewalk. She saw the bartender step sideways, just as the large albino man dropped his gun and raised both hands to his face to protect himself from what looked like absolutely nothing. She heard a death-rattled scream as the Pale Horse's door closed behind them and left her and Stepp standing underneath the large banner advertising the one-time annual purchase of a monogrammed stein on New Year's Eve.

Anya stepped from around the bar and took the bat from Baron's hands. "Get it while the eating's good, girls."

The rest of the Mushroom Cult appeared inside the Pale Horse and joined Adrielle and Cinnamon in tearing Rhino's entrails from his stomach.

"What are you doing?" Baron asked the witch and snatched the bat back from her.

"Cleaning the streets. What're you doing? Other than

providing the bad-decision-making fodder?"

"I'm trying to keep my nose clean, Anya. That's more than I can say for you." He motioned to the growing pool of blood on his barroom's floor from the decimated albino man.

"You think you're so virtuous and mighty. Just because you let that one cretin live back during the Louisiana Purchase—I, personally, would've vaporized him if he had tried to use that spell on me—does not make you honorable. We are clearly not the same, even though we stand for the same things."

"Oh no, Anya. We are certainly not the same, nor do we stand for the same things."

"I think you'd be surprised."

Baron raised an eyebrow as he motioned to the frenzy happening behind them.

Cinnamon had draped Rhino's intestines around her neck and now paraded in a circle, twirling the bloody organ like a boa as the rest of the coven chirped and clapped.

"Really?" he asked.

"Oh, they're having some fun! Plus that was her pimp. It's just a little morale-boosting retribution. Let the girls blow off steam."

"At the expense of my clean floor? You haven't changed in all the centuries I've known you, Anya."

"What's that supposed to mean?"

"Always looking out for number one. You're only as powerful as your vanity."

A ghoul's hip bumped Baron and knocked him off-balance as a gory tug-of-war competition had erupted with Rhino's innards.

"Just remember," Anya said, "I have an army, and you don't. And you don't know how powerful I'm about to become. It'll be fun to make you eat crow."

Baron was taken aback by her bravado. "What are you hiding?"

Anya folded her arms. "Girls, it's time to go. Say good bye to your toy."

A murmur of grunts and moans seeped from the blood-soaked mouths of the Mushroom Cult. The ghouls walked away from the dismembered pimp's torso lying on the floor in a heap of unrecognizable muscles and tendons.

Baron grabbed the witch by her elbow. "What are you hiding?" he repeated through clenched teeth.

Bright white filled his vision as the bar's interior disappeared. A red pentagram carved on a familiar-looking young woman's bare chest faded into view. Baron released his grip on Anya and glared at her.

"It's *her*! That girl, just now. She's the Chosen One!" Baron's eyes grew wide. "You're hunting her. You ... You even put one of your ghouls as a spy on that man she was with. These are all chess moves to get to her!"

Anya snarled and flashed three rows of razor-sharp teeth. "I'll fucking kill you!" She speared herself through the air at Baron, spinning like a missile.

He ducked and grabbed her chest as she flew by, then slammed her to the floor.

She snapped at him, like a rabid dog, her teeth clicking together with each miss of his flesh.

Baron closed his eyes and chanted. Warmth flowed through his fingers and singed Anya's black robe. White tendrils of smoke floated from the fabric.

Baron jerked his head from side to side, relief-cracking the joints in his neck. "I'll let you go. For now. But ... if you attack me or threaten me again, I won't stop until I've burned through your heart and straight out the other side."

Anya stood and brushed the ashes from her robe, waved her hand over the hole, and watched as the fabric repaired itself. "I'll get my cake and eat it too. And I won't be swayed by the likes of you."

She punctuated her statement by spitting on the floor in front of Baron's shoes and disappeared into the netherworld with the rest of her brood.

Baron stepped over the large pile of goo and splintered bone in front of the bar and hustled to the back room. He yanked open his desk drawer and removed a maroon-bound book. He blew off the top layer of dust and flipped toward the section on counterstriking an archfiend and then found the subsection on protecting the Chosen One. He ran his fingers under the ancient verbiage and closed his eyes.

He held the book against his chest as he rocked back and forth, the words of the ancient spell spilling from his mouth.

Stepp opened the passenger door of his IROC for Vicki. "You okay, Mouse? That was some crazy shit, huh?"

Vicki slid onto the seat and didn't respond. She stared dead ahead through the windshield. Stepp ran around the front of the car, and she watched him cup a fist and blow into his fingers to warm them. She darted her gaze at him when he slammed the driver's side door shut and shivered.

"Is … Is he dead?"

"Who? My client?"

She nodded as her eyes grew big.

"Look, Vic. I don't want you to worry. You need to know something about him."

"Can you tell me while we're driving? I wanna get the flip out of here. This place is giving me the heebie-jeebies."

Stepp started the car and pulled onto the roadway. He spoke as he navigated the streets toward the outskirts of town. "That guy was unstable. A maniac. Had been making violent threats to me after I stopped working on his case."

"Why did you stop?"

"It was all unfounded. Everything had been made up. He's sick and lives in a fantasy world."

"Shouldn't we call the cops?"

Stepp glanced in his rearview mirror and saw the Pale Horse disappear from sight, then noticed the gray wisps of hair of the ghoul sitting in the back seat.

"It's probably safer for me if we don't, in case he's still alive. That just might agitate him more, and then he'll come looking for me in retaliation."

Vicki nodded in understanding. "What did he think he saw? Because, you know, I kept looking, and I couldn't see anything. And then that stuff about a missing finger?"

"Crazy as a loon, kid. Crazy as a loon." He stole another glance at Pum'kin—Anya's "gift" to him—in the rearview mirror.

Vicki looked out the passenger window, accepting that answer. However, none of this helped the fact that she'd had such high hopes for tonight—the violence at the bar extinguishing her fantasy of having an exclusive night with Stepp.

Stepp returned his attention to the road ahead and felt something poke his eye. He squeezed his eyes shut and rubbed them with his knuckles.

"You okay?" Vicki asked.

"Yeah. Feel like I got a piece of dirt or an eyelash stuck in my eye."

He opened his eyes—his vision was blurry, as if he were looking underwater without goggles—and squeezed them shut again. "Oh, God. That hurts."

"Do you need me to drive?"

"Gotta be an eyelash stuck to my eyeball. I'm all teared up. Hold on." He dug his knuckles into the corners of his eyeballs and slowly opened them, testing his pain tolerance. "Looks like I got it."

He focused on the street to get his driving equilibrium back and then looked at Vicki. As soon as his gaze fell on her, his mouth went dry, and his heart raced.

"J? Everything all right?"

His intention was to say, *I'm fine*, but *I love you* came out instead. He flinched at the disconnect between his thoughts and his tongue.

Vicki sat up straighter in her seat. "You're drunk, aren't you?"

Yes, he thought. *Play that card to get out of this.* He opened his mouth. "No. It's been driving me crazy to tell you that for a long time now." He slapped a hand over his mouth to shut down whatever betrayal of his motor skills was happening here. Then, through covered lips, he added, "I daydream about us being together."

Vicki slithered closer to the center console and jiggled her bracelets to her elbow. "I feel like … like, it's been you all along who I've been saving myself for. I started to think all my little hints were just stupid and had gone unnoticed."

Stepp shook his head, warding off the impulse to talk, refusing to even try to speak anymore—how much more damage would be done with each statement?

"It was wicked hot how you stood up for me tonight with

that schizo."

The longer he kept his mouth shut, the more intense a tingling sensation grew in his groin area. Not speaking had become the equivalent to holding his breath, and the pain one would feel in their lungs was transposed to a prickling feeling in his genitals—to the point where, if he didn't open his mouth and speak, his loins would explode into a shower of rainbow confetti.

He concentrated on the specific words he wanted to say, running each syllable through his mind, so it would match what would come out of his mouth. All the while, the prickly sensation growing in his midsection became almost unbearable. He needed to speak *now*.

He reviewed his sentence once more, for good measure, in his head. *I don't know what I'm saying, Vic. I respect you highly as a woman and an associate, but I did not mean to tell you that I love you.*

He opened his mouth. "If I don't make love to you tonight, Victoria, I might just die."

Vicki giggled. "I've been waiting for those words since my first day of work. Wanna go to your place or mine?"

Stepp tried to punch the window, tried to press on the brake, tried to open the door—his movements were now also out of his control.

Pum'kin, he thought. *My designated chaperon. Has Anya done this to me?*

He glanced into the back seat. Pum'kin's eyes were closed; her mouth was open, and her head rested against the back window. She looked catatonic. He thought about how he could awaken the ghoul to help him and also to show Vicki how he did not want tonight, under these circumstances or with him, to be her first time.

Concentrate on physically hurting her. Punch her as hard as you can in the face to make her hate you, so she won't let you touch her. You can't ruin her like this.

Satisfied with the plan—although despising the thought of walloping his secretary—he removed his hand from the steering wheel and made a fist. Concentrating, he envisioned his knuckles striking her nose hard enough to splay blood across the window. He groaned as he flung his fist with all the strength he could muster at her face, and, in midflight, his hand opened and descended, landing tenderly on her bare thigh.

Vicki squeezed his hand. "I guess it doesn't matter whose place, as long as we're together!"

An uncontrollable hardness grew in his pants, and he understood there was no use in fighting whatever was happening. He succumbed to the realization that he no longer had control over tonight's agenda.

"You won't regret keeping yourself pure for me."

His hands guided the steering wheel toward a magical place the local, horny teens called Lover's Leap.

Anya's eyes snapped open from where she sat on her throne in the netherworld. She couldn't sense Stepp or Vicki or even Pum'kin anymore—*Poof!* Off the radar. She stood and paced the small room, wringing her hands.

"Someone's protecting them. Someone's cloaked them so I can't see what they're up to." She stopped pacing and tried to pinpoint Baron's location. "Candy!"

The ghoul appeared just as quickly as she had been summoned.

"Baron's gone off the grid, and I've lost eyes on Stepp, the Chosen One, and Pum'kin. Round up the troops and head out."

Candy clapped and hopped uncoordinatedly on one foot.

"Check everywhere! Start at the most obvious places—their homes, their work places, their favorite locations. Leave no stone unturned! Don't harm Stepp or the Chosen One, but, when you find Baron, bring him to me. He's all mine."

Candy chirped in excitement and vanished as Anya flung herself onto her throne, refusing defeat when she was this close to tasting immortality.

11: COVERED IN BLOOD

Candy paced just outside the portal from the living to the netherworld. A feeling of anxiety and dread—emotions she hadn't felt for decades—loomed over her. She took a deep breath through her rotted nostrils for courage and stepped through the invisible curtain.

"Ah, Candy. I've been waiting with bated breath." Anya stood from her throne, letting the silence in the room act as permission for Candy to report.

The ghoul groaned and whinnied, shaking her head.

Anya stepped forward and lifted her black veil, revealing her graying skin and yellowed eyes. "And you looked *everywhere?*"

Candy nodded and directed her gaze toward the ceiling.

"Their homes? Hotels? Bars? His office? Everywhere? You're sure?"

Candy stepped backward and hiccupped a sniffle.

"Baron has really dug his grave this time." Anya wrung her hands together. "I will not be denied!" Anya flung Candy's decayed body across the room, and it struck the far wall.

She grunted as she struck the stone floor.

"If you need something done right, you need to do it yourself." Anya retrieved the book from behind her throne and thumbed through the pages until she found the appropriate section.

Candy dusted herself off and stood stationary, her head cocked in curiosity. She startled when Anya slammed the book closed.

"Looks like we'll have to wait for Monday morning and keep our plan to pay our rookie a visit at his place of business."

Candy bowed her head and waited to be dismissed now that her priestess seemed to have regained control over her emotions.

"And you couldn't locate Baron either?"

Candy shook her head and chirped.

"I don't like the way this smells. I don't like it one bit." Anya flopped into her throne. "I want you to find a comfy place inside Stepp's house and stay put there, either until he comes home or until I meet with him on Monday morning in his office."

Candy nodded and whooped.

"And tell Nikki that I want her in the virgin's apartment. Same orders. The moment either Stepp or Vicki go home, you're to summon me immediately. Do not engage with them or let them see you. Do you understand?"

Candy clapped and hopped.

"Let's hope this cloaking spell doesn't extend longer than tonight."

Anya opened the book again and shooed Candy with one hand, Anya's gaze darting over the conjurations as she tried to find a counter spell against Baron's wizardry.

Vicki awoke Monday morning in her bed, alone, well before her programmed alarm time. She stretched and smiled, then exhaled a contented sigh. The wind howled and blustered against the glass of her windows, rattling and shaking them in their frames, but she thought she could still hear the chirping of birds somewhere outside.

She padded to the kitchenette in her apartment and retrieved her Scrappy-Doo coffee mug from the cabinet. While she waited for the coffee grounds to brew, she closed her eyes and reminisced about Saturday night. Her thoughts got lost in a swarm of images—Stepp's careful and tender hands, his delicate attention to her comfort and her nervousness, making sure she had been satisfied first before he allowed himself to finish. She scrunched her shoulders to her neck in warm bliss and poured a bowl of cereal as the last few drips of percolated coffee fell into the pot.

She moseyed to her small kitchen table and turned on the morning news. She daydreamed throughout the reporter's droning. She glanced at the clock and headed for the bathroom—unaware of the decrepit ghoul standing in the corner.

Stepp snapped awake. He wiped the crusted drool from the corner of his mouth and scanned the room to get his bearings. He rubbed his lower back and grimaced; the pain of sleeping at his office desk had done a number on his muscles. He powered up his computer and headed into the hallway. He leaned against the small amenity table in the reception area and heard the front door unlock.

Vicki entered, a gale of winter wind following her inside.

"You're early," he said as he shook a powdered creamer packet.

"And you slept here." She didn't hesitate to kiss him on the cheek. "Your bed not good enough?"

"Not a fan of being home on the weekends. The ghosts of Christmas past and all that rigmarole," he said and flapped his hand to wave off the question.

She unraveled her scarf from around her neck and hung her jacket on the coat rack before standing next to him again. "You could always stay with me."

"I appreciate the sentiment, Mouse. I really like you. I really do. But ... How do I say this? I wasn't myself Saturday night."

Vicki shook her jelly bracelets to her elbow and gazed at the coffeepot. "Oh."

"Listen." He grabbed both her shoulders, swiveling her to face him. "You are probably my most favorite person in the world. In fact, probably the only one who hasn't done me wrong in some way." He stopped to carefully choose how to phrase the words of rejection and then saw the anxiety in her eyes. "Okay, Vic. Let's take this slow and see where this goes. That's the best I can give you right now."

Hoping he hadn't noticed her blush, she clenched both fists in glee and hopped up and down when he turned to prepare his coffee. She watched him add the sugar and powdered creamer to his coffee and fantasized about making his coffee one day in their kitchen as their toddlers played with toys beneath their feet.

"Vic, you all right?"

She snapped from the image and focused on his face.

"Thought I lost you there for a moment," he said and headed toward his office.

Vicki carried her coffee to her desk and placed it next to the bronze horse paperweight. She whistled as she reviewed the week's consultations in the daily planner and then lifted the phone's receiver from its cradle, placed it to her ear, and said to the dial tone, "Detective Stepp's office. This is Mrs. Stepp. How may I help you today?" She giggled and replaced the receiver to its proper place.

She swiveled to face the radio and pressed the On button, activating the speakers and filling the room with music. She heard the front door open and close. She spun her chair front-facing and called out, "Hello?"

Melissa poked her head around the corner. "Hey, Vic!"

"Melissa! What brings you here?" Vicki asked.

Melissa flung her backpack on the floor next to the plastic gaudy Christmas tree and approached Vicki's desk without speaking. She sat down in the chair next to the desk and leaned in. "I really needed someone to talk to, and I didn't know who else to go to."

Vicki placed a hand on Melissa's. "Is everything okay?"

"My ... My ..." Melissa dragged out her confession for dramatic affect. "My ex-boyfriend found out about Benji." She cocked her head away from Vicki and stared at the ceiling, forcing a tear to form in the corner of her eye.

"What did he *do* to you?" Vicki jiggled her wrist, then

slapped her desk with both palms and stood. "Did he hurt you?"

"Please don't tell my parents," Melissa replied to sound as ambiguous as possible, using Vicki's imagination against her. "I-I don't want him to get ... arrested!"

"I'm gonna get Mr. Stepp, and we can talk about this together."

Anya leaned into Melissa's ear and whispered, "What's she saying? Are they both here?"

Melissa nodded discreetly to answer Anya and then said to Vicki, "No! Please don't. I'm really embarrassed and ashamed. I came to you because you're a woman. I just don't trust boys right now."

Vicki sat back down. "I didn't think of that. Do you want to talk here or go somewhere else? I'm sure my boss will let me ditch out for a bit. I can tell him it's a family emergency."

Anya placed a hand on Melissa's shoulder. "This dratted cloaking spell hasn't worn off yet. Can't sacrifice her if I can't see or touch her. Drastic times call for drastic measures."

Melissa twitched her head once—trying not to raise suspicions from Vicki—as a signal for Anya that it was safe to communicate the new plan.

"I'll reenter the office as Eva," Anya said. "You won't recognize me. But I think it might be a loophole. My disguise doesn't change anything about what you need to say."

Melissa nodded just enough so Vicki didn't think the gesture was affirming her suggestion about going somewhere to talk. "I'd rather chat here, if that's kosher with you."

"Absolutely. We don't open for another—"

A tall and slender woman entered through the front door, and both girls turned to look.

"May I help you, ma'am?" Vicki asked. Then, without waiting for a reply, she said, "I apologize. I didn't recognize you,

Ms. Smith. Did you have an appointment with Detective Stepp?"

Melissa furrowed her brows in confusion and shot a glance at the woman, who used an opened hand to fluff the bottoms of her impeccable curly blond locks. Eva stepped farther into the room, and Melissa admired the client's long and blemish-free legs, visible through the slit in her long skirt.

"I was hoping I could talk to him this morning without an appointment. If he's not too busy, that is." The woman winked at Melissa. "Just looking for an update on my grandfather."

"Right away, Ms. Smith."

Melissa's hands trembled as she stood a little quicker than she had meant, her chair toppling behind her. She righted the chair and closed her eyes and rehearsed the handful of words in her head that needed to be spoken, knowing she had just one shot to get it right—one shot to please Anya, and, in return, to be rewarded with all the wealth the book had to offer. She took a deep breath and opened her mouth to recite the spell that would change everything forever.

Eva's hand landed on Melissa's shoulder and squeezed like a vise to stop her from beginning the sacrificial spell.

Melissa squirmed from the pain and jerked her shoulder from Anya's grip.

Vicki turned halfway down the hallway and eyed Ms. Smith's interactions with Melissa—Vicki's eyebrows raised, and her lips pursed.

Eva's scowl spread cross her porcelain–like face.

Vicki frowned and, not moving any farther, called out, "Detective Stepp—? Ms. Smith is here to see you."

Noises came from his office, like something fell and he righted it. "Send her in!"

Eva heard his reply and half-smiled a *Thank you* to Vicki and strutted down the hallway. She wondered what he would tell her about the Wharf Killer investigation. After all, as Anya, she knew how many dynamics had changed and how much had been revealed to Stepp since Eva had first seeked his services just two weeks ago. She turned into Stepp's office as he approached the wet bar.

He paused, and she noticed his eyes taking her all in.

"Everything okay, Detective?" She took a seat, without him offering one, and removed a cigarette from her purse. She crossed her legs, making sure he could marvel at her bare skin, showing through the slit in her dress.

"With all due respect, Ms. Smith—"

"Eva. I've corrected you before. I won't do it again."

"With all due respect, Eva, but you are one tall drink of water."

Anya laughed and leaned forward to tap some ashes onto his desk and noticed his blatant gawking at the way her cleavage rose from her low-cut dress.

"All respect *due-ed*," she replied and reclined in her seat.

"I'm not sure if that's even a term," he said and sat on the corner of his desk, their ankles just inches from each other. "Unfortunately I don't have any leads on your grandfather just yet."

Anya ran her tongue along her teeth inside her closed lips. "I'm not here about the Wharf Killer." She paused to study his reaction.

Stepp scooted forward on his desk and then leaned backward so his hands propped himself up. "Oh? And why are you here, Eva?" he asked, not being discreet about where his gaze landed on her exposed milky skin.

Anya smirked and produced a small bag of white powdery substance from her bra. "I want to give you a Christmas bonus. An incentive to be the best you can be for me."

Stepp bit his bottom lip, and his gaze followed the bag all the way to where she placed it on his desk. She sat back and watched him shake the contents onto his leather desk pad and then form the powder into two perfect lines.

"Are you joining me?"

"You first," she replied.

Stepp brought his nose to his desk and snorted the first line.

Anya stood and bent forward to inhale the second line. She placed a hand on his chest and pushed him against his desk, knocking his computer mouse and Rolodex to the floor. He grabbed her waist as she swung a leg over his lap to straddle him. He moved his hands to her breasts and smooshed them together through the top of her dress. She leaned forward and pressed her lips hard against his.

He removed one hand from a breast and slid it down her torso until it found its way under the slit in her dress. He gripped her buttocks and pulled her tighter on top of him.

"You are ... the ... hottest thing ... I've ever ... seen," he said in-between kisses and used his tongue to play with hers. He ran his hands along her hips, up her stomach, and stopped when both cupped her ears. He guided her back down toward him, and she flung back an arm—like she had just pulled on a chain-saw's starter rope—and shot her opened hand into his chest.

Stepp bucked at the waist and screeched. Anya heard footfalls pattering down the hallway toward the office and swiped her finger in the air, closing and locking the door.

Returning to the matter at hand, Anya's fingers penetrated through his rib cage—splinters of bones scattered from his chest—as her fingers got tangled in the veins and arteries leading to and from his heart. Blood spewed from the gaping hole and covered both of them. The *tha-thump* of his still-pulsing heart increased with fear and adrenaline as her hand covered it. She closed her eyes and reveled in the feeling of his vulnerable muscle in her grasp.

Anya leaned next to Stepp's ear. "You cost me immortality because you couldn't keep your willy in your pants."

She yanked with all her might, detaching Stepp's heart from his body as if she were unplugging a cord from an outlet. Blood spattered across his computer monitor. He convulsed on his desk and then lay still, his eyes unblinking and fixated on the ceiling.

"I hope she was worth it," Anya spat.

The last thing Detective J. Stepp heard before eternal darkness consumed him was Vicki's high-pitched wail as she banged on the other side of his locked office door.

As Vicki leaped from her desk when she heard Stepp scream, Melissa contemplated whether she should tackle the bitch or continue playing the innocent-victim act. She decided to follow the Chosen One down the hallway and assess the situation as it unfolded.

With one fluid movement, Vicki tried to turn Stepp's office doorknob and enter the room—only her toes, knees, and face struck the door after she turned the knob to the locked door. She stepped backward, touching her nose for comfort, and pounded on the door, while wailing Stepp's name.

Melissa spied on Vicki from halfway down the hallway—not daring to get too close to either the frantic Chosen One or to the vindictive witch on the other side of the door. Melissa heard the interior office door unlatch and watched Vicki take a step backward.

Eva Smith—aka Anya—stepped into the hallway. Blood smeared her face and painted her dress in red. She haphazardly held a heart in one hand, and Melissa focused on the veins and arteries dangling toward the floor like severed electrical cords, drawing closer.

With her free hand, Anya grabbed Vicki by her lapel. "I could smell it on you as soon as I came in. Your impureness. You've been deflowered."

Vicki's eyes grew wide in realization, and she scooted past *Eva* to peer into Stepp's office. She gasped and placed a hand over her mouth when her gaze fell upon Stepp.

Melissa stood at the doorway, viewing Stepp lifeless on his desk, his rib cage ripped open and exposed as if something had burst forth from it. But Melissa stepped aside when Vicki flailed every limb in an attempt to both flee and to strike out at Eva.

Melissa ended up in the reception area to better watch the action.

Anya lifted Vicki from the floor with one hand and crammed Stepp's heart into Vicki's hair with the other. The witch lathered the dead muscle and veins as if it were a handful of shampoo and then dropped Vicki.

The Chosen One turned and fled toward Melissa, trying to run down the hallway. She screamed and slapped as much of Stepp's bits and pieces of heart muscle from her tangled hair as she ran.

Anya stepped into the hallway behind Vicki and broadened

her shoulders. "Mel, show me how you're the next curator of the cult. Everything I have is at your fingertips."

Melissa nodded without flinching and tackled Vicki as she passed by.

Vicki flexed her muscles and used all her might to roll the teenager off her body and to pin Melissa to the floor.

Anya approached the imbroglio but did not interfere. She crossed her arms and watched in delight, picking blood from her eyelashes.

Vicki, now on top and straddling Melissa, glanced over her shoulder. "You crazy woman! You just murdered my future husband!"

Melissa grabbed the nearby secretary's chair and toppled it onto Vicki, who tumbled backward with the chair. The girls had switched positions yet again.

Now Melissa scrambled to her feet and squared off with Vicki in a boxer stance.

Anya tossed back her head and roared in an animalistic growl that Melissa had never heard before. "You think you're gonna take down this cunt with a fistfight? Her impurity just cost us fucking *everything*! Kill her now, or I'll relieve you and rip her to shreds myself."

Melissa's gaze switched from Anya to Vicki. When Vicki flinched toward the exit, Melissa grabbed the bronze horse paperweight from beside the appointment calendar on the desk and swung as hard as she could.

Vicki raised her hands in defense—her jelly bracelets flinging from her wrist and landing at her feet—but Melissa's swing carried through Vicki's arms and struck her on the side of the head, the bronze horse's head embedding itself into the soft flesh of the Chosen One's temple.

Melissa stood, straddling the fallen Chosen One, as if

taunting a tackled football player with a flair of bravado. The paperweight—now dotted with pieces of hair and brain matter—was still clasped in one hand.

The radio DJ announced the next song through the speakers, and the intro to "Rebel Yell" filled the quiet office as Melissa used her forearm to swipe the speckles of blood from her forehead.

"I gotta get out of this ridiculous outfit," Anya said and morphed from the seductive Eva Smith to her normal pale-faced being— in a black robe and ghastly skinned.

"Did I kill her?" Melissa asked, placing the reddened paperweight onto the desk.

Anya approached Vicki's lifeless body and kicked her in the stomach. "Bitch deserves to die thrice."

"What does this mean? I mean, for me? And you?"

Anya pursed her lips. "Immortality will have to wait. Just as someone always replaces my curator, there'll be another Chosen One—in time. I just hope I don't have to wait two centuries again."

"Two centuries? I thought back in Vegas—"

"Rose was an error. And, if you know what's good for you, girl, you'll stop bringing that up. The last *real* Chosen One was a girl from—" Anya's nostrils flared, and she groaned in frustration. "If he wasn't so powerful, I'd skin him hide for hide for getting in the way *again*."

"Who?" Melissa asked, stepping over Vicki's body.

Anya didn't answer and walked to the front door, locking the dead bolt. She turned back to Melissa and noticed the seriousness on the girl's face. "I'd like to read minds, but I can't."

Melissa broke her daze. "I want to be next."

"Next?" Anya asked, poking a red and gold ornament on the fake Christmas tree.

"I want to take my grandfather's place. I want to prove that I can bring razor to wrist to all the shit in the world."

Anya folded her arms and glared at Melissa.

"I just fucking killed someone for you. And only because you asked. I didn't question it. I'm loyal. I've proven that. I'm my grandfather's student and so, so much more. *I* am everything you've been looking for in a guardian."

Anya turned from Melissa and headed down the hallway.

"What are you doing?" Melissa asked.

Anya pivoted to face the teenager. "If I really am relieving your grandfather of his duties and taking you on, he at least deserves one last gift."

Melissa's eyes grew wide as she followed Anya into Stepp's office. "Do I get a cool name?"

"What the hell are you talking about, child?"

"I need a cool killer name. You know? Like, Grandpapa had Wharf Killer. I need something wicked."

Anya rolled her eyes and shook her head. "So that's the most important thing to you right now?"

"I guess not." Melissa looked at the decimated detective lying across his computer's keyboard. "Can you see him? With your real eyes?"

"Now that he's dead, yes. It seems the spell doesn't work if he's dead."

Melissa circled the desk, studying the protruding bones and entrails strung about.

"Does it bother you?" Anya asked.

Melissa touched a blood splatter on Stepp's computer monitor. "I welcome it. The weak need to suffer."

Anya nodded and fell to her knees. She chanted words foreign to Melissa, and, within seconds, a kettle of vultures had formed a circle above the dead detective.

Smith hustled to the ringing phone, expecting Hank to be on the other end, wanting to discuss the shop and Roxanne. When he put the receiver to his ear and heard Anya's raspy voice, he slumped into one of the kitchen chairs.

"I felt really bad that you lost Tony."

"Sure you did," he replied, looking out the window at his bird feeder.

"I did! I just wanted to let you know that I'm gifting you with a replacement. He'll be ready in a few days." Anya glanced at the swarm of black feathers consuming Stepp's body.

"Don't do me any favors," Smith said as the drip from the melting icicle on the bird feeder's small perch hypnotized him. "I can only imagine where you found this winner."

"Oh, no. I think he'll be a fine replacement to your magical band of fools."

"With Tony gone, it's just me. Far from a *band*."

"And, Smith?"

He snapped to attention at the tone of her voice, one he had never heard before.

"Stepp has been relieved of his duties. You were right. He was an incompetent nincompoop."

Smith chuckled. "Such harsh words coming from you. Glad you finally came around to reason. I'd love to say that I told you so but—"

"Then don't. It's very unbecoming."

Wynn entered the kitchen and kissed Smith on the cheek. "I'm heading out for groceries. Be back in a jiff."

Smith nodded and waited for the front door to close before continuing with a hiss. "Anya, I am *not* getting dragged back into your sick agenda. There's nothing you can do, short of killing me, that'll sway me to return."

"Simmer down, Colombo, and stop flattering yourself. I already have Stepp's replacement on board and all in." Anya winked at Melissa when she saw the child wipe a smear of Vicki's blood from her cheek.

Smith twirled the curlicue phone cord around his index finger. "That was fast."

"I don't have time to wait for unmotivated people anymore." Anya placed a hand on Melissa's arm in a doting touch and petted her. "I have full confidence in my new partner, especially since the mission has been altered. I have new goals now, Smith. And with new goals and new endgames must come a new breed of killer. One you wouldn't have the stomach for."

"I don't want to know what your new goals are, Anya. You've fallen off the deep end, and all I ask is that you leave me and my family alone. Go have your fun. Or your revenge. Or whatever new cross you've decided to bear. I don't want to know anything. I can't be held as a vicarious liability anymore. So, if we are done here, I'd like to finish drinking my coffee and go about the rest of my life ignorant to your tyranny from this point forward. Consider this our final good bye."

"Good bye, Todd."

A shiver ran down Smith's back at the insidious sound of his first name coming from Anya's mouth for the first time—ever.

"I hope you can find the peace you're looking for in being a harebrained bystander," Anya continued, "while some of us are working to—"

Smith placed the receiver on the cradle and brought his TOP GUN FOR HIRE mug to his lips as he counted the seconds between each melting icicle drip.

Anya held the disconnected phone away from her face, looking at it and furrowing her brows. "That's the first time he's ever cut me off. I guess the honeymoon really is over. Maybe he doesn't deserve one last gift."

Melissa squinted and tried to see through the swirling black curtain of feathers and beaks. Bits of powder-pink fabric and shards of bone fragments spit into the air as the vultures performed their ritual. Curiosity bested her, and she stepped forward, closer to the perfect funnel above the desk.

"Don't get too close, child. They might do our biddings, but that doesn't mean accidents don't happen when they are focused and locked into their frenzy."

Melissa heeded the witch's warning and took two cautious steps backward. She could still feel the wind from the birds' flapping wings even with the distance she had created. "Are we gonna have to clean up all the mess?"

"The vultures will take care of that."

Melissa peered down the hallway to make sure the secretary still lie where she had been killed. "Even Vicki?"

"Even the bitch."

"What are you gonna do with her? You aren't gonna turn her, right?"

"Can't. They won't let me." Anya motioned at the vultures. "The Chosen One didn't partake in any behavior that would deem her a social deviant. The vultures are bound to that code. Plus I'm not sure I can stomach looking at her for the rest of eternity—ghoul or not."

"What about him?" Melissa nodded at the obscured Stepp.

"Oh, he has some really shiny skeletons in his closet. I'm sure the vultures are pretty zealous to turn him right-side up. He'll be an appropriate sidekick for your grandfather. Two peas in a pod when it comes to both of their respective first wives."

Melissa glanced at the towering witch beside her. "Wait. Grandpapa was married to someone else before Grandma?"

"Some closets are deeper than you can ever imagine, child. You should ask him about it one day. But don't listen to his answer. Watch the reaction on his face instead. It'll be a fun experiment in the alchemy of emotions."

Anya snuggled an arm around Melissa's shoulders and guided her to the front door.

"So, what do we do now?"

"We let the vultures do what they do best, and we go about our day. They'll take care of everything."

Anya unlocked the front door, and they stepped into the winter morning sunlight. Melissa noticed the city workers had finally hung wreaths in the trees outlining the street and had strung Christmas lights along the telephone wires.

Melissa grabbed the closing door before it latched shut. "Wait! My backpack's still in there."

"Hurry up, child. And carelessness like that can be the difference between success and skid row."

Melissa jogged across the waiting room and grabbed her book bag, taking one last gander at the spattered blood freckling Vicki's old workspace. She returned outside and waited for Anya to secure the door before speaking. "What happens to me now?"

"I'll be in contact soon. Until then, you should change nothing about your routine or behavior. Success lies in invisibility, when it comes to our line of work."

Melissa nodded, and Anya vanished. She gazed upon the festive decorations adorning the street as she headed toward school and smiled. Christmas had never been her favorite time of year—all the ho-ho-ho's and good cheer really bummed her out—but she thought this particular holiday season might truly be the most wonderful time of the year.

12: GOD CRISIS

"Hey there, Mel-o-dramatic!" Benji said, sitting next to her in the cafeteria.

"You just made that up?" she asked as she unzipped her backpack.

"On the spot. Didn't even have to put any effort into it."

Melissa rolled her eyes. "Clever." She reached in to grab her brown-bagged lunch. Her fingers grazed an added item—and then another—that she *knew* hadn't been in here during her morning classes. She peered inside the top unsealed portion of her backpack, past her lunch. She slammed her bag shut and scanned the room as she slid her bag from the table onto the floor and underneath her seat.

"Something try to bite you?" Benji asked.

"Nah. Just pissed that I left my lunch at the house. Sorry."

"I'll go grab ya something. I'm headin' up there anyway."

She nodded—anything to make him leave her alone for just a few moments.

Benji excused himself and headed toward the growing

lunch line.

Melissa stood with a grin from the table, grabbed her backpack, and headed to the women's restroom. She entered the first unoccupied stall and latched the door. She sat on the toilet and removed the now-pristine bronze horse paperweight first. *Thank you, Anya, for covering my ass.* She returned it to her backpack and next took from her bag the maroon-bound book with the triangle and eye design adorning the cover.

With each turn of the pages, her smile grew wider and more sinister. And then she found the section she felt would be the most fun to experiment with first.

Melissa opened the doors of Madam Hapney's shop and strutted across the waiting area, determination in each stride.

Madam Hapney glanced at the teenager and then at the clock. "Do we have an appointment scheduled today?"

Melissa stopped at Hapney's desk but did not sit down. "No. I came to tell you that I won't be needing your services or your mentoring any longer." She bounced once to readjust the backpack hung over her shoulder.

"Is everything okay?" Hapney stood to meet the girl's height. "This isn't like you, Melissa."

"It's not you. It's me." She slid the backpack down her arm, catching it with one hand when it reached her wrist. She opened the bag and removed Anya's book.

Hapney's eyes grew wide, and she stepped backward from the artifact and from the girl holding it.

"I know that's a clichéd break-up line, but I feel it's appropriate here too. You see"—Melissa flipped through the pages—"I'm already more knowing and powerful than you'll ever be."

"You can't possibly understand the power you're holding." Hapney raised her hands as if Melissa were trying to rob her. "And the so-called woman who gave it to you wields her power for *only* her own personal gains. She'll gut and skin you alive without batting an eyelash, if it so suits her needs."

"I've already wasted enough time chatting with you. I have a lot more important things to do now. And I don't need your pathetic little love spell to keep Graham forever anymore." Melissa stopped flipping pages and bent the book at its spine. "The vultures can do that for me. After I do what's needed, they can bring him back. Forever mine."

Madam Hapney wrapped her fingers around a hag stone lying on her desk without breaking eye contact with Melissa. She fondled the magical amulet and took a deep breath. "The vultures only serve the greater good. The only reason why they tolerate Anya is because she delivers what they perceive as stains on society."

Hapney watched Melissa's mouth open at the mention of Anya's name.

"Bet'chya didn't think I know all about Anya and her book." Hapney felt increased confidence grow inside her as she rubbed the hag stone and took a step forward. "The vultures serve many masters. Not just Anya. But they don't serve the person. They serve the *deed*. That's why little Rose Covington wasn't turned. You got another think coming if you believe the vultures will answer your beck and call just because you hold the book now. *Remember.* They serve the deed, you selfish girl."

"And you don't think statutory rape falls within their scope of needing repentance?" Melissa tapped her temple. "See? I'm smarter than the average cookie. I can manipulate any situation."

"You are vile and wicked. Get out of my face. Any cohort of that wretched woman is no friend of mine."

Melissa shoved the book into her backpack and flung the bag over her shoulder. "I'll make sure to tell her that you said that. I'm sure she'd love to know who her friends are." Melissa turned and headed for the door.

"You're playing with fire," Hapney called out, when Melissa pulled open the entrance door. "A fire you can't possibly even begin to comprehend."

Melissa spun to face the psychic, using her hip to keep the door propped open. "No, Madam Hapney. I think *you're* playing with fire."

When Melissa snaked through the door and onto the brick cobblestone sidewalk, she heard Hapney squeal from inside her shop. The teenager glanced through the windows and chuckled as she watched the psychic slap at the thin row of flames growing taller across her desk.

Madam Hapney snuffed out the last of the flames and flipped her red sign hanging on the front glass to Closed. She locked the door and slapped her palms on her jeans, trying to wipe the smeared ashes from her skin. She collected all her journals and spell books that had been turned to kindling from the fire on her desk and tossed them into the wastebasket. Then, she grabbed the handset of her telephone and dialed the seven digits with such haste she kept slipping off the three button and striking the six instead. After the fourth attempt, her hands had stopped shaking enough where she successfully dialed the phone number.

The phone was picked up the on the second ring. "Good afternoon. Pale Horse."

"Baron? It's Bridgett."

"Hold on a sec, sunshine."

Hapney tapped her foot and drummed on her chest with the hag stone as she heard Baron place the phone on the bar counter and turn off a running faucet. She heard him approach the phone and lift the handset to his ear.

"Everything hunky-dory on the wharf?" he asked.

"Anya's inaugurated a new curator to the book."

"Don't we have bigger and better things to worry about than that washed-up old shrew? I made sure the Chosen One was put out of reach and—"

"It's Smith's fourteen-year-old granddaughter," Hapney said and waited for a response before saying any more. She heard the *clink* of eating utensils hitting plates in the background, but Baron did not reply. The sound of his patrons' chitchat seemed to grow louder over the phone the longer Baron remained silent. "Are you still there?"

"Yeah, Bridgett. I'm here. I didn't think even Anya would stoop so low as to recruit a child into the fold."

"I can't help but feel it's some vendetta against Smith. You know he's never been the most loyal of servants."

"That's why I can stomach being around him when he comes to the bar. How do you know this?"

"Melissa set my reading table on fire after she bragged about being more powerful than me and showing me the book."

"Please tell me that she set it on fire with a match or a lighter."

Madam Hapney sighed. "Pyrokinesis."

"Fuck! And she's only fourteen? Did you call the cops?"

Hapney snorted. "God, no! They already think I'm some kind of fruit loop, and, to be honest, if Melissa is a loose cannon, I don't want her blowing up my shop in retribution."

"Yeah, but, if she does blow up your shop over something else, at least you could file a report on this, starting a paper trail of a person of interest. I'd think about calling them and just reporting vandalism and name her as a suspect. Get her name in the system. Sergeant Santana is a personal friend of mine. Ask for him and then name drop me, if it'll make you feel better."

"I dunno, Baron. This might be safer if it's handled in-house."

"As far as I know, none of Anya's puppets have ever been able to wield any kind of kinetic power. This is a first. And for her to be so ..."

Hapney listened to the bar's background ambiance again as Baron had trailed off and stopped talking.

"You were gonna say *young*, weren't you? And I know you're thinking the same thing I am."

Baron nodded, even though he knew she couldn't see him do it. "If she's that impressive at such a young age, and Anya has targeted her already *and* entrusted her with the book, this girl could very well be—"

"Anya's successor."

Baron snapped his fingers at the realization. "Anya's grooming this girl to take over the Mushroom Cult because Anya honestly thought she had homed in on the Chosen One and would transcend to a divinity—but that failed."

"She needs to be stopped, by all means necessary."

Baron snickered. "Which 'she'?"

Hapney swallowed hard and took a deep breath. "Both of them."

Travis confiscated Wynn's tea cup and saucer. "Would you like some more tea, Mom?"

"Nah. I think we'll get going. Your father's partying days are over, I'm afraid," she replied and squeezed Smith's hand.

"It was nice of you guys to pop by. I know Addie and Shaun always love it when you surprise them," Gwen added. "I'd like to apologize for Melissa's antisocial … aloofness, I guess."

Wynn waved her off. "She's a teenager. We were all teenagers once. I certainly didn't want to hang out with anyone in my family at that age, never mind my old-fashioned grandparents, of all people."

Travis placed his parents' plates in the sink, and the doorbell chimed. He glanced at his wife and scrunched his face in a who-could-that-be gesture.

Gwen headed for the door and peeked through the side window. "It's the police."

Travis furrowed his brows at his father in confusion and turned off the sink water as Gwen opened the front door and greeted the officers.

"Pardon me to bother you, ma'am, but are you Melissa Smith's mother?"

"Is there a problem, Officer?" Travis asked, approaching the door.

"Good evening, sir. I'm Officer Taylor, and this is Officer Raynard. We received a call about a possible vandalism. We'd like to talk with Melissa to see if she knows anything about it or can help us figure out who did it."

Travis stepped aside. "Come in. Come in."

Smith stood from the kitchen table and leaned against the counter next to the refrigerator when the two officers entered the room.

"Do you think Mel's involved or just may know who did it?" Gwen asked.

"Well, ma'am, the complainant said she saw Melissa leave the area when the vandalism was discovered."

"Did this happen today?" Travis raised an eyebrow at his wife and placed his hands on his hips.

"Sometime after school had let out," Raynard said.

"That's not like Mel at all," Travis muttered.

"Is she home? Do you mind if we speak to her here?" Taylor asked.

"Where did this happen?" Smith asked, not allowing Travis to answer the officer.

"Madam Hapney's shop. She's a psychic down on Pickering Wharf, sir," Raynard said.

"Mel vandalized a psychic's place?" Gwen retorted.

"Well, we're not pointing the finger just yet. We're just here to ask her what she might know about it," Taylor said.

Gwen placed a hand on her husband's arm. "I'll go get her."

"What kind of damage was done?" Smith asked.

"Someone set fire to the desk where Madam Hapney does her tarot and palm readings," Raynard replied.

"Or whatever kooky other things she does in there," Taylor added.

Smith noticed Raynard shot Taylor a disapproving glare.

"And you said this happened right after school today?" Smith asked.

"Yes, sir."

Smith grunted under his breath and slithered unnoticed from the room as soon as Gwen returned with their daughter in tow. The sounds of the police's introductory formalities faded as Smith snuck into Melissa's bedroom, closed the door behind him, and located her backpack. He unzipped it and yanked the two halves apart, scanning the Trapper Keeper, a pencil case, numerous textbook covers graffitied with hand-drawn band logos, a protractor, a bronze paperweight—*odd*—and ... Anya's Mushroom Cult book. His hand trembled as he reached inside the bag and removed the maroon-bound spell book.

Anya's comments during their phone conversation from this morning flooded back to him. *I already have Stepp's replacement on board and all in ... I have full confidence in my new partner, especially since the mission has been altered. I have new goals now, Smith. And with new goals and new endgames must come a new breed of killer.*

Smith's knuckles turned an unnatural shade of white, and the muscles in his arms vibrated as his fingers clenched the book.

The bedroom door swung open, and Melissa stood in the doorway. "What the fuck are you doing in here?"

Smith stood and extended the book in front of him, like an overzealous priest showing the Bible to a sinner. "It's you. My own granddaughter. So *this* is my legacy, is it? What did she offer you? Power? Control? More than you can ever imagine? She's a liar, Mel. A *lie-er*. And now you're a killer. This is *all* you'll ever be now. A killer."

She snatched the book from Smith's grasp. "Will you just shut your mouth?"

"And the cruel joke? I can't even blow the whistle on you if I wanted to. I'm sure the vultures cleaned up whatever mess the two of you made in that office. Evidence all gone. Easy peasy, spic and span."

"Mel?" Travis asked, his voice projecting from the kitchen. "Did you find his phone number yet?"

Smith and Melissa heard Travis' footsteps traveling toward them down the hallway.

Melissa shoved the book into her backpack and removed a pistol from her waistband.

"Where in tarnation did you get *that*?" Smith cocked his head and put both hands on his hip.

"A little birdie told me that Dad kept it hidden in his sock drawer." She zipped her backpack and hugged it against her chest. "And it's cocked and loaded. A girl can never be too prepared for the *big, bad world*." Her intonation on the last three words resembled someone ogling over a newborn baby.

"I'm gonna tell them," Smith said.

Melissa spun to face him. "You do, and I'll sing so loudly about how my grandfather is the Wharf Killer."

"It's time to break this cycle," Smith muttered to himself and took a breath to call out for the officers in the kitchen. "Off—"

Melissa swiped her hand across the front of his face, and Smith's lips stuck together. He throat-screamed and clawed at his mouth, trying to separate his sealed lips. She calculated about ten more paces and her father would be inside her room. She closed her eyes and flexed both elbows into her chest as she concentrated her energy.

The parked police cruiser outside the house erupted to life; the sirens activated, and the blue-and-red strobe lights spun, lighting up the street and ricocheting a high-pitched wail against the houses.

Melissa relaxed when she heard her father return to the kitchen and then follow the two officers out of the house and toward the malfunctioning squad car. She glanced at her grandfather, Smith's eyes wide in disbelief.

"Thanks a lot. If you could've just kept your big mouth shut, I wouldn't have had to do that." Melissa slung the backpack over the shoulder. "I hope you can live with yourself, knowing you're the reason why my parents—your own son—will never have a peaceful night's sleep again, always wondering where his little girl had run off to."

Smith's brows furrowed in confusion, and he tried again to speak through his spell-glued lips.

Melissa slid open her bedroom window, the winter air blustering through the room. She perched on her sill and looked over her shoulder at Smith. "Anya's gonna take good care of me. And I certainly can't let you live to dime me out."

She let herself drop onto the snow below from the first-floor window

Smith felt invisible icy fingers like claws squeeze his heart, and he grabbed at his chest. The squeezing grew tighter until black dots invaded his vision.

Anya! he screamed inside his mind.

The Wharf Killer fell to his granddaughter's bedroom floor, unable to call out for help as his heart slowed down. The sounds of the police siren faded into the growing blackness as a knocking on Melissa's door increased in volume.

Fluttering his eyelids was the only visible movement he

could muster when his son and a police sergeant burst into the room, searching for Melissa. He felt a warm set of fingers press against his neck, checking for a pulse, and allowed the darkness to consume him. He knew he was in good hands.

Then the chest compressions started ...

Baron locked the door to the Pale Horse's small office and sat down behind his desk. He massaged his thighs, feeling the relief of getting off his feet after serving the bar area and the dining room all by himself from opening time until his night staff had just arrived a few moments earlier. He slid open his desk's bottom drawer and removed a tattered gray doll. The only distinguishing markings on the doll were the black robe and matching veil covering its face. He lifted the fabric from the doll's face and closed his eyes.

Flashes of blinding light crisscrossed behind his eyelids. He squeezed the doll, trying to go deeper. The lights radiated, and an image emerged.

"C'mon, Anya. What are you hiding?" he whispered.

Even though his eyes were closed, he tilted his head to try to decipher the blurry image. He fondled the doll's material and rubbed his thumb over its featureless face. The fuzzy outline of someone crouched on a short wall sharpened. He rubbed the doll's face harder. The someone wore a backpack. Then a room came into focus—a bedroom. He realized the figure was perched on a windowsill and not on a wall, and it was a young girl. Then she fell.

He stood without opening his eyes when he realized the girl must be Smith's granddaughter. His third eye scanned the bedroom, and the hazy image of Smith grabbing at his chest and falling to the bedroom floor filled the space behind his eyelids. Not daring to lose the vision, he kept his eyes closed and fumbled to feel for the top drawer. When his fingers grazed the brass handle, he opened the drawer and removed his own edition of the book—the one designed and catered for his arts.

Holding the threadbare doll in his right hand and the spell book in his left, he recited a memorized incantation, directing all his energy and power at Smith's sprawled body on the floor.

A quick and sharp rapping on his office window startled Baron from his trance, and he opened his eyes. His gaze shot to the small window above the fax machine and couldn't see what had knocked. Then a black beak pecked at the glass again in rapid succession like a machine gun. Baron stepped backward—releasing both the doll and the book as he pressed his buttocks against his desk—when the single vulture turned and took flight from the window.

He exhaled a long breath and steadied himself, leaning both palms on his chair. He glanced at his desk and froze.

The black-veiled doll was gone.

The book's cover had a deep gash across it—like a claw mark.

Baron turned toward the window and didn't even have time to raise his hands in defense to block Anya's razor-sharp fingernails from slashing his face. He touched the wound and glared at the witch before darting his gaze to the book.

She had noticed his moment of distraction and pointed an opened hand at his desk. His desecrated copy of the spell book flew into her palm. She cradled the book to her bosom and withdrew her copy of the Mushroom Cult book from underneath her robe.

"You know as well as I do that the book is just a host,"

Baron said, lifting his chin into the air. "It's the memorized words that hold all the power."

"And I'm sure that you have this whole thing inside that noggin of yours." Anya waved his book at him.

Baron remained stoic, unblinking.

Anya returned her book underneath her robe, and Baron caught a glimpse of his voodoo doll secured to her undergarments.

He snickered. "You're all just smoke and mirrors, aren't you, oh high priestess."

Anya traced the gash adorning the cover of Baron's book with a fingertip, enjoying this moment. Then her head jerked toward Baron. She frowned, peering at him from the corner of her eye. "This is too easy. You're letting me have it." She tucked the book under her arm and stepped forward. "Why?"

A muscle in Baron's jawline flinched as his fax machine launched from its stand and struck Anya in the back of her head.

She rubbed her neck and chortled. "So, it's a war you want?" She repositioned the book in both hands. "Then it's a war you'll get." And she opened his book.

An explosion of light came.

Anya was flung against the wall.

The book dropped to the floor.

A cacophony of blustery sounds followed.

A vulture took flight.

The discarded voodoo doll fell to the floor.

Baron was on his knees.

He rose and flicked his head, toppling the nearby four-drawer file cabinet onto Anya's motionless body. It teetered as it lay across her torso, her feet sticking out, pointing to the proverbial yellow-brick road.

Baron retrieved his book from the floor and smacked it against his leg to dust off any possible contagious residue that might have transferred from the witch's touch. He knelt before her slumped body and pocketed the dropped voodoo doll. Without removing the file cabinet from her chest, he opened the book and flipped to the cardinal-red-colored section—the sacred hymns that protected the Chosen One.

The space where Victoria Jensen's name had been scribed in calligraphy was now blank. Baron relaxed and slumped against his desk to wait for the next name in line to emerge, to get notified who needed to be protected next. He shot a glance at Anya to make sure she hadn't moved.

Ink blotting caught his eye, and he returned his attention to the page's reveal of the next Chosen One. The book unveiled the letters of the new name, one by one in a scattered fashion, making Baron feel like he was a participant in the most important episode of *Wheel of Fortune* to ever air—sans Vanna White.

Enough letters had soaked through the parchment for him to fill in the missing vowels, and he gasped.

The book slipped from his hands.

Crash!

The file cabinet smacked the ground—the witch, gone.

He slammed the book shut and stood.

A movement.

He spun.

A movement elsewhere.

He spun again.

Hissing.

Hissing coming from somewhere—everywhere.

"You got your war," he muttered.

The last thing he remembered before the world spun and disappeared was the witch's three rows of fanged teeth coming at him.

And the vile sound of her hissing.

Thanks for reading Moonlight City Drive 2: Electric Boogaloo.
If you have enjoyed the Moonlight City Drive series,
check out my other books at www.brianpaone.com.

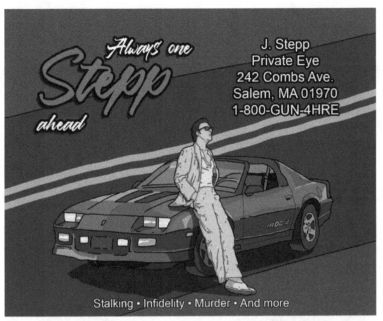